The Three Graces

Also by Phil Revell

Non Fiction

Kayaking – Heinemann Library 1999
The Professionals – Trentham 2005
The Mayflower Children – Ascribe Publishing 2011

Fiction

A Spurious Brood – Ascribe Publishing 2011
Matching Pair – Ascribe Publishing 2014
Hedgemen and other stories – Ascribe Publishing 2020

The Three Graces

Phil Revell

Copyright © 2023 Phil Revell

Cover design – Three Graces sketch by Jo Revell

The moral right of the author has been asserted.

Apart from any fair dealing for the purposes of research or private study, or criticism or review, as permitted under the Copyright, Designs and Patents Act 1988, this publication may only be reproduced, stored or transmitted, in any form or by any means, with the prior permission in writing of the publishers, or in the case of reprographic reproduction in accordance with the terms of licences issued by the Copyright Licensing Agency. Enquiries concerning reproduction outside those terms should be sent to the publishers.

This is a work of fiction. Names, characters, businesses, places, events and incidents are either the products of the author's imagination or used in a fictitious manner. Any resemblance to actual persons, living or dead, or actual events is purely coincidental.

Matador
Unit E2 Airfield Business Park,
Harrison Road, Market Harborough,
Leicestershire. LE16 7UL
Tel: 0116 2792299
Email: books@troubador.co.uk
Web: www.troubador.co.uk/matador
Twitter: @matadorbooks

ISBN 978 1803136 943

British Library Cataloguing in Publication Data.
A catalogue record for this book is available from the British Library.

Printed and bound in Great Britain by CMP UK
Typeset in 10pt Adobe Caslon Pro by Troubador Publishing Ltd, Leicester, UK

Matador is an imprint of Troubador Publishing Ltd

Prelude

It could not be. They were here, just a second ago. There were hundreds of people on the platform, but he could see no-one he knew. There was no sign of Brother Stephen's black cassock, no sign of the boys, not even Paddy's distinctive red hair.

The boy had stopped for just a moment to admire the huge locomotive breathing soft clouds of steam. For a blissful few seconds he imagined himself as the driver, with a leather cap and oil stained overalls, but then he looked around and they were gone.

On the neighbouring platform he saw some children being shepherded onto a train. He dashed over, almost beside himself with relief, only to find that these boys had blue uniform jackets, and a master who was most definitely not Brother Stephen. Horrified, he returned to Platform 8, but there was still no sign of his group and no clue to explain how they had magically disappeared.

Trembling, he imagined Brother Stephen sending the monitors to look for him, and the punishment that would follow once he was found. Paddy was the monitor he feared the most. The older boy's favourite 'tickler' was a chinese burn, where the soft skin of the forearm is twisted and stretched. But the casual cruelty was just a foretaste of what would follow when he was brought before Brother Stephen, who had emphasised most strongly at breakfast the importance of sticking together.

"And NOT GETTING LOST. Woe betide any of youse tinkers who gets himself lost. You'll be meeting the corrector that's for sure."

Brother Stephen stroked the broad leather belt at his waist, just in case any of the boys were too stupid to catch his meaning.

The boy had nodded with the rest. It had only been a month, but he knew all about the corrector. And now it had happened. He was lost and it seemed like it was only an hour after leaving Birmingham. He didn't want to cry; the other boys laughed when he cried and it invariably led to some special attention from the monitors. But he couldn't help himself; he didn't know where to look, what to do.

"Now then my lad. What's happening here?"

The thin white face looked up into the eyes of a huge man in a blue naval uniform. The outsized kitbag slung over the man's shoulders was quickly dropped to the platform and used as a seat so that the man could talk to the boy on the same level.

The sailor guessed that the lad was about eight or nine. The child was carrying a brown paper parcel carefully wrapped in twine, along with the ubiquitous gas mask in its flimsy cardboard box. Oversized grey flannel shorts reached below his knees; the boy's socks were around his ankles, and he had worn but highly polished shoes. Despite the warmth of the day he was wearing a woollen pullover over a collarless shirt. A large label secured through a shirt buttonhole announced his status as an evacuee. The eyes, which a moment ago had been brimming with tears, were focused in fascination on the sailor's badges and the legend 'Hood' on the kitbag.

"Is that a battleship? 'Hood' I mean?"

"That she is, best ship in the fleet."

The man produced a clean white handkerchief, which he used to dry away the boy's tears.

"She weighs in at 47,000 tons and we have eight 15 inch guns.

She may be slow, but we get there in the end. I've been on shore leave with my missus, and now I'm off to Scapa to rejoin. Then we'll go and sort out Hitler."

The sailor swept up the boy and sat him on the kitbag. He smoothed out the crumpled label, which announced the boy's name, home town of Birmingham and the name of his school, but said nothing about his intended destination. He stood and stretched to his full and considerable height so that he could look over the passing crowds. Temple Meads is a key station for rail traffic to the West Country, Wales, London and the North. On this September morning there were trains at nearly every platform and a mass of people, uniforms, bags and bustle.

He sighed, dropped back to one knee and rocked back on his heels to inspect the boy's face.

"Now then, I'm sure I saw a school group when I walked through the tunnel. They were going up to platform 12. Let's go and take a shufti. You ready? All polished for inspection?"

The boy nodded and stood to attention.

"Good lad," the sailor took the boy's small hand in his own and led the way to the stairs that dropped down to the station underpass.

Emerging onto Platform 12 the pair found a train stood at the platform and a red faced station official consulting a large fobwatch. A few wives and girlfriends were saying their goodbyes through open windows to the uniformed men who appeared to be the train's only passengers. The guard raised a flag.

"Passengers for Exeter and Plymouth, all aboard."

With the boy in tow the sailor strode up to the official.

"Have you an evacuee group on this train? This boy has become separated from his teachers."

"Yes, but at the back," said the guard. "In 9 and 10, but I have to get this one away now."

"Hold on a mo' will you."

The sailor looked down the long platform, and then at the nearest carriage, where two naval ratings hung out of the window. He read the names on the caps in their hands.

"Oi there, Viscount! Look after this one. His messmates are in the rear carriages."

The men on the train inspected the proffered cargo and grinned.

"Typical battle wagon," said HMS Viscount. "Expecting the destroyers to do all the work."

A door was flung open and the boy passed between hands and seated between HMS Viscount and HMS Montrose. The door slammed shut. A whistle blew. In the cab of the locomotive the driver eased open the regulator, releasing steam into the huge pistons. Connecting rods jerked into action and the wheels made their first tentative movements. A loud chuff came from the smokestack and an acrid cloud of steam and smoke enveloped the platform.

"Keep your chin up," shouted HMS Hood through the smoke, and the train pulled slowly out of the station.

On the way back down the steps to the underpass the sailor passed a boy with vivid red hair.

Paddy paused at the top of the steps and watched the departing train. Once the steam and smoke had cleared he glanced up and down the empty platform, but there was no sign of the stupid boy. Paddy knew all too well what the reaction would be when he gave the news to Brother Stephen. He cursed fluently, before running back down to the underpass to check the platforms all over again.

PART ONE

Edith

Edith was late.

There had been a hundred and one things to do that day and, at the last moment, just as she was adjusting her hat in the lobby, Mr James rang the bell from the study.

Edith took off her hat and coat and left them on the hall table. In the evening gloom of the study James Threwe stood by the window, looking out over the gardens to the long meadow and the house on the hill. He gestured towards a note on the desk.

HOW MANY?

"I don't know," said Edith helplessly. "They said it might be four or five."

Her employer's shoulders stiffened and the hands clasped behind his back writhed and twisted.

Edith hesitated by the study door.

"I have to go. The form said 8pm, they might be waiting."

For a second the silhouetted figure made no move, then he unclasped his hands and reached for the binoculars on the desk. It was a dismissal. Edith closed the study door, collected her hat and dashed out of the hall.

From Overhill to Totnes station is nearly an hour of stiff walking. Edith looked at her watch and it confirmed that she was going to be late. As she hurried down the long lane into town

Edith hoped that Mr James would not be too discomfited by the arrivals. Whatever happened it would at least be some company, for her if not for him.

Overhill lies on the east side of Totnes. It is a small country house in the Georgian style and had been built as suitably distanced accommodation for those in the Threwe family who preferred not to live at the big house further up the hill. From her bedroom Edith could look south over the Dart valley towards the distant coast; she had been housekeeper for nearly twenty years, ever since James Threwe had been discharged from the Army.

To have refused the post would have been unthinkable. From kitchen maid at Threwe Hall to running a household was a huge promotion for an eighteen year old, and a big responsibility. Then there was Mr James to think of.

"He has not fully recovered from his wounds," old Mr Threwe had explained. "He will need looking after. Not nursing you understand, but care. And we think you are the right person for the role."

Her parents had been proud and delighted, not least by the prospect of extra income. Their one concern was the condition that Edith should live at Overhill.

"It's usual, I suppose," said her father. "Housekeepers do normally live in, but …"

"There will be talk," said her mother.

And talk there was. Mr James' isolation and illness made him an object of mystery. The presence of a gardener and day maid did nothing to stem the speculation in the town, which was considerable and uncomfortable.

Local gossip received a boost three years after her appointment when the old master died and Rupert Threwe inherited the estate. One of his first actions was to slash the staff list down to six, from its pre-war complement of twenty. The reduction involved Overhill losing the gardener and the maid, leaving Edith alone at the house with her employer; a situation that some saw as scandalous. On her weekly trips into town she grew used to the stares and sudden silences that would be triggered by her entry into a shop.

"You will just have to hold your head high and ignore them my girl," said her mother. "We know the truth of it, an' that's all that matters."

The irony was that the truth, had it been revealed, would have done nothing to dampen the rumours.

In the first few years Edith was a frequent visitor to her employer's bedroom, but not for the reasons that some would have supposed. Few nights went by without her being awakened by cries and screams from the master's room.

The first night it happened she lay awake in fear, horrified by the raw distress she could hear across the landing. Wrapping a dressing gown tight, she carried a lamp into Mr James' room, and held him close until the brutal memories receded into the night. He never touched her, and acknowledged neither the nightmares nor the comfort once the dawn had broken. At breakfast he was silent as always.

In some ways the night terrors made it easier for Edith to withstand the gossips in the town. James treated her well, her life was vastly better than many. And she had a man to care for, something that many girls her age had been denied by the war.

As the years passed the night terrors became less frequent, then rare. There had not been an instance in months, but the daytime silence remained. Her employer communicated with her via notes and gestures; he made occasional sounds – a murmur, a sigh or groan, but Edith had not heard him speak since his last home leave in 1918.

As Edith made her way through the town's narrow streets she passed under the East gate as the clock struck the hour. She almost ran up the High Street and past the castle, but as she approached the station she could see the cloud of steam from a departing train and she knew her frantic rush had been in vain.

You're late my girl

The station forecourt was a buzz of activity as families from around the area collected their bewildered charges. Edith nodded to Jean Trelawney from the hardware shop, who had two little girls in tow.

A few of the children were crying, but the majority were silent and watchful, overwhelmed by the situation. Some had small suitcases, but most had a single bag held together with string or a belt.

Edith hurried on through the ticket office to the platform. A small group waited by the timetable, watched over by Mrs Mason-Jones from the WVS.

"Ah, here she is," she said, with more than a hint of reproof.

Edith apologised as the group was introduced. A tall thin man in a crumpled worsted suit was Mr Young, the headteacher of the London school that was being evacuated en bloc. Edith guessed that he was in his late forties or early fifties, but wearing well. The woman at his side was much younger, slim and attractive in a smart summer dress. She stood behind her husband and made no move to speak. Holding tight onto her mother was a little girl, with a chestnut brown pony tail held in place with a white ribbon.

"Mr Young is the Headteacher," repeated Mrs Mason-Jones with emphasis.

"This is my wife, Alice, and our daughter, Elisabeth." said the man. He looked at the little girl expectantly and she stepped forward with a polite 'how do you do ma'am'.

Alice Young smiled shyly as Edith explained about the walk up to the Hall. Her husband nodded quickly.

"The luggage is being sent on," he said. "With the things from the school. So we only have our overnight bags."

"That's a relief," said Edith. "I was worried about how we were going to get all your belongings up to the house."

Mrs Mason-Jones produced a bundle of papers and made a selection.

"These are the requisition papers. I expect that Major Threwe will deal with them."

"I expect so," Edith agreed carefully, though she knew what Rupert Threwe would do if she gave him the paperwork.

"And now if you'll excuse me, I must deal with our misplaced parcel,"

Mrs Mason-Jones waved a hand to indicate the small boy sitting alone on a bench further up the platform. The Headteacher followed her gaze. The boy appeared to be studying the nearby signal box with great interest. Mr Young turned back to Mrs Mason-Jones.

"Yes, I wondered about him. How and why is he misplaced?"

There was a critical note in his voice and Edith warmed to a man who so clearly disapproved of a child being described as a parcel. She was not surprised to see that the subtleties of tone were lost on Mrs Mason Jones.

"Oh, it's a real nuisance. He has been sent to the wrong place. He will have to be sent back. The up train arrives in an hour. It's such a fuss. I will have to stay down here at the station and arrange things, and all because someone cannot carry out a simple task."

The boy seemed to detect that he was the focus of their conversation. He gave them a quick fearful look before focusing firmly on his shoes. Alice Young took her husband by the arm and whispered a few words. He nodded vigourously.

"Excuse me," he said, in the kind of voice no doubt used to good effect at school. "You cannot send a small child into the night on his own. It's nearly dark now. He should stay here, at least for tonight. Proper arrangements can be made in the morning."

He turned to Edith.

"Would you be greatly inconvenienced to take one extra child for tonight?"

Edith explained the situation at Overhill on the walk up from the station.

"I am the housekeeper for Captain James Threwe," she began. "Mr James was badly injured in the last war. The family name is pronounced 'true' by the way, not 'through'. It's a traditional Cornish name, though they have lived here in Devon for many years."

Then she described Overhill: the six bedrooms, five acres of grounds; the stream leading down to the mill.

"It's a lovely place for children."

The Youngs exchanged a glance; they had both caught the edge of sadness in Edith's voice.

"That sounds wonderful," said Mr Young quickly. "I should make proper introductions. I am Edward, and I am Head of an elementary school in Sutton; that's south of the river in London. Alice and I met whilst she was a teacher at my school. We are hoping that she will be allowed to teach down here, though it will depend on the local board."

Edward Young explained how nearly three hundred children from the school had been listed for evacuation, with most of the teachers relocating to Devon.

"I expect we will be scattered around the town in whatever accommodation can be found."

The small group had been walking by the light of the moon for some time. They turned up a narrow lane overshadowed by trees and Edith produced a bicycle torch to light the way.

After following a stone wall for a few hundred yards they came to an open gateway and a gravelled drive. Edith led the way to the front porch, where she had left an oil lamp burning so that there would be a light to find her keys. A soft glow in the summer house at the end of the garden offered a clue as to James Threwe's whereabouts. Edith sighed with relief, James was clearly working on his latest photography project, introductions could wait 'til morning.

She opened the door and ushered the visitors into the hall.

"We have a modern range for cooking, and radiators for heating upstairs, but no electricity or gas," she said. "At the moment I am managing the house without additional help. So there is plenty of room."

The children had been absolutely silent on the way up from the station. As the adults crossed the threshold the little girl sought her mother's hand. The boy waited for a moment before joining them, standing awkwardly to one side. Edith hesitated for a moment then took his hand firmly.

"I expect that you have had a long day young man, let's find you a room and get you to bed. Would you like some cocoa?"

The boy nodded quickly. Edith turned to the Youngs.

"Mr James' injury left him unable to speak, though he can hear perfectly well. I expect he will see you both in the morning."

After cocoa and tea had been dispensed and bedrooms allocated, Edith escorted the boy to the bathroom. His parcel contained a change of clothes, but Edith took one look at the grimy underwear and decided that she would wash all his clothes so that they would have time to dry over the kitchen range overnight.

"I've run the bath; it's nice and warm. You pop your things off and I'll take them for the wash."

Edith stood by the door as the boy undressed.

"So your name is Michael," she said.

"Yes ma'am."

"And do you have a last name?"

"Yes ma'am. It's Ratcliffe ma'am."

"There's no need to call me ma'am. My name is Edith Penros; you can call me Edith."

"Yes ma'am … sorry … Edith."

Michael leant forward to put his clothes on the bathroom

stool, then turned to get into the bath. Edith stepped forward to help, then froze in shock. The boy's back was a kaleidoscope of colour, from dull mustard yellow to vivid purple. The bruising reached across his buttocks to his thighs and was decorated by a series of angry red lines.

"It's alright, I can manage," he said.

"Oh, that's …" her voice tailed off. "Excuse me Michael … I must …"

Edith fled down the corridor and knocked at the door to the Young's bedroom. There was a short pause:

"Yes, who is it?"

"It's Edith, Mr Young. Miss Penros, the housekeeper, could I trouble you for a moment?"

After a short delay the headteacher appeared in dressing gown and pyjamas. He said nothing in answer to Edith's 'there's something I think you should see'; but his expression conveyed the very clear message that night time disturbances were highly irregular and that the matter, whatever it might be, should have been left 'til the light of day.

In the bathroom Edith turned to the the puzzled man standing by the door.

"I am just going to give Michael's hair a wash," she said, as her wide eyes tried to signal a explanation.

"Could you stand up, Michael?"

The boy obeyed and Edith heard the sharp intake of breath from the tall figure in the doorway. Edward Young stepped past her and pulled up the bathroom's cane chair. He leant forward and gently turned the boy's shoulders until the two were face to face.

"Who did this Michael? Who gave you these marks and bruises?"

The boy turned to look at Edith, then back to the teacher. Fear and indecision filled the child's eyes with tears and made his face crumple. Edward leant forward until their two faces were almost touching. He took the boy's hands in his own and spoke in a voice so soft that Edith could barely hear the words.

"Don't be afraid, you are not in any trouble. You are safe here with us, but if we are to keep you safe, then we need to know what has happened."

The story flooded out, all jumbled together, a torrent of tears and tragedy. Waking one morning to find a mother on the kitchen floor, apparently unable to move nor speak. An awful day in the house alone; the neighbour's visit, the policeman and the stern woman from the Council.

Then the children's home, where he had been beaten on his very first night, seemingly as some kind of downpayment set against future misdeeds. A second beating followed a week later, the night before the council lady came to tell Michael that he would be staying at the home. The confused story of losing his way at the station in Bristol, rescued by a kindly sailor, being discovered at Exeter, when the adults around him finally realised that the little boy sharing their carriage was travelling alone.

"But why did they put you on the train to Totnes?" asked Edith.

"They didn't."

The station master at Exeter had sat him down on a platform bench and told him to stay put.

"I'll telephone and see what's what," the man had said.

But Michael had not stayed put; he'd jumped on the first train to arrive and been put off by the guard at Totnes because he had no ticket.

Edith and Edward exchanged smiles. This last piece of slapstick was easier to digest that the previous litany of pain.

At breakfast the next morning Edith introduced the Youngs to her employer. Edward Young saw a man of around his own age, perhaps a little taller, with a shock of almost black hair making a vivid contrast with skin that bore little evidence of contact with the sun. An untidy scar ran around the lower left side of James Threwe's face. The gash of shiny pink skin continued down to his collar line and was, presumably, the wartime injury that had caused the man to lose his voice. By the window stood Edith. Edward thought she might be thirty-ish; an impression that was later corrected by his wife, who reckoned on early forties.

"She has a lovely face and figure," said Alice that evening. "Put her in some decent clothes and she would make quite an impression."

Edward had not survived ten years of married life without understanding the risks inherent in remarking on other women's powers of attraction, so his reply was a neutral 'I suppose so'.

But he had wondered that morning what Edith might look like with her hair down; a thought he instantly consigned to oblivion as he dealt with the complexities of talking to a man who could make no reply.

As Edith watched the two men from the doorway her focus was on the boy upstairs, and the need for a positive reaction from James. She was nervous about how he might respond, after living in isolation for so long. The requisition letter announcing that Overhill had been allocated a group of evacuees had hardly been welcome. But, after the awkward introductions, James listened with obvious horror to the description of Michael's situation. He reached for the notepad on the desk and wrote:

We cannot send him back to his tormentors.

Edward nodded in agreement.

"He is an evacuee," he said. "And we would like him to be an evacuee with us, here at Overhill … if you would agree. I will make some discreet enquiries as to the fate of his mother, but from the boy's account of events it looks as if the poor woman has passed away. In the meantime I can add him to my school roll … we can arrange a more permanent solution once the emergency is over."

Edward paused and looked at James' pale face.

"But Overhill is your house and all this disruption must be very unsettling for you."

James reached out and touched Edward's arm. He smiled and offered his hand as confirmation of his agreement. Edith breathed a sigh of relief, and not just over Michael's future. It had been a long time since she had seen her employer smile.

There remained the thorny problem of what to say to Mrs Mason-Jones, who had promised to come to Overhill that morning to collect Michael and begin the process of finding his proper destination. The two men turned to Edith for insight.

"She will want to do what is proper, but that is not the same as what is right," said Edith. She turned to James Threwe.

"But she has great respect for your family, sir. If you were to make your feelings plain. Or even seek the support of your brother …"

James had made a sweeping negative gesture with his hands, and scribbled a note.

Not Rupert. Wait – see what the woman has to say.

In the event their nervousness was unjustified. At midday there was a ring of the bell. Edith opened the front door to the portly figure of Agnes Davy, who announced that Mrs Mason-Jones had taken to her bed.

"She says it's the 'fluenza, but that woman always spreads jam with a spade. No Edith, I won't come in; I have my own list to visit and now there's Maisie's list to do as well. I'm supposed to inspect the rooms, but who's got the time to do that, and besides, don't seem right, poking round in people's houses. Now then, where's my piece of paper?"

Agnes tapped her pockets then heaved her handbag onto the hall table.

Edith took the opportunity to attempt an interruption.

"There's a boy, Michael … Michael Ratcliffe."

"Not on the list you were given?"

Agnes scanned a crumpled register, running a stubby red finger down the list of names.

"Not on this one either. Everything's all topsy turvy. The Carters have five when they should have had three, tho' goodness knows where they are going to put them. And Mrs Trescott, she only got the one girl, and her in that big house all by herself. The boy will be another from the London school I expect."

Edith watched as her visitor rummaged for a pencil, smoothed out the crumpled paper on the hall table, and carefully added Michael's name to her list.

"Ratcliffe with 'T'? You won't know the address I suppose. I'll put the school for now, sort it out later. Is he alright … any bother?"

This was a purely rhetorical question. Paper and pencil were being stowed into the capacious handbag and Agnes was buttoning her coat for the road. A shapeless hat crammed onto a mass of wayward curls and Agnes was out of the door. After a few yards she half turned and waved.

"Give my love to your mother," she shouted, apparently addressing the flower beds.

Edith watched as the woman scurried down the drive.

"No bother," she said quietly. "No bother at all."

***

A year later Edith sliced freshly baked bread in the kitchen, and wondered whether the hens would carry on laying for a few more weeks. A morning routine had become established at Overhill over the past months. Edward Young rose early and took his breakfast with Edith in the kitchen before leaving for the school in the town. He had acquired a bicycle, and set off each morning for the Masonic Hall, where the temporary school had found a home.

"It is a blissful ride into town, and a hard slog back up the hill," he said at dinner after the first day. "It's fresh air and exercise. I'm sure it will do me good – eventually."

The town school was for the older children, 10 to 14. The local school board had considered Edward Young's request to employ Alice as a teacher, and the committee had agreed on the strict understanding that the irregularity would persist only for the duration of the emergency. The parish hall near Overhill was duly converted into a classroom and Alice installed as teacher for the younger evacuee children. A couple of local families opted for the school because it offered an escape from the long walk into town. This intermixing of town and country was unusual; the London children had acquired a fearsome and not altogether undeserved reputation. Most parents were keen to keep their offspring as far away as possible from what they saw as a collective bad influence.

Her own breakfast done Edith made a pot of coffee and took a cup through to the morning room for James, who was in the window seat with his drawing pad, trying to focus on the blue tits feeding on the dried breadcrumbs Edith had put out in the garden.

Michael appeared from the kitchen, knelt in front of the fire and began making twists from sheets of newspaper. He had already chopped sticks into kindling, and he was making ready to light the fire. This had been his morning job since the day after he arrived.

Edith popped her head around the door to check on the firelayer's progress, then returned to the kitchen.

Bureaucratic muddle and delay meant that the relocated school did not open until October, effectively giving the Young family a three week holiday, which they used to explore the Overhill grounds and local area. The little girl, Elisabeth, clearly revelled in the change of setting. She volunteered to look after the hens and it seemed to Edith that her ambition was to make them the the best fed bantams for miles around.

The two children hit it off straight away, becoming instant friends. Elisabeth was a year younger, but usually took the lead in their games around the estate. The stream was a favourite; the two disappeared for hours, returning with muddy clothes and jam jars full of samples for James Threwe to identify.

Alice Young appeared at the kitchen door.

"Anything I can do?"

Edith eyed the crisp white blouse and shook her head.

"Not in your school clothes. Michael is down, but Lisbet hasn't appeared yet."

"Oh, that child," said Alice. "She'd better not be out with the hens; her dress is clean on."

Edith smiled as the younger woman went in search of her wayward daughter.

A few seconds later Alice reappeared in the kitchen with a thunderous face and an unrepentant Elisabeth in tow. The girl had mud on her shoes and stockings, and was sent upstairs to change.

The two children attended the parish hall school; a decision that did not go down well with Elisabeth, who believed that she should be allowed to attend the 'big school' in town with her father. In Sutton she had only just moved up a class, and to be back with the little ones was a hard thing to stomach. The fact that Michael, a year older, was in the same situation made no impact on the girl's opinion.

"Besides," her father had explained. "I have to go on a bicycle, and much earlier than you would need to set off. And you would be late back as well … it's out of the question Lisbet."

Elisabeth adored her father, and the matter was clearly decided, but she expressed her disapproval in small transgressions that fell just short of wilful disobedience. These minor mutinies were almost exclusively aimed at her mother. In stark contrast the girl was a model of good behaviour with Edith, who sometimes thought that the child's acquiescence, though welcome, was yet another tactic in the battle with Alice.

Edith loaded a tray with bread, butter, jams and marmalade and took it through to the breakfast room. Michael was squatting in front of the growing fire, watching the flames.

"Enough fire worship. Go and wash those hands then come and help me lay the table."

"Yes, Edith," said the boy, as he fed another stick of kindling into the fire.

"Don't you 'Yes, Edith' me. Up you get and off you go."

In the window seat James Threwe laid aside his drawing pad, made a mock stern face at the boy, then inclined his head towards the kitchen.

"Oh alright then." Michael grinned, stood up with exaggerated reluctance, and walked into the kitchen, undoing his butler's apron as he went.

"And hang that up," said Edith. "Don't leave it on the table."

"Yes, Edith," said Michael, laughing as he shut the door.

In the breakfast room the two adults exchanged wry smiles. James turned back to his drawing pad and Edith began to lay the table. Michael reappeared and, after having his hands inspected, began to ferry cutlery from the sideboard.

Once the breakfast things had been cleared away, Alice set off with the children to school and Edith had a few moments to herself. The new arrivals had settled in far better than she had expected. The Youngs were delighted with Overhill; Alice Young confiding that their room was at least twice the size of their bedroom in London, 'and with a connecting bathroom!'

The couple seemed to approve of every aspect of their new life: the walk into Totnes, the boats on the river, the narrow streets and miscellany of shops.

The Youngs were accepting of James Threwe's situation in a way that Edith found remarkable. There was no shock, no prurient curiosity masquerading as concern, no questioning about the niceties of her relationship with her employer. It occurred to her that London people possibly had more experience of these things, and were less likely to jump to conclusions. Whatever the explanation she was grateful.

Curiously the war barely impacted on their lives. It was not that they were untouched. Edward took a newspaper and they listened to the news on the Home Service every evening after supper. There were shocks and jolts; setbacks like Dunkirk caused dismay and momentary despair. But daily life in Totnes continued as normal: the post was delivered; spring lambs arrived on the neighbouring fields; the summer of 1940 was the best that many could remember. The newspaper headlines were happening in places far away, offstage, beyond the bounds of their comfortable routine. This wasn't just Edith's view; a number of the evacuees were recalled to London over the summer break; their parents convinced that the danger from the skies had been exaggerated. Alice's class was reduced to just twelve children, and there were discussions about relocating the school back to Sutton.

In many ways the last twelve months had been the happiest that Edith could recall since she was a child. She loved the sense of being part of and surrounded by a family: sharing shopping expeditions and cooking recipes with Alice; discussing the vicissitudes of raising an only child with Edward, and playing board games on winter nights with the children.

Added to this was the joy of watching Michael peel off the layers of fear and uncertainty. Slowly, as the weeks turned into months, the tears appeared less often, and were replaced by a mischievous sense of humour that was the best possible evidence that he felt secure in his surroundings. The Youngs he treated with deference and affection, but his closest relationship was with Edith.

On a couple of occasions he had called her 'Mum' and, though she had always corrected the mistake, the word had given rise to a glow of pleasure and a sense of belonging that was achingly real. Alice often commented that Edith treated Michael 'as if he were your own child', but the attachment went much farther than 'as if'.

In Edith's heart Michael became the child she had been denied by circumstance. The fear that kept her awake at night was no longer the war, but the possibility that the inexorable creep of bureaucracy would rediscover the boy and snatch him away.

A movement caught her eye as James Threwe walked through the courtyard beyond the kitchen window equipped with walking stick, binoculars and camera. James gestured in the general direction of the river. Edith nodded and waved; Michael's had not been the only transformation.

The man who had gently chided Michael in the breakfast room bore almost no resemblance to the diminished recluse of the last twenty years. James was still unable to speak, but in all other respects the change was remarkable. In the last six months he had cycled with Edward out onto the moors, visited both the schools, started a daily constitutional walk, and re-established a proper interest in the house and its upkeep.

Edith smiled in memory at the time around Easter when James had appeared in the kitchen and requested to see the house accounts. The kitchen table was soon covered with scraps of paper as James wrote question after question. He was clearly amazed that she managed on the allowance she was given. The 'audit' provoked a visit to the Hall and a confrontation with a bewildered Rupert.

A few weeks later Edith was shopping in the town when she bumped into Frank Settle, the Threwe estate manager. Frank drew her aside and recounted with glee how Rupert had been browbeaten into making an increase to the Overhill allowance.

"And by a mute an' all. It were all done with notes on bits o' paper. A 'ruddy blizzard of ruddy scribble', Rupert called it."

One morning in May James entered the breakfast room to discover Michael in floods of tears. Opened out on the rug was the front page of the Daily Express.

'Hood Sunk' screamed the headline.

Edith walked in with a breakfast tray to find the boy in the man's arms. James met her eyes and a wave of the hand and a sideways inclination of his head told the whole story. By this time they had both become familiar with the story of Michael's meeting with a sailor at Bristol's Temple Meads station. And they both recalled the name of the sailor's ship. Hood – HMS Hood – now sunk with all hands in the freezing Arctic sea.

Edith cursed herself for the oversight that had allowed the paper carrying the news of the sinking to find its way into the firelighting box. As she gathered up the child, James took the offending newsprint and cast it into the flames.

Later that morning James escorted Michael down to the summer house, territory that had previously been strictly off limits. With curtains drawn he showed the boy the process of developing a black and white image. The film was of an owl chick that Michael had discovered on the lawn below the oak. He had wanted to rescue the fledgeling, but James had shook his head, and made him return the ball of fluff to the lawn.

Together they had set up the camera, and sure enough, a parent bird swooped down to retrieve its errant offspring. But not before James had captured the moment on film.

In the summer house James and Michael measured out the fixing and developing solutions, rinsed the developed negative, and prepared the final print. At the end of the process James clipped the finished photographs to a hanger and turned to the boy. He raised a the palm of his hand outwards, pointed to the chair, and waited until Michael sat down. Then he opened a drawer and took out a Box Brownie camera. After carefully loading a film James handed the camera to Michael and gestured towards the door.

Photography requires subjects, so closer relationships were established with Edward and Alice. Expeditions to town were arranged, to photograph castle walls and river boatyards. Elisabeth was not excluded from the activity. A journey to the Hall produced a long buried dressing up box and the opportunity to be the centre of attention. She was a natural model, establishing an instant relationship with the camera lens.

Edith and Alice were reluctant subjects for the photographers.

Alice was taken on the lawn, looking awkward and ill at ease in a crisp white blouse and pleated skirt. Michael snapped Edith overseeing the Sunday lunch, wreathed in clouds of steam. Edith thought she looked unspeakable: harassed and forbidding. But the others admired the picture and Edward requested a copy.

"It's the way he's captured the bustle of the kitchen," he said. "And the way you are surrounded by steam from the range – quite remarkable composition, though I expect that's fortuitous."

Michael was a little put out by this back handed compliment. Both he and Edith knew that the result was exactly what he intended; and that the vegetables had been overcooked as a result. It was perhaps in compensation that James took a very different kind of picture. On a fine day in June, he presented Edith with a brown paper parcel and a note that said simply:

"For a photograph, please put it on."

Edith retired to her room and opened the parcel on the bed. It contained an evening gown, and at first she dared not even touch the fabric.

There was a full length sleeveless crepe de chine underdress, low cut and gathered under the bust, in dusky pink with beautiful black embroidery around the hem. This was overlain with a three quarter length overdress in transparent black lace, with a high bodice and sleeves to the elbow. It was clear that very little could be worn underneath. Edith assumed that it had had been left behind by a guest at the Hall; it was too small to belong to James' mother.

Eventually she realised that James would be waiting. She took off her overall and dress, hesitated for a few seconds and then removed her shift. Carefully she squeezed herself into the underdress, pulled the black lace over her head and smoothed it down. She turned to look at her reflection in the mirror and coloured instantly. The dress clung to her body and showed far too much bust, even with the high lace bodice. But … but, it was beautiful. And fitted her perfectly.

Edith's first thought was to take it off. She could never be seen in such a thing, never mind be photographed. But she encountered the same problem as Rupert. It is difficult to argue with someone who cannot reply.

James

At midday James Threwe arrived back at Overhill to find a note on the hall table. Edith had gone up to the school and would be back with the children after three. His lunch was under a plate cover in the breakfast room and Frank Settle had arranged for a delivery of wood at around one o'clock.

James sighed, he had forgotten about Edith's promise to help Alice at the school. He dropped his walking stick into the rack and took his binoculars into the study. James glanced at his watch and wondered whether he had time to develop the film in his camera before the logs arrived. He decided not, but to save time later on he took the plate of sandwiches and the camera down to the summer house and prepared the fixing trays and chemicals.

James dropped the film cassette into a desk drawer to be dealt with later. He sat at the long bench munching the ham and water cress, studying the photograph on the shelf behind the door. It was Edith, in the ball gown he had retrieved from the Hall. She had been nervous and embarrassed and it had taken some time and a number of false shots before he achieved the composition he wanted. She was stood by the front door, bathed in the evening sunlight, with one hand against the stone pillar, looking down the drive towards an imaginary approaching carriage.

James was not certain when his love for Edith began. He did

know that in the past year they had grown closer, brought together by the arrival of a frightened little boy. The photograph on the shelf was tangible evidence of the change in their relationship, and he was sure that some at least of the affection he felt for her was returned. But he was her employer, and from a different class. Most important of all, he could not take her to one side and declare his affection because he had no voice to form the words.

James felt the rough edge of the long scar that ran from his forehead to his throat. It had not been an attack, or even a skirmish. One moment he had been chatting to one of the sergeants about rations and supplies. Then the shell hit and some perverse side effect of the blast threw his body out of the trench onto the open ground.

At first he thought that by some miracle he had escaped unhurt, but then he felt a warm sticky sensation on his face, and the taste of blood in his throat. When he explored the wound he was shocked to find that he could push his fingers through the side of his throat and up into his mouth. He found a cloth in a trouser pocket to hold against the wound, then he twisted onto his side so that he would not choke on the blood that was filling his mouth. A bullet zinged over his head. Voices shouted to ask whether he was injured. He tried to reply but his throat felt swollen and stiff and the words wouldn't form.

He was lying in full view of the German lines and every noise or movement produced rifle fire from the enemy trenches. His men could see him, but he knew that they would not venture out from safety until they had the cover of darkness. Over the next few hours it seemed that one of the less competent German soldiers was using his body for some much needed target practice. Bullets thudded into the surrounding mud, the wire behind him, and into his knapsack, greatcoat and body. He was hit three times in the back and legs. When night eventually fell and his men crept forward, they were fully expecting to retrieve a corpse.

James spent nearly twelve months in hospital. The wound on

his face became infected at the dressing station, requiring months of painful treatment before it healed. His shattered hip took equally long to repair. He had to learn to walk again and would always need a stick for anything longer than a stroll across the stable yard.

In May 1919, just over a year after he had been injured in Flanders, the hospital pronounced James fit to be discharged. But he could not speak. The doctors said that the vocal chords were undamaged and his voice might return.

On impulse James opened the summer house door and checked that the coast was clear. Then he sat down facing the mirror as he had done so many times before. He sat straight and breathed deeply, anxiously examining his reflection, knuckles white on the leather arms of the chair. His mind shouted the words 'Hello' and 'Good-day', but all that emerged from his lips was a rasping groan. He shook his head to dispel the feelings of bitterness, looking out of the window to the beauty of the garden.

'Summerhouse' was something of a misnomer; the building had been intended as a gardener's store and workshop, with a long potting bench and a fully glazed south facing wall to encourage the propagation of young seedlings in the Spring. It had a water supply, large sinks and an abundance of storage space. James had marked it as his territory a few days after moving into Overhill. It was a place of refuge, a sanctuary.

It was widely agreed that James' sojourns to the summerhouse were yet another manifestation of the shell-shock that had stolen his voice. Nothing could have been further than the truth. In those first few months after the war James' nights had been filled with terrifying flashbacks to the fear and pain of the trenches, but in daylight he was able to banish the images that ruled his dreams.

The cause of his daytime retreats was all too physical – it was Edith. She joined the Hall staff on leaving elementary school in the summer of 1915; she was fourteen and James two years older. Their first meeting was in the hall kitchen, when he crashed through the door following a rumour of lemonade and cannoned into the new kitchen maid causing her to drop a tray of cutlery.

James immediately apologised and dropped to his knees to help collect the scattered knives and forks. Two hands reached for the same spoon and their eyes met. James was startled by the lightly tanned face and deep brown eyes, but then Rupert came into the kitchen, resplendent in his Guards' uniform.

"What do we have here," he bellowed. "Little brother rolling on the floor with the new maid."

James and Edith rose together, hands full of cutlery, faces beetroot red.

"No need for the rouge, child," said Rupert, who was a full three years older than his brother. "I can quite see why you would want a tumble with this juicy little peach."

"Master Rupert! If you please," admonished the cook, with as much power and authority in her voice as she dared use to one of the family. She turned to Edith, anxious to remove the child from the scene.

"As for you my girl; those need to go back to the scullery and be washed over again. Quickly now."

James viewed his brother's reappearance with mixed feelings. He had always been the junior partner in their games and adventures. Rupert had always been the leader, whether it was a den to be built, a midnight raid on the kitchen or a trek up onto the moor. But the aloof stranger who returned from the army showed little inclination to share experiences. James had been looking forward to hearing Rupert's description of his first posting to France, but the response to James' eager questions was a sardonic 'soon be your turn'.

Rupert's leave lasted four days and he took every opportunity to tease James about his supposed love for the new maid. Rupert soon discovered her name, and would creep up behind James and whisper "Edith" as he passed, causing James to flush with colour all over again.

If the intended effect was to focus James' thoughts on the kitchen encounter then it was all too successful. James thought about the young girl constantly. She had smiled at him, he was sure of that. And her complexion, soft and glowing, every other female seemed pale and wan in comparison. Alone in his room James imagined ringing for her, to serve breakfast perhaps, or bring a freshly laundered shirt. He would be lying on the bed, or sitting by the window. She would knock, then walk in, and their eyes would meet just as they had in the kitchen.

And then … he had no idea. At school the dormitory conversations about girls were entirely theoretical, and usually focused on the bizarre anatomical details of other chaps' sisters. Edith simply did not belong in the same frame of reference. James strained to imagine what he might say or what she might do … but the answer was a blank, a void.

On Rupert's fourth day of leave he adopted an air of great mystery at breakfast, whispering 'wait 'til this evening'. James' father had already set in train the process that would lead to a commission in the Welsh Guards, and James was hungry for details about life at the Front. Despite the earlier rebuff, he hoped that the great secret might be a present, a pickelhaube perhaps, or a bayonet.

The evening came and Rupert refused to give any hint as to what might follow, maintaining an uncharacteristically earnest conversation with their parents about the chaps in the regiment.

At 10.00 Rupert glanced at his clock and looked pointedly in James' direction before claiming the need of a good night's sleep. James made a similar excuse and the two brothers met on the hall stairs.

Rupert took off his shoes and indicated that James should follow suit, then Rupert led the way up to the second floor, normally used when the Hall had guests. He paused at the plain door that divided the guest wing from the servants' quarters, opening the door a fraction to check the coast was clear.

To the right was the bare functionality of the servants' stairs, at the head of which was a small storeroom for guests' cases and hatboxes. Rupert produced a key and opened the door. James noticed that the hinges had been recently oiled. Rupert turned and ushered James through, a finger over his lips commanded silence. There was just enough moonlight from the window to make out the dusty shelves.

Taking great care to make no noise, Rupert moved a small case to expose a crack in the panelling. Placing the case carefully on the floor, he pressed his face to the wall for a moment, then smiled and leant towards his brother.

"Take a look," he whispered.

James leant forward and pressed his face to the panelling, half knowing what he would see. The crack led through to a corresponding hole in the adjoining wall, to one of the servants' rooms. A pair of single beds and a bedside table with a mirror. One of the beds occupied by someone who had her back to him, apparently reading a book.

James' eyes focused on the second bed, where a young girl was brushing her hair. She was wearing a shift, or perhaps it was a nightgown. Her arms were bare and the curled up position on the bed allowed the garment to ride up above her knees. The long brown hair obscured the face, but James knew who it was.

He stared, fascinated, compelled to remain with his eye pressed to the gap, despite the insistent voice in his head that implored him to 'look away, look away'.

"What can you see?"

James turned as if to answer, but a movement drew his eye back to the room. Edith, putting the hairbrush on the table. She stood and yawned, stretching her arms above her head. The bedside light shone through the thin material of her shift, silhouetting her body.

James' whole being focused on the vision beyond the wall. Rupert sensed the tension and tried to pull his brother away from the hole, causing an audible scuff as his foot collided with the small case. In the microsecond before he was pulled away from the panelling, James saw Edith stiffen, then stare at the wall, seemingly straight into his eyes.

In the following days Edith didn't appear upstairs in the house. A rumour emerged; the spyhole had been discovered by the housekeeper, who unleashed a tirade of outrage on the junior male staff. The next week James returned to school. At the end of that term he went straight on to his regiment, only returning home for his final embarkation leave.

At James' farewell dinner Edith was drafted in to serve at table. When their eyes met at the dining room door, it was as if he had been transported back to the summer before, to the kitchen floor and an electric touch of fingers over a tray-load of scattered cutlery. He had been brave enough to speak:

"How are you, Edith?"

And she had replied:

"Well enough, Sir. We are all wishing you the best fortune in France."

James' father gave a warning cough and Edith stepped back into position with her head down.

In France James' regiment took great pride in maintaining dry, well-equipped trenches, and the work that involved filled his daylight hours. He joined the battalion during the horror of Passchendaele, and led his men in just one attack, before their unit was pulled back and transferred to a quieter section of the line.

Military action on the new sector was rare, usually consisting of officer led patrols to test the enemy's defences. Orders were to 'work up' the replacements, of which there were many, in readiness for the big push that everyone assumed would follow. Along with most of the other officers James assumed that he would be killed in the next battle. Work and whisky were the usual antidotes to the depression created by the seeming inevitability of death.

In the evenings James eschewed the card games and drinking

sessions and retired to his bunk with a book as an excuse for some private meditation. Closing his eyes he imagined himself in the quiet normality of home: riding across the moor, fishing on the Dart, house parties at the weekend, music in the evenings – and Edith, who, increasingly became the prime focus of his thoughts.

Amongst James' officer colleagues it was agreed that the old conventions would be torn down after the war. Survivors, if there were any, would see a simpler, fairer world, unfettered by nineteenth century proprieties. James imagined returning home and courting the young housemaid. Sometimes this led swiftly to a rose petal strewn wedding. In other variations the pair would flee to British East Africa and raise cattle, or travel north to Gretna, returning to Threwe Hall to present his parents with a fait accompli.

This absorption with Edith grew in strength after James was wounded north of the Somme in March 1918. At his medical discharge the doctor had been confident that his voice would return. James remembered the man's exact words.

"The vocal chords are undamaged, It was your jaw and throat that needed time to heal. In a few weeks I am sure you will be talking again."

James had no reason to doubt the advice and he returned to Totnes fully expecting to be able to speak within days. The first surprise came when his father met him with the news that the decision had been taken to settle him at Overhill.

"We have engaged a housekeeper to help you recover."

In the summerhouse twenty years later James re-experienced the anger he had felt on the day. He had just spent over a year recovering. He had no wish for yet more time as a convalescent. Yet he lacked a voice to express his disapproval and had yet to develop the skill to properly communicate in other ways. And so allowed himself to be driven down to Overhill.

Then came the second surprise. At the door to meet him was Edith.

This was not how James had imagined their reunion. He had envisaged any number of scenarios, but a silent encounter between patient and nursemaid he had never foreseen. He attempted to speak on that first day, but it was too soon, and the resulting discomfort simply confirmed everyone's view of him as cruelly afflicted.

Over the next weeks and months James found himself trapped inside a relationship that others had decreed. As each day passed the possibility of expressing any of his feelings to Edith became more and more difficult. Paradoxically her night-time ministrations made the situation worse. She was caring and thoughtful, but as a loyal and dutiful servant, not as a prospective lover.

The result was that his throat tightened every time he came close to her. It was as if his vocal chords had been tied in a knot. The solution was to take himself away as much as possible. He adopted the summer house as his personal retreat, and cultivated an interest in photography, partly because he had been left a camera in the effects of an officer colleague, but also because the necessity for absolute darkness during the developing process gave a rationale for his solitary confinement.

In the last year there had been a warming in their relationship, he had been able to look Edith in the face and smile, and see the smile returned. He was spending more time in the house, and occasionally they sat at breakfast together. This was entirely due to the presence of their guests, and he dreaded their departure and the return of the cool formality that had been the norm.

A buzzard dropped down onto the lawn and began to tear at the young squirrel held in its talons. A pair of magpies alighted alongside the big bird and began to dance around the feeding predator in the hope of joining the feast. James opened a drawer and reached inside for his camera. Belatedly he remembered that he had finished the cartridge and would need to load a new film. He looked into the garden only to see the buzzard take flight with the magpies in pursuit.

The loud clatter of a lorry turning onto the courtyard cobbles jolted James out of his reverie. It was Graeme from the estate, with a load of logs for the store. James left the summer house and walked out into the yard. He liked Graeme who, along with most ex-servicemen, understood the hidden scars left by the war and demonstrated an empathy that was conspicuously absent in most civilians.

Graeme's son Malcolm sat grinning atop the lorry's load wearing what were obviously his father's cast offs: a collarless shirt and battered corduroy trousers held up with a broad belt. He smiled and waved. At fourteen it was his first September since bidding farewell to school, and he was enjoying the freedom.

"Usual place, Mr James?" Graeme shouted.

James nodded and watched as the lorry was skilfully navigated into position by the wood-store. Graeme jumped down from the cab and Malcolm started passing the logs down to his father.

A sudden roar caused all three to look to the sky; three black shapes flying down the valley.

"Dad, look," shouted the boy. "They're bombers. I think they're German! JU 88s. Look! You can see the black crosses."

The aeroplanes followed the path of the river out to sea. In a few seconds they were gone, but there was enough time to see the the glass nosecone, the twin engines, and the black crosses on the fuselage. And then there was a fourth, with the same profile and markings, but higher in the valley than the others, and trailing a thin plume of black smoke.

"It's going to come right over us," shouted Malcolm.

A new engine note overrode the dull drone of the bomber. A higher note, growing in intensity until the shape of a smaller aircraft could be seen, diving down from the clouds, seemingly on a collision course with the lumbering black shape of its enemy.

"It's a Hurricane," screamed the boy: "a Hurricane."

The wings of the newcomer twinkled with yellow sparks and

James heard a noise like a football rattle; an all too familiar noise, despite the twenty odd years that had passed since he had last heard the sound: machine guns.

"Shoot," screamed Malcolm, jumping up and down with excitement. "Shoot!"

The fighter turned away, and was lost in a second over the brow of the hill. The three watchers transferred their attention to the bomber.

"He must have hit it," said the boy. "He must."

And it seemed that he had. The plume of smoke trailing from the right hand engine thickened and turned to flame. The aircraft dipped first to the right, then left as the pilot fought the controls. Finally, just as it was about to disappear over the rise, there came half a dozen black dots from the centre of the fuselage. Tiny, insignificant, and soon lost to view.

At first it seemed that the small black eggs must fall in the field beyond the house, but their trajectory took them towards the familiar buildings on the rise beyond the stubble fields. They saw the flash first, white then red, followed by a growing black cloud. Then came the noise and shock of the explosion. James calculated distances, but the results simply confirmed what he already knew. It was the school; the bombs had hit the school.

Malcolm was still drunk on the excitement of the moment.

"The Hurricane did get him. I knew he would. He'll not get far though, not on one …"

"Go to the Big House," shouted a hoarse and unfamiliar voice. "Get them to telephone. They must send the brigade and ambulances to the school."

Father and son stared at James in amazement. He tried again, speaking calmly and with as much authority as he could muster.

"Malcolm. Go, now. To the Big House. They must telephone for help. Graeme. Turn the lorry round, we must get to the school. Smartly now."

Perhaps it was the parade ground 'smartly now' that shocked the other man into action. Graeme turned to his son.

"Get down and do what the Master says. Quick as you can."

Malcolm hesitated for a second and then began to run to the house on the hill. Graeme jumped into the cab, started the engine and turned the vehicle around. James dashed into the kitchen and reappeared with a handful of tea-towels.

"Best I could do." he said as he climbed into the cab.

"Let's hope we don't need them, sir," said Graeme.

James fingered his scar. His voice had been returned to him, but at what cost? He looked ahead to the school, but the high hedge-line obscured the view. Forcing his hands down onto his knees, he tried to control his emotions. He would be no use to Edith or the children in a funk. Graeme glanced sideways.

"Almost there, sir."

Seconds later Graeme swung the old lorry into the school yard, and any hopes the two men may have harboured were quickly dispelled. There was an eerie silence: the air was full of tiny pieces of paper falling slowly back to the ground. Two bombs had bracketed the parish hall, landing harmlessly in the stubble fields either side of the buildings. One had landed in the corner of the playground and another had smashed through the tile roof, exploding in the confines of the improvised classroom.

The hall had been transformed into a shattered ruin: roof gone, walls reduced to a few feet of brickwork. Only the doorframe remained, bracketing an empty space. A fierce fire burned where the small oil tank had once stood in the corner of the school yard.

James jumped down from the truck and headed for the empty shell of the classroom. There were no bodies, nothing that was recognisably human, but it was clear that most of the children had been inside. Scraps of clothes, splashes of blood, other things that he found it difficult to focus on: fingers, feet, faces. In one corner lay a larger form that might have been Alice. Certainly it looked like her skirt. He approached close enough to identify what had once been a crisp white blouse, then turned away. Edith was here somewhere.

A shout took him outside.

"Tourniquet … I've nowt to use." Graeme had found a child.

James took off his belt and held the remains of an arm whilst Graeme threaded the buckle and pulled it tight until the blood stopped flowing. The little girl was unconscious, white faced and cold to the touch. Her clothes had been blasted away. James thought for a moment, then ran to the lorry and brought the old blanket that Graeme kept in the cab for his collie dog. Together they wrapped the girl tight then Graeme held her in his arms. In the distance they could hear the fire engine's bells.

"Soon be here," whispered Graeme to the unconscious little girl, and then to James.

"Anyone alive in there?"

"No," said James. "The bomb must have exploded inside the room."

His eyes searched the yard.

"I've checked this side," said Graeme. "Not been over there though."

He pointed to the corrugated iron outhouse that served as a privy. James picked his way over the debris. The lavatory was in the far corner, and had been knocked sideways by the blast. The roof was off and the door swung by one hinge. James checked inside and then looked around. The rubble was worse here; the blast had destroyed the school's gable end, scattering blocks of stone across the yard.

Something made James look behind the privy, in the tiny corner against the boundary wall. Sensible shoes, bare legs and a familiar blue dress. Edith was huddled against the wall, shielding a child. Blood trickled from the little girl's ears and nose. James knelt down, pulled the hair away from her face, and put his ear next to the small mouth – nothing at first, then the faintest of breaths.

With a clamour of bells an ambulance turned into the yard, followed by a fire engine. Uniformed men jumped down from the vehicles and stood and stared at the destruction.

"Over here," yelled James. "This way, in the corner."

An ambulance man arrived, and the two men managed to prise the child away from Edith's grasp.

"This one's alive at least," said the medic, before carrying the child away.

James moved Edith into a sitting position and put an arm around her shoulders. Someone brought water and a cloth and James trickled some of the liquid over Edith's face and into her mouth. She responded, shuddering gently before opening her eyes and attempting to stand.

"No," said James. "Stay put for the time being."

"There was an aeroplane," she said, looking dazedly at the devastation. An engine roared and bells sounded as the ambulance left the playground. In the distance James could hear more bells climbing the hill from the town.

"Mary, is she alright? I tried to hide; I thought it was going to crash."

Beyond the wall James saw Graeme's boy Malcolm approaching across the field with Michael and Elizabeth. James shook his head violently and, with a perception far beyond his years, the fourteen year old steered the children away from the school before they had chance to see over the wall.

"We've to go back to Overhill," he said, ignoring their protests and leading them back down the hill.

James looked at Edith.

"Mary is fine," he said.

Edith's eyes met James' and she seemed to focus for the first time.

'It's James … and you're talking. It is you, isn't it James?"

"It is," said James. "I thought you were dead."

"I can't hear very well," said Edith. "My head is buzzing."

James leaned forward and kissed her forehead, then leant back so that she could see his lips.

"I love you."

"And I love you," she said drowsily. "I'm so pleased you can talk again."

Nicole

A line of students queued to present identity documents and ration cards, in exchange for a thick folder of paperwork, including a timetable that had been out of date before it was printed. It was admissions day at Camberwell and Nicole had been roped in to help with the new intake.

No-one could have missed Libby, by far and away the most colourful figure in the room. Her definition of 'make do and mend' comprised a pair of sailor's trousers cut off below the knee, with a bright red breton style top and a blue spotted headscarf tied as an alice band. Nicole prayed that the queue would deliver this wonderful creature to her desk.

Which it did. She was seventeen, and enrolling on the art foundation course. Her name was Elisabeth Young. Once the formalities were done the girl lingered.

"Can I help with anything else?" asked Nicole.

Libby leant forward.

"Thing is … I've nowhere to stay."

Nicole looked at the admission form.

"But your address here is given as …"

"Sutton. Yes I know, but it's too far out, and anyway – that's where my father lives, so obviously I don't want to live there. Anyway, he's just got married. I thought I'd share, but Christina –

we went to school together – she says she's already got a flatmate, so now I've got nowhere to go."

Nicole looked at the girl, with her guileless, too bright eyes, and found herself whispering.

"I have a spare bed, you could stay with me."

It was strictly against the rules, and the pair had to finalise the details in the ladies' loo outside the admissions hall. But, by the end of the day, Libby, together with her surprisingly extensive wardrobe, was successfully installed in Nicole's Peckham flat. The first item to be unpacked was a battered doll called Treacle, given pride of place on Libby's pillow.

That evening Nicole heard Libby's story, about her mother's death in Devon, the return to bomb damaged London, her father's decision to marry again, and the ambition that led to Camberwell.

"I just feel that there's something inside me, to do something, be someone."

Nicole nodded, hardly hearing the words, focused instead on the animated face and boyish figure of her new friend.

"There was some family money that came to me when mummy died," continued Libby. "So I can pay towards the rent, and I can help out and cook a little."

Nicole wanted to kiss her. She had never known an attraction so strong. She felt impelled to cross the room and take the girl in her arms.

"I expect we'll work things out," she said, nodding sagely, in what she hoped was a mature, experienced way. The reality was that she was barely three years older than Libby, and had been in London for less than six months. Nicole had never had a true girlfriend, or any close friend at all. Men found her cold, women seemed to think that she was too intense, or not intense enough. The nearest she had come to a real friend was Annette at secretarial school in Ipswich.

"It's not your fault," she'd said. "But you're so buttoned up. You come across as if you were their nanny, or an older sister. It's not what girls want."

Nicole found the comment unhelpful and irritating. She knew she was stiff and formal. She was painfully aware that girls found her stuffy and tiresome. She wanted to be a good sport, but didn't know how.

Applying for jobs in London was an attempt to rectify the situation. She would begin again, make the effort to be more outgoing, less of a frump. But in the three months since she started work at Camberwell she had been out in company on just three occasions. Once with an aunt who lived in Greenwich, once with another new starter in Camberwell's accounts department, and once with a man she met at the library, who invited her for a Sunday afternoon walk on Peckham's common, then tried to put his hand up her skirt.

Nicole tried to be patient and philosophical about the lack of success, especially about Suzy the new starter, who fled back to her family in Abergavenny the following day, but she had to admit that it was discouraging.

And then providence dropped Libby into her lap.

In that first week the two girls went out almost every evening, doing the kind of things that Nicole would never have done on her own. They ate at a rather dreadful cafe, watched an incomprehensible play in Chelsea, crammed into a scruffy Soho basement to listen to some strange American music, and joined a group of Libby's student friends at the Camberwell Arms, where Libby, who was six months underage, persuaded Nicole to try a vodka and tonic.

By the end of the week Nicole had spent nearly ten pounds doing things that she would never have chosen to do – but she didn't mind at all. Libby, it seemed, did not find Nicole boring, or stuffy, or tiresome, possibly because she was young, and finding her way, but mainly because Libby craved attention, and Nicole provided that in abundance.

This wasn't one-way traffic. On their free evening Libby

dismantled Nicole's wardrobe, sorting items on the bed whilst exclaiming 'you can't wear this' and 'this will have to go'. Or simply giving an eloquent sniff as another innocent garment hit the growing pile of rejections.

After considering Nicole's workwear Libby rejected a blouse that buttoned to the neckline in favour of a looser, simple design that she pulled out of the capacious trunk the two girls had dragged up the stairs when Libby moved in. The blouse was styled like a man's open necked shirt, and in Nicole's view, showed too much chest.

"But you have a great bust, you should make the most of it. And besides, that blouse is too big for me," said Libby. "And your hair, you should wear it straight, like Veronica Lake."

"Where do you find all these clothes?" wondered Nicole. "When I go shopping everything's utility, that's if I have enough coupons to go in the first place."

Libby's answer was to take Nicole to the Saturday market on Portobello Road, where there seemed to be no shortages at all.

"But you said this was a second-hand market," whispered Nicole as they passed trestle tables groaning under the weight of goods. "A lot of this is new."

"From the docks," winked Libby. "I won't tell if you don't."

Libby re-organised the flat, putting the beds closer together and moving Nicole's alarm clock to make space on their shared dresser for three framed photographs. One showed Libby as a child, wearing a gossamer creation that was clearly intended as a fairy costume. The others were of her parents. Her father had been taken in a schoolmasterly pose, alongside Libby in a new school uniform. The third picture was in a black frame, and showed a pretty young woman in a crisp white blouse and long pleated skirt. She looked anxious and reluctant.

"That's my mother. She was killed in the war."

Libby hesitated, completely focused on the picture:

"I should have been killed as well, but I'd bunked off with my boyfriend."

Nicole reeled for a moment, torn between amazement that Libby had possessed a boyfriend at the age of ten, and shock that she had been cutting school at the same time.

Libby turned away from the framed picture.

"That's when I decided I was going to be an artist. I suppose it's always been with me, Art I mean. It was the only thing I did well at school – much to daddy's shame."

After the expedition to Notting Hill and the Portobello market Libby and Nicole celebrated their purchases with a half bottle of vodka and a bottle of Schweppes. They sat on Nicole's bed whilst Libby chattered about the college, the students, her lecturers and the shining career that awaited.

"A designer, I think. We were talking about design this week. It's something I have a real feeling for … I'm sure I could do it."

Nicole had never had more than two alcoholic drinks in succession, and she began to feel light headed. Libby decided that they would try on the clothes they has bought, including some exotic underwear snapped up from one of the stalls.

As Libby stripped down to her knickers Nicole tried to find an alternative focus for her attention, but her eyes were pulled back to the slim figure, with its boyish rear and petite breasts. When Libby posed for her attention Nicole looked away, blushing furiously, afraid of being discovered.

"Oh, you're embarrassed, you silly." said Libby. "There's no need to be, there's nobody here but us girls. Now come on, try this camisole."

Nicole blushed again, shaking her head.

"Not now, Libby, perhaps later."

But Libby was not about to be denied. Ignoring Nicole's feeble protests she pushed the bigger girl onto the bed and removed her blouse.

"Gosh," she said. "Look at these … much bigger than my little things," she cupped her own breasts in comparison. Nicole hardly dared to lift her head.

"Oh no, Libby, yours are perfect."

"Nicole, that's sweet of you, thank you," said Libby. "You are a love. I'm so lucky to have found you."

She leant forward and kissed her new friend on the mouth. It was a mere touch, a brush of the lips. And Libby immediately followed the kiss by easing the camisole over Nicole's head. But the effect was enormous, cataclysmic. Nicole was unable to move or speak. Her one desire was that Libby should kiss her again.

Libby failed to notice the earthquake that had happened before her eyes. She was more interested in the effect of the camisole. She pulled her friend over to the small mirror.

"See, it does suit you. I knew it would."

The moment was lost. Libby decided to pour herself another drink. Nicole declined.

"I'm a bit woozy, Libby. I think I should go to bed."

As Nicole retreated to the bathroom Libby gathered the things they had bought and stuffed them into a bag. She picked up a large book titled 'Twentieth Century Design' and settled down to plan her future.

One of Libby's first actions at the flat had been to remove the blankets, leaving her sleeping under an eiderdown and sheet. She slept naked except for a pair of knickers.

"I get too hot in bed with blankets and stuff," she explained. "Daddy says I'm exothermic, he made me look it up; it means 'a surface that radiates heat'."

Nicole found the nightly striptease disconcerting, and it was just as unsettling to undress in front of Libby's cool gaze. Nicole's solution was to get ready for bed in the bathroom, only emerging in her winceyette nightgown when she was certain that her flatmate was safely under the covers.

Once the lights were out Libby was soon asleep, but Nicole often lay awake into the small hours. She turned on her side and watched the face of her sleeping flatmate, the pale face framed by nut brown hair spread across the pillows. Libby sometimes talked in her sleep. On the first occasion Nicole crossed the room and stood by Libby's bed, unsure as to what to do. The girl was mumbling softly, but the words were meaningless.

A week after the visit to Portobello Road Nicole was awakened by the unmistakeable sounds of distress. Libby was deeply asleep, but she had kicked off the covers, her fists were clenched as she writhed from side to side, calling 'Mummy, stop, no' over and over again. Nicole left her bed and crossed the room. She shook Libby's shoulders, gently at first and then with more force.

"Libby, it's me, Nicole, you're alright. It's a dream."

Slowly the agitation subsided. The eyes opened, confused and unseeing.

"You're alright, it was a dream," repeated Nicole, holding her tight. They lay together, Nicole's arm around Libby's bare shoulders.

"I'm sorry," said Libby after a few minutes calm. "I get these nightmares."

"That's alright."

"I'm glad you were here."

"I'm glad too."

Nicole looked down at the pale face, inches from her own. Tentatively she kissed the soft skin, first on the cheek, then lightly on the mouth. Libby looked up in surprise and for one horrifying moment seemed about to break away. But then she snuggled closer.

"That was nice," she said. "I think you can do that again."

Nicole complied, more firmly this time. After a second or so Libby responded, leaning into the kiss and opening her mouth, hands reaching up and pulling Nicole into the embrace. After a deliciously long interval Libby broke away, looked up and grinned mischievously.

"Well, really!" she said, kissing the tip of Nicole's nose. "That was very naughty of you, and rather lovely ... but it's three o'clock, and I have an essay to finish in the morning ... so back to bed you go."

The older girl disengaged herself and returned to her own bed, where she lay awake until dawn, besieged by conflicting emotions. The joy of the encounter was uppermost, but underlain by a nagging fear that Libby would regret the embrace in the morning. They had gone too far, Libby would tell her friends, or even the authorities. Nicole would be labelled a lesbian, a pervert, a dyke. She would lose her reputation and her job.

She tried to reassure herself with sensible advice. Libby, after all, had just as much to lose. But the worries remained, and were only dispersed on the edge of sleep, when Nicole's thoughts returned to the kiss itself: wondrous, electrifying, bewitching. It was her first, and she would remember the moment for ever.

***

In the morning at breakfast Nicole was at first relieved and then a little disappointed when Libby made no reference to the night's events, a situation that continued for the rest of the week. The following Saturday Libby planned a trip into London to see Deborah Kerr's new film at the Odeon in Leicester Square. She was to go with her student friends, but the arrangements fell apart, and Libby and Nicole travelled up to the West End alone.

Kerr played a nun sent to set up a school in the Himalayas, and Nicole expected to see a story about poor peasant children being rescued by the saintly sisters. The first surprise came in the queue, comprised as it was, of the kind of people that Nicole imagined belonged to the Bloomsbury set – loud, strident, extravagantly dressed. The kind of people that would normally cause Nicole to shrink away, lest her Suffolk accent and plain clothes became a cause for comment.

The film was a revelation. Nicole sat transfixed, on the edge of her seat, focused on the shocking events and vibrant colours on the screen. At the terrifying climax, on a surreal Himalayan cliff edge, Nicole could barely watch. Her hand sought Libby's, and the two girls held tight as the nuns struggled for survival.

They made the journey back to Peckham in almost total silence. Their heads were full of things they could not say on a crowded bus. When they reached the safety of the flat it was if a dam had burst.

"I couldn't believe the end," said Nicole.

"The colours! I've never seen a film so – so luminous," said Libby. "And the lipstick scene – did you notice Sister Clodagh wearing lipstick at the end."

"She tried to wash it off, but it was there."

"Do you think they slept with each other?"

"The film people couldn't, not with nuns – I mean, it wouldn't be allowed."

"They couldn't show anything, silly. But that's what we were intended to think. 'I will stay with you' she said. And then they looked at each other."

Libby began to get ready for bed. Nicole retreated to the bathroom to undress. On this night in particular she didn't want to be faced with Libby's body. When she returned to the room the lights were out. She crept to her bed, only to find it already occupied – Libby – wearing bright red lipstick.

"Take that silly nightdress off and come here."

The following morning it was again as if nothing had passed between them. Nicole didn't know what she expected, but she expected something, and Libby's failure to acknowledge what had occurred was both confusing and disorientating. When Nicole looked at Libby she saw a lover, a soulmate, someone she could entrust with her heart. But the Nicole reflected from Libby's eyes was a flatmate still; a girlfriend, but not in the way that Nicole wished for.

As the nights passed without a repetition of their coupling Nicole began to believe that Libby regretted what had occurred. Perhaps Libby hadn't enjoyed their touching, or maybe Nicole had done something wrong. The easiest explanation was that Libby had simply found her unattractive in the flesh: too big, too tall, too bosomy. In the end Nicole decided that it was safer to pretend that nothing had happened. Until ten days later, when Libby crept into her bed.

This set the pattern for the next few months. The two girls were flatmates, friends and occasional lovers. Nicole ached for the affection and shared sense of belonging that she imagined should follow from lovemaking. But Libby remained distant. There were rare traces of something more; an occasional kiss in the morning and genuine concern when Nicole had a fall from a moving bus. But these were not the norm and Nicole eventually reconciled herself to a love that was reciprocated sporadically, if at all.

***

As the summer of 1948 approached Nicole began to experience a sense of panic. Foundation Art at Camberwell was a one year course, and would soon be over. Libby had completed her portfolio, and been congratulated by her tutor, only the end of year formalities remained. Libby would soon move on: to work, or to a university on the other side of the country, out of London, out of Nicole's life.

In the last week of May these worries were rendered irrelevant by three events over successive days. On the Monday Libby announced that she had been offered a place at nearby Goldsmiths to study Art & Design. The following day she started a summer job as a runner for Poppies, a model agency with offices near Tower Hill. On Wednesday she returned to Nicole's flat insisting that they must go to the Goldsmith's evening lecture.

"But I was going to wash my hair," protested Nicole.

"I don't want to go on my own. I won't know anyone, and everyone else is busy, so you just have to come."

The lecture subject was Libby's latest focus of interest: film and the film industry. The speaker was to be Carol Reed, director of 'The Fallen Idol', which the two girls had seen the previous month. But when they arrived at the college they found the director had sent his apologies, and the talk would be given by someone from the college film society – a photographer called Robbie O'Neill.

The substitution led to an audible groan of disappointment from the crowd, followed by a drift to the exit. The visibly embarrassed would-be speaker had to wait as more than half the audience left the hall in search of something better to do.

O'Neill was in his mid-twenties, dressed in shirt and black trousers, no tie or jacket. He turned out to be a confident speaker, and gave his depleted audience an entertaining account of the various roles to be found on a film set, from the 'talent' to the 'best boy'. He spoke without notes, moving around the front of hall, making eye contact and smiling easily at his audience. Nicole thought he looked like Montgomery Clift; Libby thought he looked wonderful.

"It's confusing, on my last film the 'best boy' was a girl." he said. "I'm actually the stills cameraman, but I assist the director of photography, who works under the film director, two very different jobs."

At the end of the talk Libby dragged Nicole down to the front of the hall to join a small group waiting to ask questions. The college caretaker hovered by the door, jangling a bunch of keys.

"Look's like we're being thrown out," said Robbie, looking at Libby as he picked up his motorbike jacket. "Do you mind asking your questions on the run."

Libby didn't mind at all, and Nicole followed behind as the pair exchanged differing views about monochrome versus technicolour film-making. On the pavement next to the college railings was a

BSA Gold Star 500cc motorbike. Robbie swung a leg over the machine and leant back.

"Are you a student here?"

Libby nodded. It was, after all, almost true.

"It's just ... no, you probably wouldn't be interested."

"Interested in what?"

Robbie looked at her again, this time with a professional air, appraising, judging. He explained that he had been given a commission 'photography, not film'. He had to find three girls for a portrait: two brunettes, and a blonde.

"The brunettes need to be petite ... slim and attractive."

"Attractive?"

"Definitely. You fit the bill to a 'T'. But it's probably not your thing."

Nicole watched as her friend pretended to consider the matter carefully.

"Why shouldn't it be my thing?" said Libby. "I work part-time for a model agency."

"Great," said Robbie. He ferreted for a pen and paper. "Look, here's my address. Could you come over on Saturday morning? About ten, we could talk about it then. Can I give you a lift home?"

He looked up at Nicole.

"I'd offer you a lift," he said. "But I wouldn't get you both on board."

Libby looked back at Nicole as if seeing her for the first time. Robbie kick-started the bike, revving it noisily before settling the engine down to a low growl. Libby stepped over the saddle onto the pillion, and put her arms around Robbie's waist.

"Hold tight," he said, and they were gone, the bike turning right at the end of the street before the blue exhaust smoke had cleared from the air.

When Nicole arrived back at the flat Libby flourished the note.

"Look at this."

Nicole read the address that Robbie had written: Cheshunt Gardens, Belgravia.

"That's good," she said, as her heart shrank and twisted in her chest.

On Saturday Libby spent an inordinate amount of time choosing clothes, before settling on work trousers and a plain white blouse topped by a smart jacket she had found in a second hand shop.

After one last check in the mirror Libby gave Nicole a quick peck on the cheek and rushed out of the flat. She arrived back late that night, slightly tipsy and full of excitement about her day. Nicole listened as Libby talked about the other two models, Debbie and Michelle, and the rehearsal shoot in Robbie's studio.

"It's going to be a portrait based on 'The Three Graces'. That's a sculpture by Antonio Canova. It's famous. Thing is, there's a bit of a problem …"

Nicole waited for the request that she knew would follow.

"It's just that Michelle, you know, that I told you about … well she can't make the session, something about a row."

Libby avoided Nicole's eyes as rushed out the conclusion.

"So I said that you'd do it, the session I mean."

Ignoring Nicole's horrified expression Libby persevered with the detail.

"You're blonde and just the right height, and Robbie has a deadline for the commission."

Libby glanced up at Nicole's stony face.

"Oh, don't be silly, it's just a few hours … it's not as if you are doing anything else today."

***

It was not quite as awful as Nicole had expected. Robbie was charming, Debbie dispensed vodka and tonic and was talkative and funny if a little shocking at times. The three girls began the session draped in muslin sheets, but as Robbie worked and the vodka glasses were refilled the material covered less and less until all three were completely nude. As the two acolytes Libby and Debbie had to pretend to caress Nicole but, as the session developed, the touches became less and less of a pretence and Nicole found herself in a position of exquisite discomfort; her acute embarrassment subdued by the pleasure of the moment.

In the following days Libby made several return trips to see Robbie, and on the Friday she went to a party with her new friends. Nicole waited up, but Libby didn't reappear until late Sunday morning. She'd had a 'wonderful' time.

"And there's another thing …"

Cheshunt Gardens had a spare room.

Libby spent the afternoon packing her things. Robbie appeared at five on the BSA, accompanied by his brother driving a small Bedford lorry. The two men manoeuvred Libby's trunk down the stairs, whilst Nicole followed with overflowing bags. Libby carried Treacle, the battered doll. On the pavement she gave Nicole a peck on the cheek, then climbed onto the pillion of the BSA.

"Bye Nicole, thanks for everything. See you around."

Nicole couldn't speak. She forced a smile and waved until the motorbike reached the end of the street. There was no answering wave. Libby's attention was on the road ahead.

Michael

Over the last six months Michael had settled into a daily routine. He set off walking from the dingy room in Munro Terrace and usually managed to board a 22 'bus before Sloane Square. He liked to sit upstairs, all the better to marvel at the spectrum of humanity offered up by London's streets.

Michael left the 'bus at Piccadilly, cutting his way north through Soho's narrow streets and alleyways. In the mornings he weaved through the bustling street market, dodging barrow boys, handcarts and delivery vans. In the evening there was a different kind of trade; city gents and businessmen scuttled furtively through the alleys, scrutinising the display cards pinned to the open doorways before dashing up steep stairs to the curtained rooms on the upper floors.

The Patten Photographic Agency occupied a jumble of offices above an Oxford Street shoe shop. At least the letterhead said Oxford Street, but the narrow staircase led up from a nondescript entrance in Berwick Street, causing endless confusion for delivery men.

The reception had two adjoining offices, the largest being the territory of Graham Patten: owner and principal photographer. Patten's speciality was portraiture, and he made a steady living from out of town debutantes whose mothers were reassured by the Oxford Street address. He also did occasional work for fashion designers who were a step below haute couture.

On the second floor there was what Patten described as a technical studio, where his partner Oliver Lance did high resolution work for advertising agencies. Packets and tins of household essentials were arranged and photographed against a selection of roll down backdrops, ranging from 'south seas beach' to 'modern kitchen'. Michael was occasionally detailed to help, a job he found indescribably tedious. Unfortunately it was work he could not always avoid, and today he was scheduled to assist Mr Lance in the careful arrangement of some tins of corned beef.

Michael squeezed past a loafer at the entrance and skipped up the stairs to the frosted glass door on the first floor landing.

"It's no good running up the stairs. If you want to be on time you should do your hurrying at the start of the journey."

"Good morning, Mrs Perceval."

"There's nothing good about it."

The woman behind the reception desk made a noise that was half snort, half sigh. Mrs Perceval was in her early forties, with a seemingly permanent scowl, tightly permed auburn hair, and half frame glasses on a neckband. She wore matching check jackets and skirts, white ruffed blouses buttoned to the neck, and large pearls that Michael assumed were fake. She exuded a powerful scent of lavender. Michael had no idea of her first name and did not expect to be told.

He grinned, partly to annoy, because she seemed to find his good humour irritating.

"What's the panic today then, Mrs Perceval?"

"I do not panic young man, when have you ever seen me panic?"

She inclined her head towards the closed door to her right.

"Others may panic, I just get on with my job."

She opened the huge diary on her desk.

"There has been a double booking," she sniffed again, howsoever such a thing had occurred, it had not been her doing.

"Mr Patten is in the country: Norfolk, near Kings Lynn. He will be there all day, returning tomorrow evening. It's a debutante portrait and it's been in the diary for months."

There was a heavy and significant pause.

"But he left a note on my desk."

Michael smiled. The word 'note' was pronounced with utter distaste. Mrs Perceval didn't like notes, proper communications arrived on headed paper.

"It seems that there is another booking, which was never put in the diary, an agency job in Chelsea. Mr Lance cannot do it; it's not his kind of work and anyway, he has a full day. I will have to cancel, which is just …"

She searched for a suitably horrible word.

"It's appalling, that all I can say. Appalling. We never cancel. It's just not done. And …"

She picked up the note as if it were a particularly unpleasant piece of rubbish.

"And this doesn't even give a proper address. I've telephoned the client and they don't seem to know either."

She peered at the note.

"Fashion shoot. Libby. Barok. Chelsea. 11am. That's all it says. How, I ask you, are we supposed to find anything from that?"

Michael adopted his most polite and helpful expression.

"It's a coffee bar on the Kings Road … 'Barok' I mean. There's a photographic studio on the first floor above the bar. I expect Libby will be the booker."

Mrs Perceval looked at him and, for a second, Michael imagined the faintest trace of a smile. Then it disappeared.

"Of course. You have digs at that end of town don't you. Well, it seems that you are useful for something."

Mrs Perceval reached for the telephone directory and flicked through the pages. She made a careful note of a number, picked up the 'phone and dialled. She listened for a while but the lack of reply was evident. She looked at her watch and sighed.

"Nine fifteen. You would imagine that a coffee bar would be open by now, would you not?"

Michael shrugged carefully. 'Barok' rarely opened its doors much before midday, but he saw an opportunity approaching and was reluctant to give too much away.

Mrs Perceval thought for a moment then came to a decision.

"We need to contact this Libby person. You will have to go. Tell them we can't do it, offer to rearrange."

Michael grinned again. The day had just become immeasurably better. He picked up his bag and made for the door.

"You won't be needing that," said Mrs Perceval, with a significant look at the blue RAF satchel.

"But, it's got my lunch and a flask," lied Michael.

"And your cameras?"

"Well, yes but …"

"Get out of here before I change my mind. And don't go getting ideas above your station."

"Yes, Mrs Perceval."

***

The journey back to Chelsea gave Michael an opportunity for some much needed thinking. The job at Patten's had not turned out as expected. He recalled the interview back in January. Under Mrs Perceval's appraising eyes he had sat in the reception area for half an hour until the door to the inner office finally opened and Graham Patten appeared.

The proprietor of Patten & Co was a slow moving round faced man in his fifties, with watery blue eyes and an expression that reminded Michael of a fish on a slab. Patten's three piece pin-striped suits struggled to cope with a considerable paunch. A waistcoat fob watch only served to emphasise the straining fabric.

"Public school?" he'd asked. There was a quizzical tone to the question, as if Patten felt that Michael was unlikely public school material.

"Yes sir, Blundells – it's in Tiverton – that's Devon."

"I know where Tiverton is."

Patten glanced down at Michael's summary.

"You have just finished at Chelsea College of Art."

Michael nodded.

"A design course, but it was a broad introduction, and we did a fair amount of photography."

"And before that, you were in the RAF," said Patten. "Straight from school. And as a regular, not national service?"

"I wanted to join their photographic unit, and national servicemen don't get much choice as to the unit they join."

"So I've heard," Patten looked down again. "So what did you do with the RAF? It doesn't say here, just gives your Berlin posting and the dates."

"I'm not allowed to say."

Patten looked up from the summary and seemed inclined to challenge the answer, but Michael met his eyes.

"I gained quite a lot of experience. With a wide variety of equipment."

"So I see."

Joining the RAF had been the solution to a series of communications from Blundells, whose tutors had reported, with increasing exasperation, how Michael was failing to take his studies seriously and was therefore unlikely to gain a place at Oxford. He was fluent in French, mainly as a result of James and Edith's decision to offer accommodation to a French refugee during the war. But Michael had no interest in following a university course in the language. The thing that really captivated his mind was photography.

A family conference resulted and the answer, strangely enough, had come from Rupert, now a Brigadier at the War Office. Rupert's inter-services liaison role had obviously highlighted a need.

"The RAF needs photo-chappies, and he will get a good training. Suit him down to the ground."

Michael was keen from the start, but it took some time for his parents to come around, largely due to prejudice based purely on the source of the advice.

"So you were an airman for how long … five years?" said Patten, once more working his way down the summary. "Not tempted to stay on? You were promoted pretty smartly."

Michael had anticipated this question, and had his answer ready.

"I signed up for the training, which was very good. But the opportunities were limited; we did virtually no portrait work for example."

Patten nodded approval.

"I see you were in Berlin for the airlift. That must have been interesting. Or is that another thing you are not allowed to talk about?"

"No sir, or rather, yes, it was interesting. Although I think we were all working so hard that we didn't realise the significance of what was happening at the time."

And that's putting it mildly, thought Michael. He had barely finished his training when he was sent to Germany. For a few hectic months, Michael's job was to unload the constant stream of transports landing and, in quite a few cases, crash landing, at the city's Templehof airfield. The 'noddies' were needed to do the unloading because the regular troops were manning the city's meagre defences against the expected Soviet invasion.

Graham Patten looked across the desk expectantly; Michael realised that he had been asked a question.

"You were based in Paris after Berlin?" repeated Patten helpfully.

"No sir, the unit was based at Rocquencourt, just outside Paris, but I was able to get into the city quite often, leave and so on."

"That sounds a little better than Brize Norton."

Patten smiled, the first time he had done so, and Michael smiled in return.

"Yes sir. It was."

"And you were adopted as a child? I see that Ratcliffe is not the family name."

"No sir. It's my mother's name. I was evacuated to Devon in 1939, and my guardians adopted me at the end of the war."

Michael remembered the moment in the spring of 1945. They had walked into Totnes for the VE celebrations. Edith and James had been full of a secret, and on the way home Edith had asked him whether he would accept them as his parents. It had been one of the happiest days of his life.

Patten noted the faraway expression on Michael's face, and correctly identified the cause.

'They must have been very special people."

"Yes sir … they were. And still are."

Patten smiled again, then the telephone rang and a frown of irritation wiped the smile from his face. He picked up the receiver and the irritation was replaced by a mask of oily charm.

"Oh yes, of course I will. Put her through."

Patten covered the mouthpiece with his hand.

"Important call, give me a few moments will you."

He waved towards the door and Michael returned to the reception room where Mrs Perceval nodded towards a chair before returning to her typewriter.

And that had been it; the job was his: assistant photographer, on five pounds seventeen and sixpence per week. But the six months since the interview had seen very little camera work. Graham Patten believed that photography was an art that could only be acquired by diligent study alongside a suitably experienced mentor. Michael's RAF training was seen as almost irrelevant, and his year at Chelsea discounted as a waste of valuable time.

Michael worked in the developing lab, he set up backdrops and arranged tins and packets for Mr Lance. In Patten's studio he worked the lights, took measurements and readings, and make tea for visitors. He hardly touched a camera except to load and unload film.

"You may have experience young man, but debutantes are not aeroplanes, and studio photography requires a great deal of skill."

***

Michael caught a moving bus at Leicester Square and climbed the stairs to the top deck. There was a morning paper on the nearby seat, the banner headlines screaming indignation following Nasser's seizure of the Suez canal. Michael pushed the paper to one side and sat down. Glancing at the satchel he wondered whether the morning errand would be an opportunity to use his cameras.

The passage of six months had been quite long enough for Michael to forget how he'd celebrated when offered the chance to work at Patten's. Michael held strong views about photography; views that he had kept well hidden from his employer. A particular dislike was for the carefully arranged portraiture that was Graham Patten's speciality. Photography, in Michael's view, was a spontaneous activity, with the photographer encumbered by as little equipment as possible.

Soon after passing through Sloane Square Michael glanced out the window and realised that the bus was stationary, with a seemingly endless line of traffic ahead. He decided to get off and walk the remaining few hundred yards.

The cause of the hold up soon became obvious. A policeman stood in the middle of the road, directing traffic past a motley collection of water board vans. A pneumatic drill began its ear splitting roar, smothering all the other sounds on the street. A group of workmen in overalls and leather jackets smoked and chatted, seemingly inured to the racket.

'Barok' was more than a coffee shop, as Michael discovered soon after enrolling at Chelsea. He had been invited to a jazz evening, in what appeared to be a private members' club. In a cramped room a jazz quartet played Bix Beiderbeck classics to a diverse crowd of students, artists and lecturers – with a few city gents and debs thrown in for good measure.

It was only in the daylight of the following day that he discovered that the 'jazz club' was actually a coffee bar; the atmosphere of genial amateurism explained by the lack of the necessary licences for either alcohol or music. The place became a regular haunt, not least because it was also popular with a variety of pretty girls.

The upstairs studio ran on equally anarchic lines, more like an informal club than a business. Several well known photographers used the facilities, but the studio was just as likely to be booked by Chelsea college lecturers for photography workshops, or by amateurs, whose work was often indistinguishable from the professionals. For life models the photographers hired girls from the Chelsea Palace; a struggling theatre that specialised in song and dance reviews played out against a tableaux backdrop of nude girls.

Several of the Chelsea Palace models doubled as waitresses in the coffee bar, serving Polish vodka and cheap red wine in coffee cups and mugs. After several visits to the theatre in the name of research, the general consensus amongst Michael's friends was that the girls were sexier at the cafe with their clothes on.

On arrival at the shop Michael tried the side door leading upstairs to the first floor studio only to find that it was firmly locked. The was a 'closed' sign in the coffee shop window, but the door was ajar, so he pushed it fully open causing the bell above the door to jangle.

"We're closed," said a voice.

Michael stepped inside.

"I said we're closed. And shut the door against that horrible noise."

The speaker was Debbie, one of the Palace dancers who doubled as a model in the upstairs studio. At the same table sat a stern faced blonde wearing a plaid shirtwaister dress with a broad belt. Next to her was a slim girl with amused sparkling eyes. The other tables were piled high with cardboard boxes full of clothes. One girl in a pencil skirt and short sleeved sweater sat apart, disengaged from the group and looking beyond the room to the passers by.

Michael guessed that these were the agency models, and that the older man was the booker. He closed the door carefully. The road-drill muffled down to an unpleasant background roar.

"I'm from Patten's. We've been booked for the studio upstairs, but the door's locked."

"You're our snapper," said the man, getting to his feet with a broad smile and thrusting out a hand.

"I'm Archie, Archie O'Neill." he gestured to the group. "This is Libby, from the agency, Nicole, who's giving up her day off to help out. Debbie, and – ah, last but not least …"

He indicated the girl by the window, clearly having forgotten her name. She pulled her gaze away from the street outside and glanced at Michael.

"Annabel," she said, before resuming her scrutiny of the stationary traffic.

O'Neill was in his early forties, with an expensive but badly creased suit that looked a size too large. Michael realised that they had met before, both at the photographic studio and at the cafe. He decided that O'Neill must be the owner of the cafe or the studio, possibly both, which meant …

The girl that O'Neill had called Libby interrupted this thoughtful speculation.

"I'm sorry," she said. "But we will have to cancel I'm afraid. We've no power for the lights, the workmen have cut the cable in the road."

Libby bore a strong resemblance to Audrey Hepburn: brunette, with a slim figure and an urchin fringe over wide eyes. She had dressed to emphasize the resemblance, in dancing pumps, black slacks and a close fitting long sleeved black pullover.

"That's a pity," said Michael, looking at the summer light streaming in through the shop window. "Although it's such a beautiful day that we could almost do the shoot outside."

"What a marvellous idea." said O'Neill, looking out onto the broad sunlit pavement. "He's right about the light; we could do it right here."

"We can't do it here," protested Libby. "We haven't the room."

"Not here, silly." reproached O'Neill, pointing to the pavement outside the window. "There!"

They both looked at Michael expectantly. He made a series of quick judgements, first absorbing the fact that the pair were seriously proposing to do the shoot on the pavement outside the shop. Following this perception came the recollection that he had somehow failed to mention that he was not in fact the photographer, merely a messenger sent to re-organise dates. Finally he conjured a mental picture of Graham Patten's reaction to a daylight fashion shoot carried out on the Kings Road pavement.

He'll sack me

Michael quickly concluded that he didn't care one way or the other. He had two cameras with a half a dozen films for each, It would have to do.

"It's perfect, let's get started."

Half an hour later he was photographing Annabel and Debbie against a backdrop of coffee shop tables and chairs. Archie had carried the cafe furniture out to provide what he described as a 'continental flavour'. Inside the shop Libby and Nicole presided over a mountain of clothes and empty cardboard boxes.

Michael's guess about O'Neill's ownership of the two businesses proved correct, the clothes were from a shop further down the Kings Road that was due to open the following week.

"We need some publicity stuff," explained O'Neill. "Posters, flyers, that kind of thing."

The clothes were a mix of smart student fashion and what O'Neill described as 'teddy girl chic'. The collection was totally unlike anything Michael had seen on the newspaper fashion pages. There were denim work trousers rolled up above the ankle, three quarter length Edwardian jackets, circle skirts with hemlines dangerously close to the knee, what Debbie called 'Jane Mansfield' blouses and a couple of dresses that had clearly been inspired by Marilyn Monroe's recent visit to London. There was a complete absence of formal evening wear. Neither were there any hats, gloves or what Libby contemptuously dismissed as 'useless knick knacks'.

O'Neill oversaw the operations on the pavement. As time went on this involved managing a growing crowd of bystanders. The attraction was partly the novelty of the spectacle, but also the fact that the lack of suitable space meant that Debbie and Annabel's costume changes were taking place just the other side of the coffee bar window. Nicole attempted to hide the changing girls by pulling down the blind, but she only succeeded in jamming the mechanism with the blind half drawn. The result was a impromptu burlesque show, featuring tantalising glimpses of legs and stockings.

Neither Debbie nor Annabel appeared bothered by the situation, quite the reverse. Annabel's aloofness disappeared as soon as the shoot was underway, whilst Debbie made a beeline for the 'Monroe' dresses and obviously enjoyed being the centre of attention.

Michael used the twin lens Rolleiflex when he wanted the girls to hold a pose, but most of the pictures were taken with his 35mm Pentax. He knew that the medium format film in the Rolleiflex would deliver a better quality image, but the smaller camera was so much easier to focus. He could sometimes get off a couple of shots whilst the girls were arranging their clothes.

He was completely relaxed, enjoying the freedom to shoot the kind of pictures he had always wanted to take, secure in the knowledge that Graham Patten would almost certainly re-arrange the session and that the pictures were unlikely to be used. Besides, once his employer discovered the facts he would probably be sacked anyway.

A taxi pulled up alongside the small crowd. A small man in a tired grey suit bustled out and told the driver to wait. Elbowing his way to the front of the appreciative bystanders the man took in the tableaux with a glance and then worked his way round to O'Neill.

"Alan Seymour, Express picture desk," he said cryptically. "Fashion shoot?"

"Yes," said Archie. But his attention was on the police constable further down the street, who had begun a slow stroll in their direction.

"Nice girls," said the newcomer. "Who's the snapper?"

"He's from Patten's," said Archie. The policeman was still strolling, but his gaze was clearly focused on the crowd and he appeared to be unbuttoning a pocket with a view to extracting a notebook. "I say, do you mind, but we may have to …"

Archie's brain caught up with events. He turned slowly and looked down at Seymour, who was watching Michael with a professional interest.

"Did you say Express – Daily Express?" said Archie.

Seymour took in Archie's distracted air and glanced down the street to identify the cause. He waved a hand at the crowd watching the girls.

"This looks interesting. Something we could use, would you be OK with that? Shared use? With full attribution?"

Archie had only the vaguest idea what was being proposed, but he recognised the name of a national newspaper. He nodded, then glanced nervously at the approaching constable, who had almost reached the edge of the crowd.

"Don't worry about the plod. I'll sort him." said Seymour. Archie looked on in admiration as the pint sized bundle of energy pushed his way back through the crowd to the policeman and flourished a press card.

"Seymour, Daily Express. Can you do something about these people, officer? They are blocking the pavement and our photographer is trying to work."

The policeman's notebook paused in mid flourish, and then was slowly returned to the breast pocket.

Seymour pressed his advantage; he waved at the girls.

"Frankly I'm surprised your sergeant didn't send someone earlier; we told them that Miss Hepburn would be here with her co-stars."

The officer looked first at Seymour's press card, then at the models. Libby had joined the group and Michael was arranging the three girls in a new setting. Libby was sat on the coffee table, and had changed into a simple black dress, with a low neckline. Debbie and Annabel occupied the two adjacent chairs and pretended to drink cups of coffee. Libby put a foot on the vacant chair and crossed her legs, causing the hem of her dress to ride well above her knee. She looked at the policeman and smiled. The man pulled his eyes away from her legs.

"Right-oh sir," he said. "Would you like me to clear the pavement completely?"

"Oh no, we can't do that. Just make sure they keep a respectable distance."

Seymour pushed his way back through the crowd as the voice of the Law began its work.

"Patten's?" he said to Michael "Is that Graham Patten on Oxford Street?"

Michael nodded.

Seymour examined Michael's cameras.

"What film are you using?"

"Kodak 400 in the Pentax, down to 50 in the Rollei – black and white obviously."

"Good. We might use these as a feature spread, could be good for you. Have the film ready for 6pm – on the dot, both formats, negs and contact sheets. I'll send a despatch rider. It will be interesting to see how the 35mm turns out."

Seymour made for the waiting taxi, then turned back.

"Oh – and we'll need some notes about the clothes, designer's name and so on. And make sure you get the crowd in the picture … and the plod if you can."

He caught the apprehensive look on Michael's face. "Don't worry. The client's on board, and you'll get your credit if we use the pix."

Seymour glanced at Libby, then leant in to Michael and dropped his voice to a whisper:

"She really does look like Hepburn in that dress."

***

An hour later Michael and Libby were installed in a taxi for the journey back to Patten's.

"Libby should go with you," O'Neill had said. "She'll know the proper names of the clothes. I wouldn't have a clue."

To Nicole's clear displeasure she was tasked with repacking the clothes into the mountain of cardboard boxes. Debbie disappeared to work her afternoon shift at the Palace. Annabel had been collected by a smart young man driving an open top Mercedes.

In the taxi Michael was preoccupied with the problem of how to explain events on his return to Patten's. He thought of several plausible explanations, but was not given the opportunity to use any of them.

"I've had the Express on the 'phone," said Mrs Perceval as he walked through the door.

"This is Libby, Mrs Perceval," said Michael as the girl followed him into the room. "The booker, from Poppies Model Agency. She's come to do the notes for the photos."

A series of expressions crossed the older woman's face. It was clear that she had a great deal to say, but it would not be said in front of Libby. She nodded at the girl and then turned to Michael

"We'll discuss this morning's events later," she said ominously. "The Express said that a despatch rider would pick up the negatives at 6pm, so get yourself up to the darkroom."

"Yes Mrs Perceval," said Michael "I'll get right on it."

The darkroom was on the third floor, above the studios, and reached by a staircase even more narrow than the one that led up to the main office. Michael showed Libby into an outer room decorated with Oliver Lance's latest commission; 10x14 prints showing cans of soup set against a series of unlikely backgrounds.

"I should take a seat," said Michael, pointing to a chair piled high with magazines. "It will take a while to set things up."

Libby picked up the magazines. "Where …?"

"Oh anywhere," said Michael "On the bench there, next to the chemicals. Don't get the stuff on your clothes; it wouldn't do that dress any good."

Libby shrank into her seat and crossed her legs. Michael found himself looking at the swell of her breasts, which reminded him of the constable's reaction that morning.

"After all, you need to be careful with that dress, in case Miss Hepburn wants it back."

Libby smiled and looked around the room with interest. Waist level workbenches lined the walls, cluttered with a variety of trays and equipment. Bottles of chemicals and packs of photographic paper occupied shelves above the benches. In the corner was a deep sink and a door leading to the dark room proper. The sound of busy traffic on Oxford Street rumbled in the background behind a fully drawn blind.

She watched as Michael measured out chemicals into jugs, laid out photographic paper, and rinsed developing trays with clean water. He carried the jugs into the darkroom. Back in the lab he consulted a wall chart before setting a mechanical timer.

"I've never been in a darkroom, and I don't know anything about how a photograph is produced. It's a bit like baking," said Libby.

"I wouldn't know," said Michael. "That's the darkroom beyond the curtain; this is the lab. Most of the work happens in here."

Michael crossed the room and reached behind Libby for the light switch. He had to lean over her and, for a moment, their legs touched. He was acutely aware of the physical contact, and of her proximity and perfume. In one movement he turned the overhead light off and the red wall light on.

"We need to be able to see in here, that's why we use a safety light. You have to develop the film in total darkness. You put it into a special tank with a chemical that brings out the image on the film. That's the tricky bit, because if you make a mistake you ruin the film … OK, we are ready, I think."

He picked up the used film cartridges and went into the darkroom, drawing a thick curtain behind the door.

"How on earth do you manage?" Libby called from the studio. "I can barely see in here."

"It's just something you learn to get right; a bit like a soldier loading his rifle in the dark."

In the pitch darkness beyond the curtain Michael loaded the films into the developing tank. Then he reappeared and set the timer.

"Twelve minutes."

"How does it all work?" asked Libby.

Michael hesitated. His usual answer assumed that the question had been posed out of politeness. He would say that the chemicals 'worked like magic'. If the questioner was half way serious he would add that the fluid changed the composition of the film. He looked at Libby. The soft red light emphasised the contrast between the dark fabric of her dress and her pale skin. She was leaning forward, waiting for his answer.

"Photographic film is made from a plastic surface covered with a coating of silver crystals. It doesn't have to be plastic, you could use paper or even a piece of wood. It's the crystals that are important. When you press the shutter on a camera you expose the crystals to light, and that changes their composition."

He looked up to see her reaction, but he couldn't see her eyes properly in the half darkness. He decided to plough on regardless.

"If you leave the film open to the light the crystals turn completely black. The trick is to expose the film to a tiny amount of light, just enough to leave an image. In the darkroom we make that image permanent. First we develop the latent image, then we fix the image as a negative."

"But what about the print, isn't that the final process?"

Michael smiled. She had been listening.

"Not to a photographer. The important thing is the negative. Once you have that you can make a small print for an album, or a 10x14 like those." He gestured at the line of prints hanging from the ceiling. "Or you could enlarge all the way up to a street poster, all from the same negative. But without a good negative you can't do a thing."

He carried on working, repeating the process until he had developed all of that morning's film. Libby offered to help and he gave her the seemingly endless task of running warm water through the metal developing tank, explaining that it was necessary to remove all traces of processing chemical from the finished negative. Finally he extracted the developed film strips and hung them over the bench top to dry.

Libby stood alongside him and peered at the results.

"It's back to front," she said. "No, not back to front, reversed, what's the word?"

"It's a negative; the white bits turn out black and the dark bits white. We turn it round when we make a print."

"Are you going to send all the film to the newspaper people? I was hoping to be able to take some prints back to the agency."

"I don't know if we will have time to do that today," said Michael. "I will work up a full portfolio tomorrow."

"But won't the newspaper people want to see all the film?"

"They might, but we risk losing all our work if they mislay the film. Really they only need to see a few frames. Better to send a selection and a contact sheet. Besides, we haven't the time to write up the notes for all that film." He waved at the strips of drying negatives.

"What's a contact sheet."

"It's a proof copy; a single sheet with all the frames from a strip of negatives, but the images are positive."

Libby's blank expression indicated that this explanation had missed its mark by some distance. Michael was about to make a second attempt when there was a knock at the door. He shouted: "it's OK to come in" and Mrs Perceval appeared.

"It's the agency. Someone called Nicole has been ringing them. She needs to talk to this young lady. I said we would ring her back."

Libby disappeared down the stairs and Michael got on with making contact prints. By the time she returned he had laid out half a dozen completed sheets on one of the benches.

"Sorry it took me so long," she said. "Nicole is still at Barok. She's not very happy. She says that Archie has disappeared somewhere and the evening staff want to open up."

Michael had a clear picture of Nicole alone at the cafe surrounded by piles of boxes. He grinned and Libby's tense expression softened into a smile.

"She doesn't know where to take the clothes. It took me three 'phone calls to find Archie. And then I couldn't get back to Nicole because the line was busy. I was on the 'phone for ages. Mrs Perceval started tapping her watch."

Michael's grin widened and Libby thumped him lightly on the arm.

"It's alright for you; safe up here with your contact thingies. I was the one dealing with the dragon downstairs."

Libby picked up on the sheets of photographic paper and looked at the tiny images

"Are these the ones?"

"Yes. Think of them as miniature proof copies."

"This is Debbie on her own," said Libby, squinting at the tiny figure on the picture. "She looks really good in that dress; she has the figure."

For the next half hour the pair used a tripod magnifier to work through the contact sheets, selecting and rejecting, noting down the frame numbers and adding some basic description of the clothes.

They were working under a spotlight at one of the benches. Libby sat on a bench stool, with Michael stood alongside. As they passed the magnifier back and forth their hands touched, at first momentarily, and then for a split second longer than was absolutely necessary.

As Libby wrote the notes to accompany the selected pictures Michael was free to study her body: the fairness of her skin contrasting with the dark hair, the small hollow in the nape of her neck, a thin strand of underslip momentarily exposed across her shoulders.

Libby gave one sheet of contacts a cursory examination and then pushed it to one side. Michael reached for the magnifier. One frame stood out from the rest. It was Libby, as he suspected it would be. She was sat on the coffee table, looking straight into the camera, bracketed by Debbie and Annabel, legs crossed, with her hands on her knee. A half smile played on her lips and her eyes sparkled with mischief. A few men from the watching crowd had elbowed their way into the frame; they were all looking at Libby.

"We have to use this one."

Libby looked up from her writing and saw the sheet he had chosen.

"No, we can't," she said quickly. "I was just there to be the background for Debbie and Annabel. I'm not a model … and …"

He put his hand on her shoulder.

"And everyone is looking at you because you are gorgeous, and lovely, and the best thing in the picture."

She looked up in surprise. He leant forward and kissed her lightly on the lips. Then, having survived the first attempt, he pulled her to her feet, wrapped his arms around her slim body and kissed her again.

There was a light knock on the door. The pair separated quickly. Mrs Perceval was framed in the doorway with eyebrows raised. Michael wondered how long she had been there.

"The despatch rider is here."

Mrs Perceval

The following morning Michael endured an uncomfortable quarter of a hour with Mrs Perceval, who listened to his account of events, expressing disapproval and displeasure with her usual skill.

"Let's begin with the simple things. You were supposed to be assisting Mr Lance. Not gallivanting with models in Chelsea. He had to manage on his own all day."

"But you sent me," protested Michael. "You told me to go."

Mrs Perceval ignored the interruption and held up a second finger.

"Two … You were sent to Chelsea to pass on a message to the client, not to indulge in art house antics on the Kings Road pavement."

A third finger appeared.

"Three … we don't do informal work. It's not what our clients want to see, and it's not the kind of photography that Mr Patten likes to do. And before you mention the Daily Express …"

"Me? I didn't say anything." Michael put his hands to his chest. "What did I say?"

"You may not have said anything," snapped Mrs Perceval. "But you were thinking that a national newspaper is going to publish your pictures, and that must be good. Well, it may or may not be good for you, but it isn't good for Patten's. The Express is not a serious newspaper. Your pictures will be chip shop wrapping next week, but we have to maintain a reputation with our clientele."

"OK ... enough ... guilty as charged, where's the bloke with the rope?"

Michael put his head in an imaginary noose, jerked his tie into the air and pulled his head to one side. Mrs Perceval maintained an expression of absolute inscrutability, and Michael wondered for a moment whether she ever played poker. He abandoned the pose, raised his hands in surrender, and waited to hear her verdict. She leant back in her chair.

"Mr Patten will not approve," she said in a softer tone. "You'll be lucky to keep your job. The one thing that might save you is the fact that the client seems happy, but then they haven't seen the pictures yet. You are going to take the portfolio today?"

Michael nodded. Mrs Perceval busied herself with the paperwork on her desk

"Did you see her last night?" she said casually, without looking up. "The booker I mean, what was she called, Libby?"

"Yes, and no. She is called Libby and I didn't see her last night; she was busy."

"Well see her tonight; you could do worse."

Michael grinned.

"Don't look at me like that; get up those stairs and do some work ... Oh, and a Mr Oldfield rang."

Michael paused on his way to the stairs. Mrs Perceval consulted her diary.

"He would like you to ring him today. I said you were busy this morning and it would have to wait 'til lunchtime ... I don't know what it's about," she added, in response to his puzzled expression.

Mrs Perceval waited until Michael had gone up to the darkroom, then she looked down at the diary, where the name 'Oldfield' and a telephone number were written next to the words:

'Empire News Agency'. She smiled to herself, then reached for some paper to feed into her typewriter.

***

By the time he finished the portfolio it was one o'clock and Michael's shirt was damp with sweat and sticking to his back. It was another hot day and the top floor lab and darkroom were stifling. His tie felt like a noose around his neck, a reminder of his play acting with Mrs P. It had been childish, he thought, self-indulgent and juvenile. He resolved to try and behave like an adult.

As he descended the steep stairs his one thought was to walk the short distance to Soho Square and spend his lunch hour doing nothing at all in the sun. Mrs Perceval had an alternative plan.

"I've been speaking to the client," she said. "Mr O'Neill, lovely man. His company are holding an event this evening at a house near Belgrave Square."

She paused and selected a piece of paper from her desk.

"You are invited, I can't think why. This is the address. I asked about dress code and he laughed, so it would seem that it is not black tie."

Michael looked up sharply, but her face was as impassive as ever.

"I understand that the young lady is also invited. Stop grinning young man. And The Express telephoned."

She paused. Michael tried to maintain a disinterested silence, but abandoned the effort after a few seconds.

"Alright … what did they say?"

"They will print the pictures in tomorrow's edition."

Michael hesitated, and glanced at the door to Graham Patten's office in what he hoped was a meaningful way.

"What on earth is that expression you are making? It looks like indigestion. If you wish to use Mr Patten's telephone you simply have to ask. Is that so terribly difficult?"

Michael asked, and Mrs Perceval nodded in the direction of the door.

"I'll time the call," she said.

Once inside the office with the door safely closed Michael almost ran to the desk and dialled the number for the model agency. There was a long wait whilst someone went in search of Libby. Michael listened to a listless typewriter and two voices discussing the hot weather, before approaching footsteps, and a whispered 'I think it's the photographer from yesterday', heralded Libby's voice.

"Michael," she said, with what he hoped was genuine enthusiasm. "We're looking forward to seeing your pictures."

"That's good. Look, Libby … I was hoping …"

"And we are all invited to Archie's birthday party, his fortieth apparently. It will be a bit of a bash … think the Chelsea Arts Club Ball, but without the parade. It's fancy dress, what will you go as?"

Michael had no idea.

"What are you wearing?" he said.

"Now or for the party?"

"For the party."

"You will have to wait and find out."

Michael's sigh of irritation was more audible than he intended.

"Don't be like that," she said. "I know … you can be an angry young man, like John Osbourne's play."

Michael confessed to not having seen the play.

"Neither have I, but everyone else seems to have. It's grim northern reality: boots, braces and vests. That should be easy."

Michael was sure that he was being teased, and did not know how to respond. He looked at his watch, aware that Mrs Perceval might put an end to the call at any moment.

"Look … where shall we meet?"

"The party starts at eight, but I'm meeting the girls to get dressed up," she said. "I have a job to do this afternoon, so I will see you at the party … got to go. Bye."

Michael looked at the receiver and swore quietly. The conversation had not gone according to plan. He had anticipated a quiet evening where he would have Libby all to himself. He did not welcome the prospect of sharing her with other people, and especially not at a fancy dress party. He wondered whether it would be worth ringing back and asking her not to go, but then he imagined Mrs Perceval's eye on the clock next door.

He sighed again, then dialled the second number on the paper, trying to recall if he knew anyone called Oldfield.

"Empire News Agency."

Michael froze in astonishment. He had applied for a job with Empire News a month ago, and received a curt, dismissive reply.

"Can I help you caller?" said the operator.

"Mr Oldfield?"

"Putting you through."

The receiver was picked up almost immediately.

"I was asked to ring this number," said Michael quickly.

"And you are?"

Michael gave his name and began to apologise for the delay in returning the call, only to be cut off in mid flow.

"It's alright, got you now. We'd like to offer you a job … if you are still interested."

After a second of stunned silence Michael managed to establish that he was both interested and able to meet Mr Oldfield that evening.

"St Ermin's Hotel, near Victoria. I'll meet you in the lounge … 6.30?"

Michael said 'yes' but the line was already dead.

"Well, bloody hell."

"There is no need for profanity, whatever the cause," said Mrs Perceval from the doorway. "That was eleven minutes. Sixpence. I'll dock it from your wages."

Oldfield

With a few minutes to spare Michael walked through the revolving doors of St Ermin's Hotel. The hours since midday had passed in a blur. He delivered the portfolio to Libby's office near Fenchurch Street Station, enduring two stifling journeys on the Tube, including an escalator breakdown at Bank.

Back at Patten's he completed the afternoon's work, before Mrs Perceval had, much to his surprise, sent him home at 4.30pm. The early finish meant that he had a head start on the Friday rush hour, but it was still approaching six o'clock before he had changed his clothes and caught the bus back into town.

The hotel lounge was busy. Michael stood by the entrance for a few moments scanning the crowd until a tall bearded man appeared carrying a copy of the 'Evening Standard' with the banner headline: 'Suez Crisis'.

"Ratcliffe?"

Michael nodded, then followed the man to a corner table occupied by a rotund, red faced man, holding half a pork pie in one hand and a cigarette and scotch in the other.

"Sit, sit," he said, waving the pie at the empty chair. "I'm Oldfield, this is Mr Webster, one of our partners."

The tall man nodded, and eased himself into a chair, eyeing the rapidly disappearing pie with some distaste; an expression that did not go unnoticed.

"It's alright for you lot on the fifth floor. I haven't eaten since breakfast."

Oldfield turned to Michael.

"Your letter said you speak French. Is that schoolboy or fluent?"

"I'm pretty fluent," said Michael. "We had a French refugee billeted with us during the war. I speak some German as well."

"Well you won't need that. We are not planning on going to war with them in the near future." Oldfield turned to the taller man. "That is right isn't it? Two nil, no replays?"

The older man gave the impression of someone who had heard all of Oldfield's jokes, and didn't enjoy them the first time around. Oldfield turned back to Michael.

"It's this Suez thing. Looks like it might get interesting. We need someone out there in case it does."

Michael could hardly believe his ears. This was the kind of work he fantasised about whilst arranging tins of soup at Patten's.

Oldfield mistook the silence for lack of interest.

"It's a staff job, not freelance. You'd be joining our correspondent in Nice at first. We'd move you to Cyprus if things kick off."

Michael tried to gather his thoughts and construct an intelligent question.

"And if nothing happens? If Suez doesn't turn into anything?"

Oldfield glanced at his colleague, who nodded.

"We have a vacancy," said Oldfield. "A job that requires a French speaker. You would be in line for that if things go well."

Michael wanted to jump into the air and punch the ceiling, then kiss the unappealing Mr Oldfield on both cheeks whilst singing the Marseillaise. But he confined his response to what he hoped was a laconic assent.

"That sounds good. When do I start?"

Five minutes later he was out on the street, beaming happily at passers-by, having arranged to drop into to Oldfield's Holborn office the next day to finalise arrangements. He skipped down the hotel's short drive, bumping into an older woman at one point and apologising with a theatrical bow.

In the lounge bar Oldfield watched Michaels's progress with a dour expression. He finished his scotch and stood to leave. The taller man reached for a bowler hat and umbrella.

"What do you think?"

Oldfield brushed bits of pastry away from his trousers.

"He's green. He has no news experience, and the recommendation came from the spooks. Other than that I think he's wonderful."

"Our contact says he's a good photographer. Nobody on your list spoke French, and Ratcliffe has security clearance from his time in the RAF, which will make it much easier to get him close to the action."

Oldfield sighed.

"I find that hugely reassuring,"

Archie

Eight o'clock that evening found Michael approaching the portico, pillars and imposing front steps of 19 Cheshunt Gardens, one of the Georgian mansions overlooking the tiny triangle of green space that is the junior relation of Belgrave Square. He was wearing what he always wore in the evening; black trousers and a white shirt. After five years in uniform Michael only wore a tie if the occasion made it absolutely necessary, and the evening was far too warm for a jacket.

He began to have misgivings about the choice of clothes as he approached the front door, where two large men in evening dress loitered purposefully. A cowboy approached, accompanied by a 1920s flapper, complete with an improbably long cigarette holder, tasseled skirt and cloche hat. The cowboy produced a card from his leather waistcoat as he approached the door and the burly doormen waved the pair through.

Michael hesitated; he had no formal invitation. A pair of Pierrot clowns arrived, produced cards for the doormen, and disappeared inside. A taxi drew up and disgorged an Arab dancing girl, followed by Tony Nevis, one of the photographers from the Kings Road studios.

Michael was relieved to see that Nevis was not in fancy dress.

"Hullo Tony."

"Michael!" The man turned to his partner. "Darling … this is Michael, a fellow snapper. Salome – Michael, Michael – Salome."

The girl nodded at Michael, but was obviously more concerned with keeping her various veils strategically positioned.

"Tony!" she pleaded.

The man glanced at her and grinned.

"Yes, we'd better get inside before it all falls apart … coming Michael?"

The couple walked up the steps with Michael following, and the doormen nodded all three through the entrance into a marble floored reception hall flanked by twin oak staircases decorated with a variety of costumed partygoers. A gorilla wandered around the hall, trying, without much success, to frighten the guests as they arrived. At the far end of the hall people crowded around huge double doors. Ragtime jazz spilled out from the room beyond.

Two chorus girls stood by to take hats and coats. They quickly realised Salome's costume difficulties, and the three disappeared into a side room for some essential repairs. The gorilla goosed a passing slave girl then approached Michael and Tony beating his chest. It really was a very convincing performance, even at close quarters. Michael wondered how hot the costume would be to wear, then the gorilla wrapped an arm around his shoulders and began to pick imaginary nits out of his hair. Michael struggled, but the gorilla had a surprisingly strong grip. Then the gorilla abandoned his victim, grabbed Tony and began to dance.

Michael took the opportunity to escape and look for Libby. He drifted into what he guessed had once been the morning room. A makeshift bar occupied one corner, complete with rows of optics and a cocktail waiter mixing drinks.

A small group stood by the bar, two huge men in dinner jackets, surrounded by a small crowd of admirers, like small boats greeting ocean liners returning to port. Michael recognised a well known actress and a radio star amongst the group. None were in fancy dress. The girls hanging on the mens' arms had over wide smiles and tight fitting dresses with the kind of necklines that did not encourage anyone to look into their eyes.

"And then the filth turned up, and Jimmy Boy here scarpered."

The speaker had the sallow complexion of someone whose work keeps them out of the sun. He glanced to his left and the second man nodded sagely.

"But with the goods, Frankie, with the goods, so I got me priorities right."

"Depends which side of seven years you were on. Still …"

The man paused and looked straight at Michael; his expression cold and unsmiling.

"Can we help you, squire?"

Michael shook his head.

"No, just passing through."

He wandered through connecting doors into the next room. Two uniformed waitresses guarded a long trestle table covered with paper tablecloths that were presumably hiding some kind of buffet. Couples taking a break from the music littered the sides of the room.

So far the only familiar face had been Tony Nevis at the door. Michael had no better luck through the next double doors, where another trestle table groaned under the weight of crates of beer and cases of wine. Drifting blue smoke filled the air and the room was packed with a mainly male crowd of drinkers, busy making serious inroads into the booze. Few were in fancy dress, although there were a couple of Tarzans and a circus weightlifter complete with moustache, weights and leotard.

Michael elbowed his way to the table, commandeered a bottle of pale ale and followed the music through into what he supposed must have been the ballroom, where a jazz quintet played 'Satin Doll' to an appreciative audience.

He looked around at the people sat on the floor and realised what was missing in the room, and from the other rooms in the house. There was no furniture: no chairs or tables, sideboards or cabinets, no carpets on the floor, no chandeliers or light fittings. The trestle tables and bar furniture looked out of place for that very reason; they had been imported, brought in just for the evening.

Michael joined the crowd in front of an improvised stage, watching the jazz players for nearly an hour until they finished their set. The arrival of a skiffle trio forced a swift return to the reception hall, where the gorilla was hanging precariously from the balustrade of one of the staircases.

More and more people were arriving, including Kaiser Wilhelm complete with pickelhaube, three more dancing girls, and several naval ratings who may even have been genuine. There was still no sign of Libby, and Michael decided to explore. Returning to the beer stores he picked up a new bottle and took it through a swing door to the rear of the house. This was, as he expected, the servants' area.

He walked into a huge kitchen dominated by a massive table, piled high with empty crates and food trays. Circling the room, he tried doors at random and found what he assumed to be the butler's pantry, followed by the cold store and buttery. The last door opened onto a staircase, with whitewashed walls and plain wooden stairs leading up the the next floor. Switching on the light he followed his nose up to a door that opened onto a broad gallery. This was the house proper, the long corridor lit by a solitary pool of light.

Feeling almost like a burglar, Michael walked slowly down the gallery. Bare patches on the walls revealed where family portraits had once been displayed. Through the windows to his left he could see a garden bathed in soft moonlight, to his right a series of doors.

He opened the nearest, stepped into the room, then froze. Naked on the bed lay one of the men from the cocktail bar downstairs, a vast expanse of soft white flesh. Less than a yard away an armchair faced the bed, its occupant unseen but for a cloud of cigar smoke. The man on the bed was flanked by two of the girls, now stripped down to their stockings and suspenders. One girl was patiently fellating the man's semi-erect penis. A light from a bedside table illuminated the tableaux.

Michael took a step back and a floorboard creaked softly. The girl pulled her mouth away, looked up at Michael, then winked before returning to her task. The wink alerted the watcher, and the armchair was pushed back violently to reveal the second man from the bar. He looked at Michael then slowly withdrew the cigar from his mouth.

"You can fuck off now," he said quietly, before returning both the cigar and chair to their original positions. The man on the bed hadn't moved at all.

Michael retreated to the corridor and closed the door. He was shocked, not by the sex, but by the cold aura of violence that had overlain the scene.

He ignored the next two closed doors, smiling at himself as he did so, because he thought it unlikely that the scenario would be repeated. But the final door before the end of the corridor was open. He glanced inside the room and the contents caused him to step inside and switch on the light. It was a photographic studio, complete with roller backdrop and lighting rack. A professional tripod stood in the middle of the room. There were work benches, a lighting table, storage for chemicals and equipment and the connecting bathroom had been turned into a darkroom.

He wandered around, adjusting the tripod, trying the roller action of the backdrop, opening doors and cupboards. Most were empty. He found no cameras, no other equipment. In the darkroom it was a similar story. There were no developing tanks, no rinsing trays – nothing but the sink in the corner.

He returned to the studio and to a drawer chest he had not been able to open. There had been a similar chest in the photographic laboratory in Berlin. Similar to a naval chart table, it had a plain glass surface over a series of wide shallow drawers. On first try the unit appeared to be locked. Closer examination revealed that there was only a lock on the topmost drawer. Even so, none of the drawers would open.

Michael recalled that the key to the Berlin table had once gone missing, and that the duty sergeant had solved the problem by removing all the drawers from the bottom up. The sound of Lonnie Donegan's 'Cumberland Gap' drifted up from the floor below.

"Two minutes," Michael said to himself. "I'll give it two minutes."

Starting at the bottom he jiggled the brass handles gently and eventually succeeded in removing the whole drawer. It was empty, but with one drawer removed it was easy to reach inside the unit and push the next drawer out. That was also empty. He laughed at himself.

He reached inside the unit for the next drawer, and then the next. Both were empty. Two drawers remained. He struggled with the penultimate drawer, but was encouraged by the weight. This one, he thought, would reveal something.

"Probably a load of old newspapers," he whispered to the empty room. A burst of applause from the room below offered the hope that the skifflers had finally finished their set..

The drawer slid out and Michael eased it onto the glass table surface. There were two portfolios tied with tape.

"Bingo."

Opening the first he discovered dozens of photo enlargements, often of the same negative. Some were landscapes, others scenes in London. Michael recognised a series that were obviously taken in Paris, and some that looked African in origin. Morocco? He admired the skill of the photographer. Studio or al fresco, landscape or close up, the pictures were taken by someone who really knew how to use a camera.

The final drawer was still locked. In Berlin the sergeant had reached inside and somehow released the lock. Michael felt underneath, and found a simple latch mechanism that swivelled sideways. He pulled the drawer out onto the table. More portfolios, portraits this time, all of women, and mostly nude. He leafed through, noting ruefully that the photographer also knew how to arrange his subjects. Michael opened the final folder. This contained more pictures alongside a some rough sketches. The first enlargement was a treatment of Canova's 'The Three Graces', wonderfully done, with three beautiful models.

Michael caught his breath, carried the picture to the light and studied it again. He didn't really need a second look, but wanted to be sure. The pose was faithful to the original, with one girl bracketed by the others. The central model, looking a touch uncomfortable, was Nicole from the previous day's photo session. On her left was Debbie. The right hand model, with her hand cupping Nicole's breast and her head resting on Nicole''s shoulder, was Libby. It was Libby with long hair, but definitely Libby.

The rest of the portfolio confirmed the fact. Most of the photographs were of Libby and, towards the end of the folder, she appeared with shorter hair. Michael spread a selection out on the tabletop. It was a magnificent set; a series that any professional model would have treasured beyond worth.

Libby

"I thought I might find you here."

Libby stood in the doorway, framed by the light from the corridor, a half full tumbler in her hand. She was dressed as Tinkerbell, complete with wings and tiny ragged-edged skirt.

"Golly," said Michael. "You look … um .."

"Magical?"

"Yes, well, I was going to say 'gorgeous', but 'magical' will do for now."

Libby smiled; she put the tumbler down on the floor, fluttered her hands and spun on her heels, before taking a bow.

Michael applauded.

"Did you walk here dressed like that?"

"No – we all came together in a taxi. The costumes are from the Palace; Debbie smuggled them out. I've brought a raincoat to wear on the way home."

Libby picked up her drink and stepped into the room. She saw the spread of pictures and stepped quickly over to the table. The smile disappeared.

"He said that these had been thrown away … he said they were gone."

The words were not directed at Michael, but at the pictures, and her gaze was not on the tableaux spread out on the table top, but into the middle distance. She was clearly close to tears, and the crumpled face contrasted sharply with the light hearted costume.

"Who said?" asked Michael "These are wonderful pictures Libby. You shouldn't be ashamed of them."

She turned in shock.

"Ashamed! I'm not ashamed …"

She was obviously about to say more, but she looked away, put the tumbler down on the table, took a deep breath, and started again.

"These are Robbie's pictures. Archie told me that they had been lost or thrown away. I'm actually very pleased to have found them. It's just a bit of a shock. Where were they? Not spread out like this surely?"

Michael explained about the locked cabinet.

"Who is Robbie?" he asked.

"Robbie is … was … Archie's younger brother." she looked away again, focusing on the far wall.

"We were going to be married. We met at Goldsmiths, at a lecture, he was five years older than me. He was different and special … I fell head over heels …"

She picked up the tumbler and took a drink, before turning to face Michael.

"He was a photographer, a good one, you would have liked him."

Libby spread out the 'Three Graces' enlargements. She had herself under control now, and she smiled at the memory.

"These were for a commission. I don't model, not tall enough and I don't have the figure. But he asked, so I did."

"They're wonderful," said Michael, hoping she would hear the silent 'and so are you'.

"He was just beginning to get his stuff noticed when he crashed his bloody motorbike."

Michael must have looked as shocked as he felt.

"Sorry," she said. "It's brought it all back."

He reached out and held her shoulders, drawing her into his arms.

"Careful with the wings," she looked up and smiled, making no particular move to draw back. They stood entwined for a while, then Michael kissed her, a series of tiny touches that began on her neck and edged up to her lips, until she opened a mouth that tasted strongly of gin. For a few seconds he concentrated on her lips and tongue, then he pulled back and looked at her with a mock stern expression.

"This is a darkroom … but you said …"

"Oh I lied," she said easily. "I wanted to talk to you, or rather to get you to talk to me. You were much too quiet in the taxi. I thought you were shy. And then you kissed me, just like that. All part of your cunning plan I suppose."

They kissed again, with more intensity than before. Michael's hands began a slow exploration of her body. His right hand began in the middle of her back, then travelled down across her buttocks. The caress was light, soft, electrifying. For a second Michael thought that she would surrender to his touch, then she gently broke away.

"Not here," she said. "Not now."

Visibly, she composed herself and looked down at the table top.

"I'm glad you found the pictures. But we can't leave them spread out like this. Let's put them away and I'll collect them later."

Michael smiled his understanding, then helped her put the photographs back in the drawer. Hand in hand they left the studio and made their way back down the main staircase. As they passed the bar Libby refilled her tumbler with an inch of gin topped up with lemonade.

In the dining room the jazz band were back on the tiny stage, this time playing frenetic rock and roll. Four girls close to the stage were hand jiving. At the rear of the room, a small appreciative crowd watched a pair of dancers demonstrating their skill at lindy-hop, with the girl showing most of her underwear in the process. The floor was full of an eclectic mix of ages and dress styles; evening gowns and dinner jackets jostled for space with fancy dressers, boppers and what Mrs Perceval would have described as 'student scruff'.

A few feet away two sailors locked in a deep embrace. Michael looked around, but the scene was attracting no especial attention. He had encountered homosexuality at school and in the RAF, but he had never seen a couple act with such blatant disregard for the consequences. He looked away, in case anyone would think that he was staring, then groaned as he saw the gorilla approaching. He tried to pull Libby away, but she reached out to the gorilla and began a playful dance. They circled Michael a couple of times before the gorilla released its grip. Two hairy paws reached up to the neck and began to pull. The head came away, revealing a red faced Archie.

"Christ, it's hot in this bloody thing."

"Michael was upstairs in the studio; he found Robbie's portfolios," said Libby.

"That's good," said Archie. "Trust a snapper to know where to look, eh?"

A slave girl appeared with a bottle of beer. Archie received it gratefully and drank half the contents.

"Needed that. I think I'm going to take this thing off. Didn't expect it to be so hot. Look, I'm glad I found you both."

He reached out and wrapped huge hairy arms around their shoulders. There was a strong smell of camphor and sweat.

"The Express is going to do a feature, that's a bit of luck isn't it? I've arranged for a bundle to be sent round. Apparently the first edition goes to the railway stations just after eleven. I suppose it's obvious really, if it has to get to Cornwall and places like that. I'd never really thought about it."

The hug tightened, Michael felt his ribs creak and, for one ridiculous moment, wondered if wearing the suit conveyed some kind of special strength to the wearer. Archie took another pull of beer, upending the bottle in disappointment after a couple of gulps.

"Anyway, spoke to a chap at the paper and he seemed to think it would get here before midnight. I need another drink, and I'm going to get out of this suit. Enjoy yourselves."

Michael watched as Archie weaved his way through the crowd.

"Is this Archie's house?"

"He lives here. But it belongs to his mother. She moved back to Somerset when his father was killed in the war; she's not been back since. Too many memories apparently."

"Of what?" said Michael looking around at the bare walls. "The place has been stripped."

"Ah well …" she smiled knowingly. "Archie's money doesn't actually cover his expenses, so he has been selling stuff to pay the bills."

"Was there much to sell?"

"Oh yes … there was a Titian, and a Monet in the gallery. This room had a Sheraton dining set. Archie sees it as an advance on his inheritance, especially so since Robbie died. There's no-one else, and he's worried that his mother might leave the lot to a cats' home, or the Salvation Army or someone."

"Is that likely?"

"I don't know. I've never met her … let's dance shall we, before those awful skifflers come back on."

She took his hand and dragged him onto the dance floor. Michael had been taught to dance at school, on winter Wednesdays when the weather was too awful for sport. The lessons encompassed the waltz, foxtrot and gay gordons, and required the boys to take the female role on alternate dances.

Since leaving school he had strived to avoid dancing, largely successfully, but he managed not to trample on Libby's toes until a red cloaked figure crossed the floor to join them. It was Debbie, allegedly dressed as Red Riding Hood. Alongside Debbie was Nicole, in a modest Peter Pan costume that Michael guessed had not been borrowed from the Chelsea Palace wardrobe department.

At one stage in the dancing the band slowed the tempo and Michael found himself in a slow, close foxtrot with Debbie. She had abandoned the red cloak to the care of Nicole, which left her wearing a tiny skirt and a dancer's stiff basque; a garment that did not so much support her breasts as present them on a shelf. She held him close, arms wrapped tight around his back. Michael soon felt his body react and attempted to pull himself away. But she held on, and pushed their hips together.

"Oh Grandma," she breathed in his ear. "What a big cock you have … oh shit!"

She pulled away and spun around so that she was no longer facing the door.

"Nicole! Cloak! Quickly, my cloak."

Once she was safely covered up, Debbie turned to face the door and waved enthusiastically. She winked at Michael as she made her way across the room.

"Is it my turn now?" asked Libby, as she joined him on the dance floor.

"She had me prisoner. She wouldn't let me escape."

"I didn't see you struggling to get away. I wondered whether you prefer women with a fuller figure."

Michael decided to ignore this line of conversation. Claiming a need for some respite he left Libby and Nicole on the dancefloor, and went in search of drinks. Returning with a tray he found Libby sat on the floor with her back against a pillar. In the hall doorway Debbie waved before giving a balding man an affectionate hug. Michael sat down and offered Libby a beer, but she produced another half full tumbler. She snuggled up to him and took a swallow.

"Gin," she grinned, her eyes sparkling.

"What was the problem just now? Is that her father?"

Libby giggled.

"God no. That's Gerald; he's her patron."

"Patron?" said Michael in confusion, then the penny dropped and he laughed. "You mean he's a sugar-daddy, that Debbie is a …"

"Don't be melodramatic. Lots of girls have special friends. Look around you."

"So these girls are … well, prostitutes?"

Even as he said the word Michael felt ridiculous. The girls at the party bore no resemblance to Berwick Street's hollow eyed tarts.

"No, of course not," said Libby, shifting her body until they were no longer touching. "Gerald doesn't pay Debbie to sleep with him. I'm not even sure that she has. He buys her presents, jewellery, clothes, that kind of thing. He's some kind of businessman."

"And in return?"

Libby rolled her eyes and sighed.

"And in return … Debbie is nice to him. She goes with him to parties, country weekends … lots of rich men have girls in town. The man with Gerald is something in the government."

Michael focused on the group. Gerald's companion was dressed in an old fashioned double breasted suit and looked like a provincial bank manager. He was talking animatedly to a striking blonde in a low cut evening dress who was apparently captivated by every word her companion uttered.

"I've met Gerald," said Libby. "He's quite sweet in an old fashioned way … and before you ask. The answer is no. I do not have a patron, or sugar daddy, or whatever name you choose."

Michael was about to reply, but hesitated, unwilling to spoil the evening with an argument. He was rescued by Archie, who reappeared, having shed the gorilla costume in favour of white painter's overalls.

"They've arrived," he shouted.

Michael pulled Libby to her feet and the three returned to the reception hall, where Nicole handed out copies of The Express. Debbie joined the group, as did Annabel, with a tall, blonde dinner-jacketed escort in tow.

"Page eleven," said Archie. There was a concerted rustling of paper.

"Gosh," said Debbie. "It's a whole page."

This wasn't quite true. The story spread over two thirds of the page, with a quarter page shot showing all three girls being admired by the crowd, one of Debbie in the Monroe dress, and one of Annabel demonstrating cool professional poise. The headline was 'Pavement Style', and the text burbled about the impromptu fashion show that had stopped the traffic in Chelsea.

Michael's focus was on the picture byline, with the legend *photographer: Michael Ratcliffe* in tiny print. The next few minutes were a confused scrum of handshakes, kisses and congratulations, mostly from people that he didn't know. He had the smaller of two centres of attention, with the larger group cluttered around Archie, including Gerald, who was pumping Archie's hand and announcing that the coverage was 'better than any advertisement' and would be 'good for business'.

Whilst her beau was thus occupied Debbie took the opportunity to offer her own congratulations to Michael; a long embrace interrupted by Libby, who elbowed her way into his arms and assaulted his lips with her own, only breaking away to threaten dire reprisals if he 'smooched that hussy again'.

"She was smooching me," he protested. He led her away from the crush, cupped her chin, lifted her mouth and kissed her gently.

"Debbie is not my type, you are. Cross my heart. I am yours for the rest of the night."

Looking only slightly mollified, she took his hand and dragged him back to the bar to celebrate, then to the dance floor, where they danced until she lost a shoe and stumbled heavily. Michael caught the fall and held on as she refitted the shoe. She leant against him, her head on his shoulder:

"Too much gin," she whispered. "Take me home will you?"

***

The half hour walk through the cool deserted streets cleared Libby's head and, by the time they crossed the Ebury Bridge, she was well enough to joke about living on the wrong side of the tracks. Her bedsit was in Pimlico, in a run down cul-de-sac backing on to the main railway line into Victoria.

She had been largely silent on the walk, happy to listen to Michael chattering about wild parties in Berlin. As they reached the weatherbeaten door she reached for her keys and held a finger to her lips.

The bedsit was on the top floor. Michael had to negotiate three flights of stairs, a number of creaking floorboards and then endure a long wait while Libby found the correct key to her room.

"Does your landlady not allow visitors?" he asked, as soon as they were safely inside.

"Landlord," corrected Libby. "And I don't think he cares, but we need to be quiet because Peter on the first floor works at Billingsgate, and has to be up at three."

She pulled off her raincoat and threw it on the bed, then changed her mind and hung it behind the door. She looked at Michael, who was standing just inside the door carrying the photo portfolios and a bag containing the costume wings.

"Just put those things down somewhere ... over there by the chest of drawers."

He did as instructed, and then waited again, unsure of what to do next. For a second Libby looked equally uncertain.

"Before I do anything else I need to get out of this costume."

Michael smiled and raised his eyebrows. Libby returned the smile, then turned her back to him.

"Don't jump to conclusions, this thing is cutting me in two. Just do the zipper will you?"

Michael pulled the zip down and watched as she flexed her back gratefully, then she picked a dressing gown off the bed and made for the door.

"Back in a 'tic."

Michael watched the door close, smiled to himself and looked around the room, which was bigger than his place in Chelsea, but not noticeably tidier. It had the essentials of bed, sink and two ring burner, with an electric fire set into a chimney breast. Worn lino covered most of the floor, with a battered square of carpet between the bed and the sink. Stockings and underwear hung from a line over the sink, clothes and shoes spilled out of the open wardrobe. The only real colour came from a sunflower patterned quilt on the bed, where a red suited doll lay face down on the pillow.

Framed photographs covered a dressing table, with more on the wall behind. A long haired Libby on the back of a motorbike; Libby holding an abstract painting, Libby on a beach that looked like Brighton. The same young man featured in most of the pictures: a slimmer, younger version of Archie, fair haired and lean with a James Dean half smile. There were some family pictures: a serious faced younger Libby wearing school uniform, Libby with an older man that Michael guessed was her father, and a woman in a pure white blouse and severe skirt that reached almost to her ankles.

Something about the pictures triggered a sense of recognition; a memory shadow that refused to rise to the surface. The door opened before Michael could focus on the cause, and Libby was back in the room.

She was wearing the dressing gown, which covered her from head to toe.

"Look," she said, striking a pose. "The belle of the ball."

Michael stepped forward and took her hand.

"Step forward Miss Pimlico 1956."

He led her over to the bed and sat down beside her.

"Don't sit on Treacle," she said, picking up the doll and giving it a kiss. "He's the love of my life."

"That's a great name," said Michael moving the battered figure to one side. "But dolls have their limitations."

Gently he kissed her. As she responded, he loosened the ties of the gown and slid his hand inside, delighting in the discovery that she was wearing nothing beneath.

His hand found the small hard point of her breast, and eased her gently onto her back. He opened her dressing gown and admired the slim, neat body for a moment as she watched and waited. Then he smiled and began the slow and tender overture to making love.

***

A few hours later Michael awoke, confused at first, before the warm body alongside combined with the delicious ache in his loins to provide a reminder of events. The morning sun had just began to light the room through the thin curtains. In the nearby sidings a steam locomotive began its asthmatic preparation for the day ahead.

Libby mumbled something in her sleep. She stirred, tiny movements of distress, as if she were tied down. Michael rose on one elbow and looked down at her face, which was agitated and disturbed.

"No, no," the words were a whisper, barely audible. "No … Mmm. Mo .. No."

He had heard that it was unwise to wake someone from a nightmare, but he could not listen to her distress and do nothing. He touched her shoulder.

"Libby ... Libby it's me, Michael."

"No. Stop ... Mother, please, stop. No!"

The last word was a shout, and Michael abandoned caution and shook her by the shoulders. Her eyes jerked open and she stared into space as the dream receded, before turning to the wall and rolling herself into a tight foetal ball.

"Libby. It's gone, whatever it was, it's gone."

He held her shoulders and slowly she relaxed and unwound, turning towards him and laying her head on his chest. After a few minutes she sighed and gave him a hard grateful hug.

"It was just a dream. I get them sometimes."

She raised her head and gazed at the untidy hair flopped over blue eyes that were soft with concern.

"I feel safe with you."

He grinned in response and she kissed him quickly.

"And I ... I like the way you do that. Like a Cheshire Cat."

She had been about to say 'love'. She liked his ready smile and wiry strength. The easy self assurance that fell just short of arrogance. She liked the way he kissed her neck and throat, and the gentle way he had opened up her body. She felt a connection from the very first moment in the cafe. In the studio at Patten's she had wanted ... no, not just wanted ... expected him to kiss her. At the party she wanted to be touched and taken, but appreciated the respect and understanding he had shown when she lost her nerve.

"Do I pass muster?" said Michael, and she realised that she had been staring down at his body.

"You'll do," she said. "Though there are bits that I've not inspected."

She moved her hand down under the covers. Michael enjoyed the soft exploration without moving for what seemed a long time, then he turned her onto her back and moved his head down between her legs.

"Treacle," she said, turning sideways to look at the doll. "I'm not sure that you should be watching this."

Michael moved his position slightly.

"A little higher," said Libby, arching her hips. "There … mmm, yes, just there. Oh gosh … Treacle, I think you may be out of a job."

Michael woke for the second time just after eight o'clock. He dressed quickly and crossed the landing to visit the bathroom. Returning to the half light of the flat he used Libby's hairbrush to beat some order into his hair whilst he examined the pictures on the dressing table. The same feeling of recognition returned, but he still couldn't pin down the cause.

"Libby …?" he began.

A tousled head appeared above the sheets for a second, then returned to the warmth of the nest. Michael looked at his watch and decided to ask about the pictures later. Gently he shook a lump on the bed that he guessed was a shoulder.

"Libby, I've got to go. I have a meeting in Holborn."

The head re-appeared and he kissed her quickly.

"See you tonight?"

She nodded drowsily and disappeared beneath the quilt.

"I'll ring Poppies, leave a message," he said, as he closed the door.

Libby listened as he negotiated the stairs and left the house. As she heard the front door close she moved her hand over the warm impression he had left in the bed, then rolled face down into the hollow, luxuriating in his warmth, his masculine scent and the memory of his body on hers.

When Robbie had been killed she thought that she would never again experience this feeling of belonging, never find anyone who might fill the gap he had left. But she felt completely at ease with Michael, as if they had known each other for years.

She kissed the faint impression left on the pillow. A deliciously warm thought appeared inside her head: silly, unwonted, ridiculous. It was much too soon to be sure.

"I love you," she whispered, sounding out the words. And then louder and with more confidence; the words addressed to the battered doll propped up at the end of the bed.

"I love you, Michael."

***

Michael walked towards Victoria thinking of where he might go with Libby that evening and what they might do at the weekend. He frowned with the realisation that he had promised to travel down to Devon to see Edith and James.

I could arrange a photo shoot in the garden

A memory exploded, like a thunderflash on Guy Fawkes Night, stopping him abruptly on the pavement, and forcing the woman behind to detour into the road.

The picture on Libby's dressing table … A green lawn on a bright spring day.

How many years ago, fifteen?

His first camera, a box brownie given as a present by James Threwe. The dressing-up box brought down from the Hall. Alice Young not wanting to have her picture taken, and finally posing awkwardly in her schoolmistress's crisp white blouse and long pleated skirt. Lizzie standing impatiently as she waited her turn, dark hair loose and down to her waist. Lizzie, his best and only friend, with her sparkling eyes, and mischievous sense of adventure.

"Lizzie!" said Michael to the street at large, almost shouting the name in bewildered amazement and disbelief. He looked back, wondering whether he should return and share the knowledge. But then a nearby church clock struck the half hour.

I will see her tonight – and tell her then.

Kings Road

Libby emerged from the bathroom after spending far too long on her hair and make-up. On the bedside chair the waiting black skirt and white blouse mocked her careful preparation.

"It's what most shop assistants wear," she pantomimed in front of the mirror, a parody of Nicole's well intentioned advice.

"And do eat something for breakfast – you don't know what arrangements they will have for lunch."

To back up the suggestion Nicole had left a Weetabix biscuit in a bowl on the small table, next to an apple, because fruit is 'good for you'. Alongside the cereal bowl a note wished Libby 'good luck', with a postscript request to get some more milk on the way home.

Libby glared at the neatly set table, with its simple check tablecloth and beaded cover for the jug – in which she knew there would be just enough milk for the cereal and a cup of tea.

"Sensible Nicole, kind Nicole, understanding Nicole – too bloody perfect Nicole."

Libby felt her eyes welling up and dashed to the loo to save her make-up with some toilet paper.

"I will not cry. I will not, that's over, finished." She checked her face in the mirror. "There will be … No … More … Crying."

Libby gathered her resolve, put on the blouse and skirt, and told herself that she would be the best shop assistant in London bar none. She boiled some water and made tea, then sat at the table and forced herself to eat the cereal. She washed up at the small sink, put the apple in her handbag, checked her purse to ensure she had the correct fare, then carefully locked the door and walked the ten minutes to the underground station at Notting Hill.

***

At the end of August, once she felt fully recovered, Libby returned to London and threw herself into the jobs market. In a series of dispiriting interviews she was told that she was unlikely to get the kind of job she was applying for. The rejections had been cold and brutal. Employers highlighted the lack of references and gap in her resume. She could almost see them adding two and two before they turned her down.

With increasing desperation she turned to anything she could find in the 'Standard', but with no greater success. One man suggested there might be a job if she was prepared to have a second 'personal' interview later that evening. A typing pool supervisor said she was too posh:

"You wouldn't last ten minutes with my girls," the woman said. "Been out of circulation have we, dear?"

After a month of rejections Libby presented herself at Cheshunt Gardens and virtually begged Archie to help.

"Of course, love," he said. "Anything I can do, you know, just anything. Though I don't know why you left the agency. You've tried them I suppose?"

One glance at Libby's face revealed the answer to that question.

"I'll ask around, see what I can do." Archie reached for his wallet. "You all right for money? I could let you have twenty, just to tide you over."

Twenty pounds was three month's rent on the Moscow Road flat. Libby nodded quickly.

"That would be really good of you."

Her ready acceptance took Archie by surprise. The hand, which had not actually reached his jacket pocket, continued its journey and extracted four white notes.

"Sure?" he said, as he watched the money being folded into Libby's purse. "Girl like you, bright, attractive – you could do any job. People are stupid aren't they? Look, friends arriving soon. Can you give me a ring in a few days."

Three days later she walked round to the call-box outside the shops on Pembridge Road. Interminable ringing, then a breathless Archie.

"Oh. Yes … Libby, how are you? No, of course I haven't forgotten."

There was a long pause.

"Look – this is the best I can do, you might not want to …"

Another pause, Libby heard whispering and a muffled answer. She imagined the hand over the mouthpiece, then Archie's voice returned.

"Anyway, here goes, best I can do … Laura needs someone to help … you know Laura? I'm sure you two have met. No? Well, she's running the shop on the Kings Road. No, not the coffee bar – it's called …"

Libby heard a bang as Archie dropped and retrieved the handset, then the noise of rustling paper.

"Sorry about that … it's called 'Sublime' … opposite Wellington Gardens, on the north side. Laura's running the show, after Caroline left. Laura Mills-Johnson, Teddy's sister. You know, from Oxford. Are you sure you haven't met? Anyway, she's been left in the lurch, could do with some help."

***

Libby stood on the Kings Road. The shop was fifty yards away from the Barok coffee bar. This was presumably the establishment the publicity shoot was intended to promote. Memories crowded into her head and she fought down an urge to flee back to the flat.

Sublime's window display was a hotch potch of badly dressed mannequins, sun shrivelled price labels and dusty clothes samples decorated with a scattering of dead flies. The window glass was cluttered with promotional posters, including some that she recognised from the year before. The overall impression was one of neglect; her mouth pursed in disapproval.

She pushed the door, a bell jangled and a woman with honey blonde hair interrupted an animated telephone conversation with an invitation to 'look around please' before returning to her call.

Libby wandered the room checking out the clothes rails, making her usual assessment of any clothes shop. Did it have anything she might like, and was it available in her size? For the first question the answer was a definite 'Yes', but the rails were full of the larger sizes. It was not just that there was nothing in her size that she liked. There was nothing in her size at all.

"Can I help you?"

"My name's Libby Young … a friend of Archie's, about the job."

The woman looked puzzled for a couple of seconds, before smiling with recognition.

"Oh, great, that's wonderful. Yes, it was today wasn't it? Do you know, I had completely forgotten."

Laura emerged from behind the small counter and began a tour of the shop. Dresses and jackets on the rails, blouses on the display shelves, underwear in a multi drawered unit alongside the counter. Stocks, it seemed, were a little low, but orders were on the way. Fridays and Saturdays were the big days, there was a loo upstairs, and a storeroom – which, Libby noted, appeared to be devoid of stores.

Libby's duties were to serve customers, clean up, manage the rails, open up and close when necessary, and to fill in for Laura when she was unavoidably detained.

"Six pounds a week. We close Mondays and half day Wednesdays, and we open late until seven on Fridays and Saturdays."

Libby soon discovered that Laura often used the word 'we', when she actually meant 'you'. By the end of the first week it was obvious that her employer ran the shop as a hobby, on a strictly part time basis. Orders were based on what Laura liked, and what she thought her friends would like. Which might, thought Libby, be a reasonable way to run the business, were it not for the fact that Laura and her friends preferred to borrow clothes, rather than pay for them. The paying customers were subsidising Laura's social life.

Late on Friday morning Laura requested a 'little word', just as Libby was about to disappear upstairs for much needed loo visit followed by a sandwich.

"You have made such a good start," began Laura, reminding Libby of a teacher about to bestow a gold star. "I've decided to demonstrate a huge amount of trust, because I just know that you can handle the responsibility."

She handed over the keys and intimated that she might be a touch busy over the weekend. Libby worked the rest of Friday and the whole of Saturday on her own, and seemed to send a great deal of that time explaining to customers that items were on order, or out of stock. By six thirty on Saturday she was exhausted. As she flipped the door sign to 'closed' she recalled Archie saying that Laura had been left in the lurch.

"Left in the lurch!" she said to the disordered clothes rails. "They walked out, you silly cow."

She eyed her reflection in the shop's full length mirror.

But that's not an option for you, is it my girl?

For a second she almost allowed a wave of misery to overwhelm her, but she pushed the feelings away and started the process of totting up the day's takings prior to locking up and starting the journey back to Moscow Road.

Libby found the Saturday night journey home particularly depressing. She was desperate to kick off her shoes and wallow in a hot bath. The streets were busy with people whose working week had finished hours ago, if it existed at all. Sloane Square tube station was full of partygoers and people travelling into Town. A year ago Libby would have been making the same kind of journey; now she was dressed in her shop girls' clothes and the highlight of her evening might be to share a tin of salmon with Nicole.

The pair had settled into a comfortable routine, washing each other's hair, sharing the shopping and cooking, going to the cinema on a Monday, and listening to Nicole's records on her neat little suitcase player. Libby missed the glamour of working at Poppies, and the social whirl that went with the job.

Not so Nicole, who had never been comfortable with Libby's job at the model agency.

"People think it's all sex parties and dirty old men," she'd said, not entirely inaccurately.

Nicole worked as secretary to the boss of an export business near Marble Arch, a convenient couple of stops down the Central Line. The work was routine and predictable, which Libby presumed had been the attraction.

Her flatmate's solid common sense could be wearying at times, but Nicole always came to the rescue when it mattered, first after Robbie's death, and then with the pregnancy. The bolt hole at her aunt's little terraced house in Suffolk had been the ideal place to go to have the baby. After the adoption Libby returned to London with no place to stay, and Nicole offered to share the Bayswater flat. And she was company in the evenings; a captive audience for Libby's frequent grumbles about the shop.

"Girls like that walk on water," Nicole had said, after hearing of Laura's latest piece of ineptitude.

Libby looked up in surprise, Nicole rarely expressed a strong view about anything. Her usual approach was to listen to Libby's caustic opinions without comment; a tactic Libby assumed was designed to avoid making any kind of decision as to the rights and wrongs of the situation.

"What do you mean?" she asked. "Laura's a disaster waiting to happen."

Nicole paused in her ironing to consider Libby's furious expression.

"Everything is given to that kind of girl on a plate. She doesn't need the shop to succeed because she doesn't need the money. Nothing matters, the shop is just a hobby until the next thing comes along. If something goes wrong she can waltz back to Daddy for another handout. It's not a career. It's not even a job. It wouldn't be like that if a man was running the shop."

She selected a blouse from the washing basket and picked up the iron.

"It's just the way things are, Libby. There's no point getting all annoyed about it. It's a man's world. Girls like us just have to buckle down and make the best of things."

***

Libby usually collapsed into bed around nine o'clock and was asleep almost before her head had touched the pillow. But not tonight. At midnight she was wide awake and staring at the ceiling. She seethed with anger, partly because she had accepted a shop assistant's job instead of holding out for something better. But mainly over the ridiculous situation.

She, Libby, could run that shop. She could make it work: sort the orders, pay the bills on time, provide what people really wanted to buy. But she wasn't in charge, Laura was. Laura! who was complacent, inept and apparently blind to the idea that a clothes shop is where people expect to find nice clothes. The train of thought looped around her head for what seemed like hours.

When she did fall asleep it was to dream of the shop on a crowded Saturday. Customers were rampaging through the rails, strewing clothes over the floor. Libby was on her hands and knees, desperately tidying up as an immaculately dressed Laura towered over her.

"Libby will do that, ask Libby, Libby will get that for you …"

***

Libby worked through the winter at the shop, effectively as the manageress, as Laura rarely appeared for more than half a day at a time.

Tuesdays and Wednesdays were reps' days, and Libby was an interested spectator as Laura was persuaded to buy things that she knew would not sell, whilst being denied sufficient quantities of stock that was flying off the rails.

"They always say that," she complained after one rep had left the shop.

"Say what?" asked Libby innocently.

"He says he can't give me more than a dozen of the 'Starburst' dress, and most of those will be the wrong sizes."

Libby had sold the last small size "Starburst' on Saturday, and had promised at least three other customers that stocks would be in that week.

"So how many 'small' size?" she asked.

"Two," said Laura gathering her coat and bag. "I'm just out for a coffee. Hold the fort can you, there's a love."

Just before lunch the following day Laura popped her head around the door and announced that she had an 'important meeting' and could Libby be a sweetie and deal with the rep from Mattesons who was due that afternoon.

"What do I say?" asked Libby. "We are almost out of their dresses, I suppose we should be thinking about their summer collection."

Laura paused at the door; there was a taxi waiting and she was clearly anxious to leave.

"Really? Gosh, yes. I suppose we should, but I don't think that is what he is calling about."

And then she was gone, leaving Libby staring at the door.

What else could he be calling about?

The answer came about an hour later when the rep appeared. Libby explained that Miss Mills-Johnson had been unavoidably called away and the man laughed.

"Chickened out of seeing me more like."

He leant over the counter and the smile disappeared.

"Tell Miss snooty Mills-Johnson that there is no more credit. She has to return the goods or pay the money she owes by the end of the month. And returned goods must be in good condition. The last lot she sent back had been worn – one dress had stains all down the sleeves."

He looked Libby up and down.

"You look like a sensible girl. If I were you I'd look for another job, 'cos this place is going down the pan."

Laura laughed when Libby offered an edited version of the rep's dire threats.

"He's said that before. I'll pay them when I'm ready."

Libby nodded quickly, and was rescued by a customer who came in to look at scarves. But she thought that the rep had summed up the shop's likely prospects with remarkable accuracy. The place was indeed going down the pan – and her job with it. Her weekly wages were paid from the till, as were most of the rest of the bills. During one of Laura's many absences Libby dug out the order book and compared it with the ledger. It took most of the afternoon, but by the end of the day she had established that the 'unpaids' amounted to over two hundred pounds. Some of the bills were months overdue.

In the back of the ledger were some rough calculations and a list of names and addresses, including Caroline Quinn, whose clothes Libby had modelled the year before. Laura had been evasive when asked about Caroline.

"We lost touch," she said. "I think she moved, to Poplar or somewhere awful like that."

Libby carefully noted down the address, which was indeed in Poplar. She told herself that she would not allow the shop to fail. If she worked really hard perhaps Laura might make her the manageress … and then one day … perhaps she might run a shop like this herself.

Look around you girl, anyone could do better than this.

The following day she asked Laura's permission to re-design the window display, and gave up an entire Sunday to clear out the dust and flies, and provide the mannequins with a much needed wash. She brought in a couple of straw bales from the local rag-and-bone man, and a wheelbarrow from the hardware store further down the road. She made a scarecrow, dressed the mannequins, and arranged them around the bales, with one sat in the wheelbarrow.

On Tuesday Laura arrived around mid-morning and stared at the display in horror before pushing her way through a crowd of customers.

"Libby," she said sternly. "About the display."

Two young girls turned away from a sizeable pile of purchases and giggled.

"Isn't it wonderful," said one, in the kind of penetrating voice that can be heard clear across a crowded arena at the Berkshire show. "Everyone's talking about it. Such a crazy idea. We love the scarecrow, don't we Sam."

Whatever Laura had been about to say remained unsaid. After lunch she made her usual excuses, but before disappearing she pulled Libby to one side.

"Your display seems to be very popular, but do ask me about these things in advance. I could have made some suggestions."

Libby was tempted to ask what Laura might have suggested, but the door had already closed.

On her next day off Libby took the District line to Bromley-by-Bow, then asked a newspaper seller for directions to Morris Street.

"Over the cut, you mean?"

"I suppose so," she handed over the scrap of paper with Caroline Quinn's address.

"Poplar Feeds?" he asked.

Libby nodded.

The man pointed. "Round the corner, down the main road, right into Devas Street, for about ten minutes or so. Left into Violet Road until you cross the cut. T'other side of the bridge is Morris Street. Poplar Feeds is on the left."

He looked her up and down.

"Take you about a half hour. There's no bus, and you won't get a taxi round here."

Libby hesitated.

"Do you know what this place is – Poplar Feeds?"

"Used to make animal fodder out of mouldy wheat and fishheads. Stank to high heaven. Don't rightly know what they do there now, full of wogs nowadays, women wearing curtains an' stuff. Like bloody Bombay."

It took a little over half an hour, through streets where Libby's smart clothes stood out like a sore thumb. Finally she crossed the Limehouse canal – the cut – lined with warehouses, the nearest of which had the name 'Poplar Animal Feeds' emblazoned in faded paint across its brickwork. Shabby double doors led into an even shabbier hall with a metal cage lift next to broad well-worn stairs. A wooden noticeboard had slots for the names of the building's tenants. Quinn Designs was on the second floor.

***

"They are from Bengal mainly. That's Pakistan, since '48 anyway."

Libby looked over Caroline's shoulder to the noisy shop floor, and the women working at the rows of sewing machines.

"They are wonderful machinists – wonderful."

Caroline looked nothing like the smooth ex-model that Libby remembered. She was dressed in work boots and jeans, a man's shirt, with her hair tied up in a scarf, like a factory girl from the war. The small office overflowed with fabric samples and bolts of cloth. Two tailor's dummies stood in the corner, alongside an angled drawing board.

One of the shy neat women came in with a dress for Caroline to inspect,

"No, this won't do," said Caroline. "Tell her to start again."

She put the half finished dress on the bench, and turned to Libby. "What brings you out to the Limehouse wastelands?"

Libby explained about the job and about her frustration with Laura. Caroline nodded with understanding, and Libby was encouraged enough to reveal her dream that Laura might fade into the background and allow Libby to run the business.

"She might," said Caroline. "We were going to run that shop together. The plan was that Laura would run the shop and I would supply the clothes …"

"But it didn't work out?"

"You guessed. I wasn't cut out for the retail side. It took too much time when what I really wanted to do was make things, but that wasn't why we split up. That day last summer when we had the photographs done, you modelled didn't you? In that Hepworth dress? On the day of the shoot I was supposed to work with the photographer whilst Laura looked after the shop. But she double booked herself, so I had to be at the shop and Archie filled in at the studio. It's amazing the pictures turned out as well as they did."

Caroline picked up the dress and looked at the stitching again. "I might be able to do something with this," she turned back to Libby.

"That kind of thing happened all the time. Laura could never remember what she had ordered, and she missed payments. I can't afford that, so I stopped supplying. I sold my flat, and took the lease on this place. I started with two machinists I found at the local cafe. That was Panya just now, they're my supers – they speak English, and they know how to handle the girls."

Libby picked up a blouse with a finely worked neckline. On the next bench was a skirt with side pleats and broad waist loops for a belt.

"These are nice … who is your buyer now?"

Caroline sighed. "I sell some direct, mainly to shops where friends have put a word in for me. But most of what we make goes to a wholesaler – Solly – he has connections all over the place …"

"But …"

"Yes, you guessed again. He does pay, but he drives such a hard deal that I'm hardly making any money. Solly's very conservative about what he buys – and very secretive about who he is selling the stuff on to. I think I'm being diddled, but I don't know enough about the business to challenge him, not yet anyway."

Panya reappeared with another version of the same dress. Caroline inspected the stitching and then explained the modifications she wanted done to the previous dress.

"I'd better go," said Libby.

Caroline looked up and nodded.

"Good to see you, glad you dropped by. If you do end up in

charge I for one would be really keen to be a supplier. You have a feel for what people are wearing, you always did."

***

The following Saturday at the shop, Libby was surprised to see Laura appear, and even more surprised when her employer stayed after lunch, working hard, making sales, dashing to greet customers, and at one point even making Libby a cup of tea.

At seven, as Libby was tidying the rails and replaced dislodged price labels, Laura flipped the door sign to 'closed' and approached with an ominously bright smile.

"Libby," she began.

It seemed that things had not quite turned out as Laura intended. She was just 'so busy' and the shop was just 'so much' hard work.

"So I've decided to let it go. The rent is paid until the end of next month, and we still have quite a lot of stock, but at the end of August the shop will have to close. I thought I would tell you now, so you could look for something else, although …"

The smile stretched a little and Laura put her hand on Libby's arm.

"I'd be really pleased if you could stay on until the end."

Nicole had gone to Woodbridge for the weekend to see her mother, and Libby's time off was initially spent brooding over the sheer injustice of events. She followed this with an enjoyable interlude where she imagined a series of suitably gruesome ways to murder her employer. Finally, and more productively, she planned how she might take over the shop.

When Nicole returned on Sunday evening she had barely made it through the door before Libby presented her with sheets of calculations. Libby had to contain her impatience as Nicole sat at the small table and carefully worked through the figures.

"There are a lot of unknowns," she said eventually. "The rent for example – you have it as a monthly, but the landlord might want three months in advance, or even six."

She paused and looked at Libby.

"It's an awful lot of money Libby. Three hundred and fifty pounds; that's more than some people earn in a year."

"But do the figures add up, have I missed anything?"

"Yes and no," said Nicole, smiling. "The figures do add up, and no, I don't think you have missed anything."

Libby laughed in delight and kissed Nicole on both cheeks.

"Can I take my coat off now?"

On Monday Libby went to the shop and spent most of the day doing a full stock-take. She made an appointment with her bank for Wednesday afternoon. She rang the shop's landlord, who was out of town until Wednesday morning.

"Do you wish to leave a message?" asked his secretary.

"No, no message," said Libby, who did not want the landlord ringing the shop when Laura might pick up the call.

She left the shop at three and made the long journey across town, first to London Bridge and then down to Sutton. Libby had not seen her father since before Christmas, and she had only seen him a half dozen times since he had remarried five years before.

The new Mrs Young was a widow. Her name was Maureen and she had made disastrous attempts to befriend Libby, attempts that had left both women wary of each other's company.

Libby walked up the neat path just as the nearby church clock was striking six o'clock. She felt no connection to the house. She had lived there for only a few months before starting college at Camberwell. After that she had always managed to have a place to call her own, even if it was only a bed-sit. The solid three bedroomed semi belonged in another world.

Maureen loved ornaments and decoration, and the house had been filled with china animals and crystal vases. Framed scenes from Dickens were scattered around the hall, every chair-back had its antimacassar and the windows were hidden behind ruched lace curtains. Libby found it difficult to conceal her contempt for the décor, and the curtains had been the subject of an early row when she had compared them to french knickers. She found it difficult to believe that her father liked all this rampant frippery, but then she found it equally incomprehensible that Maureen had caught his eye in the first place.

Libby endured a light supper of ham and salad, follow by Battenburg cake and weak tea. There was some stilted conversation about Maureen's two sons, who had taken – in Libby's view – the sensible option and emigrated to Canada and New Zealand.

"When did you get back from France?" said her father, after safe topics had been thoroughly exhausted.

Libby had not confided in her father about the baby, and had explained her disappearance by claiming to have been working for the agency at their non-existent Paris sister company. Nicole assisted with the deception, arranging for a French cousin to forward letters to Woodbridge.

Libby explained that she had been back for a few months, but had changed jobs.

"Which is why I came really," she took a deep breath. "I've been given this wonderful opportunity to start a business."

She explained about the shop, glossing over her actual role, painting a soft focus picture of a magnanimous Laura recognising her retail limitations and encouraging Libby to take over a flourishing enterprise.

"Three hundred pounds," said Maureen in shock, when Libby finally worked around to putting a figure on the costs. "That's a fortune."

Libby ignored the pinched expression and concentrated on her father.

"It would be a loan, and I'm absolutely certain I could pay it back. Obviously I'm not asking for the full amount; I'll be using the money that Mummy left me. And I have made an appointment at the bank."

Edward Young looked at his daughter and tried to put out of his mind the very many times as a child when she had made promises and failed to deliver. He had little confidence in Libby's fairy tale opportunity, and he knew that the true nature of her business venture was not the only matter being carefully concealed. He had discovered in February that Poppies Model Agency had no sister company in France, and that Miss Young had, in any case, left their employment. There was also the uncomfortable fact that Libby had made no effort to build bridges with Maureen, quite the reverse. But she was his daughter …

"Lisbet …" he paused for what seemed to Libby to be a very long time. "I'm not sure you understand our situation. Three hundred pounds is, as Maureen says, a very large sum of money. Our main responsibility …" he glanced over to Maureen. "Well … it has to be to make sure that we have enough funds for our retirement."

"And for our grandchildren," added Maureen. "One day you will get married my girl, and have children. Then you will realise what's important and what's not."

Libby left the house with a cheque for fifty pounds, a sum that was only offered after she had submitted to a long lecture about the folly of living beyond her means. Edward signed the cheque with a heavy heart, only too well aware that the money was a gesture that would please neither of the two women.

***

On Tuesday Libby willed her employer to break her previous pattern and arrive before lunch. But it was two pm when Laura breezed through the door, and nearly closing time before Libby felt able to deliver her well-rehearsed speech.

"Laura, about the shop … A friend and I have been thinking about taking it on. We were wondering whether you would allow us to buy the unsold stock."

The raised eyebrows were really answer enough, but Libby ploughed on with her script.

"Or even whether you might think of allowing us to pick up the business now, taking on the lease."

Laura made an unconvincing pretence of giving the idea some consideration.

"Well, that's a surprise. And very enterprising of you, but do you really think you have the skills, or the contacts?"

These were obviously intended as rhetorical questions, and Laura smothered Libby's attempt at a reply with a wave of the hand.

"So it's a 'No' I'm afraid. But really plucky of you to come up with the idea. I'm impressed."

Debbie

The day after Laura's not unexpected refusal Libby closed the shop at midday and dashed back to Moscow Road to change. She put on new stockings, a black pencil skirt and cream blouse, and finished it off with paisley silk scarf. She powdered her nose and put the tiniest dab of colour on her lips. Then it was back on the tube to the Sloane Square branch of City and West. She arrived a full twenty minutes too early, and strolled up and down Kings Road trying to keep her heartbeat under control.

A couple of minutes before two o'clock she went through the big revolving doors, took at seat at a table, and tried to look like someone who knew how to open a shop and make lots of money. A balding middle-aged man arrived and took the seat opposite, nodding to Libby nervously before putting his battered trilby on the table. He selected one of the desk pens, looked at the attached chain with puzzlement, made sure it would reach to his side, then picked out a form from the rack. He studied the paper as if it was written in Sanskrit, then glanced over to Libby.

"It says there are two kinds of accounts," he whispered. "Current and deposit."

Libby nodded.

"What's the difference? It's just that our firm has just decided to pay us monthly – and we've got to get a bank account. Never 'ad one before."

Libby had barely started an explanation of the distinction between accounts when the frosted glass door marked 'Manager' opened and a tall man in a pin-stripe suit appeared. He looked around the waiting area, before striding confidently towards Libby's table.

"Mr Young?" he said to the man opposite Libby, presenting his hand to be shaken.

The bald man half stood, tentatively offering his hand, before looking round in confusion.

"I'm sorry," he said. "But I'm Clegg, Arnold Clegg."

Libby stood up. "My name is Young. I have a two o'clock appointment."

Now it was the manager's turn to look confused.

"I have an appointment with a Mr Young," he said, with an emphasis on the 'mister'.

"Well, I am definitely a Miss, as you can see," said Libby.

The manager hesitated for a few seconds, then shook Libby's extended hand.

"You had better come through."

Inside the office Libby accepted the offer of a chair and took the carefully prepared papers out of her bag. Safely behind his desk the manager looked at his appointment book and then at an account sheet.

"Yes," he began. "Your account is in the name of Elizabeth Young, but my secretary told me I would be seeing a Mr Young. Most odd."

His eyes travelled further down the document.

"And I see that you have requested a business loan for the amount of three hundred pounds."

"Yes," said Libby. "I'm planning to open a business on the Kings Road." She offered the papers from her bag. "I've prepared an outline of the anticipated expenses, and a summary of the potential monthly income. I work there at the moment, so I am pretty much certain that these figures are accurate."

"You work there." There was a pause as he looked at Libby, then he took the papers and put them on the desk. "And Mr Young – is that your father? A brother? You did say 'Miss', so it is presumably not your …"

"It is 'Miss'. I am not married. There isn't a Mr Young, not attached to me anyway."

The man hesitated again, then leant back in his chair. "I'm afraid there has been some kind of mistake. We don't give business loans to young women, and certainly not loans of this amount."

"But I filled in the form … I've had an account with this bank since I was seventeen. I've never been overdrawn. There's nearly a hundred pounds in my deposit account. Isn't that – what's the word – security?"

The manager stood and handed Libby her sheaf of papers.

"As I said, there has been some mistake. You should not have been given an appointment. I'm sorry if we have wasted your time."

Libby stood her ground, ignoring the proffered papers, trying to look the man straight in the eye. But he was moving towards the door.

"Aren't you even going to look at the figures?"

The manager opened the door.

"I can only repeat, there has been a mistake."

He took Libby's arm and escorted her to the revolving doors.

"Take my advice young lady," he said in a fatherly tone, as he pushed her gently through the doors. "Keep your savings for your bottom drawer."

Libby found herself propelled out onto the street, and on to the pavement, where she swore violently, causing a young mum with a pram to steer her child away.

Libby turned towards the underground station and walked straight into a familiar statuesque figure.

"And who is the 'bloody smug bastard'?" said Debbie, smiling at first, and then concerned as she saw the distress on Libby's face.

"Oh dear, you look as if you've had some bad news." Debbie glanced at the bank entrance. "Been to see the manager?"

Libby nodded.

"No surprises there then. After all, it doesn't rhyme with wanker for nothing. Come and have a cup of tea, and I'll tell you my problems, it always helps to be told that someone else is just as deep in the shit."

They found a corner table in a nearby cafe, squeezing past a trio of well heeled women enjoying a cream tea with cakes. Debbie explained that she had travelled half way across London for a non-existent shift at the Chelsea Palace.

"But I thought you'd stopped," said Libby. "I thought Gerald didn't like you working there."

"Gerald is no more. He's moved on. Wife found out, run out of money, I don't know which, but it's 'goodbye Gerald, hello Chelsea Palace'. Except it isn't, they're closing down. No more tits and bums, who'd have thought?"

She made a clown's sad face, then grinned across the table. "See, you're feeling better already."

"What will you do?"

"I won't starve. There's modelling and waitressing. I might try the Windmill. There are other Geralds, the world's full of 'em. If the worst happens I might work the clubs – a girl's got to live."

Debbie looked at Libby's cup. "You've not drunk your tea. What was it with the bank? Have they bounced a cheque?"

Libby took a deep breath and explained about Laura and the shop, and the seemingly ridiculous idea that she might take it over. She had, she explained, been in in to the bank to ask for a three hundred pound loan. Debbie whistled softly, drawing disapproving looks from the trio of women in the window seat.

"And the bastards said 'No' didn't they?"

Libby nodded.

"But golly, Libby … three hundred quid!"

"Yes, I know, but … I could make that place work. I know I could."

"It all sounds too much like hard graft to me. You need a Gerald, you can have mine. He's goin' free at the moment," she laughed at the thought.

Libby smiled weakly, then the smile disappeared, and she leant across the small table.

"Why not? Why not a Gerald? If they are two a penny?"

Debbie's grin faltered as she saw Libby's serious face.

"Don't be silly. That's not for you, not in a month of Sundays."

"Why not?" said Libby, piqued and a little insulted by the amazed expression that faced her over the table. "I'm not stupid. I know what I would have to do."

Debbie's surprise morphed into an amused smile, and Libby's irritation became embarassed indignation.

"Don't you think I could do it? It's just sex; I can do that."

"Yes, and look where it got you last time."

The two women glared at each other. Debbie gave in first, and made a face at the trio in the window, who had abandoned their conversation in favour of listening to something much more interesting. Debbie turned back to Libby.

"It's not about whoring," she said, with no attempt at a whisper.

"And even if it was, three hundred quid is an awful lot of money, and the Geralds of this world didn't get rich by paying that for a girl. It's more about being a trophy they've won at the fair. It's a performance. You have to be there for them, when they want a girl on their arm. It means weekends away, and afternoons at the races. There is money, but it's small change compared with what you need. It can be fun … being taken to nice places, being bought clothes and presents. I like all that, the glamour and so on … but you have to pretend all the time, because the men are boring, boring, boring."

The cafe manageress whispered to the waitress, who made a

nervous start towards their table. Debbie put a shilling next to her cup.

"It's alright, we're leaving." As she passed the open mouthed trio in the window she posed for a second with one hand on her hip.

"I suppose you think your men are at work."

Once outside the door Libby and Debbie marched rapidly away from the cafe before collapsing into giggles outside Peter Jones.

"Their faces!"

"Did you see the manageress? I thought she was going to explode."

Libby smiled at her friend; the earlier row forgiven if not forgotten.

"Look," she said. "I want to do something with my life, not just get married to the next bloke that comes along. And I really don't want to be a shop assistant or a typist for the rest of my days."

She saw Debbie about to speak and put a finger to her lips.

"Let me finish. I can make a success of that shop, I know I can. I went to see Caroline Quinn and she will supply me with her designs. You remember that 'Monroe' dress? That was one of hers. I know it's a lot of money, but I'll pay it back. It will be a loan not a gift. Surely someone in business would understand. And I may not need three hundred, I have some money of my own …"

A thoughtful expression tracked across Debbie's face and Libby stopped in mid flow.

"You know someone! You do, don't you? You know someone."

Debbie stepped back, wondering if she could disavow the knowledge that Libby had seen on her face.

"I don't know him," she began. "At least, we've not … you know … it was awhile ago and he's not really my type. But we've met … and I know that he has helped girls out …"

She stopped, clearly reluctant to go on.

"Well … who is he? Have I met him? Does he have a name?"

"*You* haven't met him." There was an emphasis on the 'you' that Libby didn't understand until much, much later.

"He's a bit … unusual," continued Debbie slowly, as if the words were being dragged out of her mouth. "You'd have to be very careful."

"Yes, but what's his name?"

"Simon Lombroso – people call him Sly."

Totnes

The British European Airways Vickers Viscount from Nice landed in London at 9am, but it was nearly three o'clock before Michael arrived at Paddington, and seven in the evening before he staggered off the train at Totnes.

James was waiting with the Ford Anglia. It was raining, and on the way up to Overhill the windscreen wipers slowed to a leisurely crawl, forcing James to peer at the screen, like a sea captain navigating in fog.

"Thanks for coming down, Edith is really pleased, she's cooked a full roast, with all the trimmings, so I hope you're hungry."

Michael smiled weakly. He had been hungry, having eaten nothing since snatching a hurried cafe-et-croissant from the boulangerie outside his apartment in Nice. But he had succumbed to hunger pangs as the train shuddered through Reading. In defiance of logic he had swayed down to the buffet car and eaten a couple of dry and tasteless British Rail ham sandwiches, followed by an apple tart composed of leaden pastry and very little apple.

On arrival at Overhill he feigned a ravenous appetite and managed a generous portion of lamb and a second helping of crumble. Feeling heroically stuffed he pleaded the genuine need for a comfortable bed and was asleep seconds after his head had touched the pillow.

Just before five in the morning he was awakened by the morning sun, diffused through the drawn curtains. As the room came into focus he felt a glorious sense of familiarity and belonging. Home again, in his room, to the right off the landing, with its Avro Lancaster model hanging from the ceiling, the air rifle and cricket bat on top of the wardrobe, the prized collection of fossils in a shoe box under the narrow school desk.

Michael opened the curtains to the panoramic view down the river valley and out to sea. At sixteen he had been desperate to chase that horizon. His one ambition had been to escape from Overhill's beguiling comforts and the humdrum delights of Totnes' narrow streets. He shivered to exorcise the teenage ghost and climbed back into the warm bed.

Viewed through the wide angle lens of experience, the room and its contents shifted form and became a sanctuary from the harsh realities of adult life. The four walls were the distillation of safety and security: steadfast, immutable, cosy and snug.

He drifted back to sleep, waking three hours later to find a cold mug on tea on the chest of drawers. Dressing quickly, he poured the mug out of the window and wandered down to the empty kitchen. The table was set for one, with bread and jam waiting, through the kitchen window he could see Edith hanging washing in the courtyard. He filled a kettle and put it on the range to boil.

Edith appeared at the door with the empty washing basket.

"You're down then."

"Yes, sorry … dropped off again … thanks for the tea. I'm making another pot, would you like some?"

"Mmm, yes, I'll join you," she began to slice the bread. "Sit yourself down and have some breakfast. James has gone into town, some Council meeting, he'll be back for lunch."

She watched him eat for a while, marvelling as always over his ability to make food disappear.

"This new job …" she began hesitantly. Michael had broached

the subject of the posting the night before, and the news had been received with dismay, as he had suspected it would.

"It's not certain yet … there'll be a lot of things to consider."

Edith sighed.

"We've barely seen you these past two years … and you were only across the Channel. How often will you get back from … where is it? Singapore?"

Michael looked across the table at the anxious face and wondered whether he could eat another slice of bread.

"It could be Hong Kong, I'm not sure."

"That's even further isn't it?"

Now it was Michael's turn to sigh.

"Mum. I don't know. It's like I said, I'm not sure yet. There's to be another meeting when I get back to London. I'll know more then."

He reached for the bread knife and cut another slice. Edith smiled and slid the butter dish and jam across the table. James had warned her against pushing for information about the new job. She decided to change the subject.

"That girl you wrote about before you went out to Nice … what happened to her? You sounded really keen in your letter."

Michael tensed, "We lost touch," he said quickly, getting up from the table. Edith realised that she had made yet another wrong step on the endless parenting tightrope. She began to clear the breakfast things away.

"I'm going to take a walk up to the hall," said Michael. "It's not been sold yet, has it?"

"No. It's still for sale. Your boots are in the scullery, under the sink."

Michael picked up his camera and checked the telltale to ensure that it was loaded with film. It was a warm day and he went out in shirtsleeves, crossing the cobbled yard and through the archway into the gardens. He stopped beyond the archway to take in the many changes that had been wrought to Overhill over the past ten years. There were additional greenhouses and the kitchen gardens had been extended until they almost encircled the house. The darkroom where James had presented Michael with his first camera had been converted back into a potting shed.

This was all part of the project that James and Edith had begun since he left home – a market garden business that thrived on James' green fingers and Edith's hitherto undiscovered hard nosed business sense. The business had recently been supplemented by the introduction of bed and breakfast accommodation at the house. A small arbour had been fitted into the rose garden, as a peaceful place for guests to enjoy a welcoming pot of tea.

"We have six bedrooms," Edith had explained. "It's a shame not to make use of them."

The rose gardens were James' pride and joy, and Michael was enveloped in their scent as he walked past a battalion of blooms. He followed a gravel path to the beech hedge, leaving the ordered splendour of the gardens for the steep slope down to the stream.

This has been their route down to the dingle, all those years ago, Lizzie in her battered sandals and muddied knees. Her gingham dress dirty almost before they'd started to play.

***

It had all gone wrong after the party. He'd returned home to find a letter with a travel warrant to Gibraltar, and a short note from Oldfield asking him to ring the office.

"Bit of a flap," Oldfield had said. "We need you to fly out today, from Croydon. You'll be picked up when you get to Gib."

The stream looked smaller than he remembered, and years of rain had washed away any evidence of the civil engineering works that had been their favourite activity: no dams, walls or dens. He turned upstream, following a well used bridleway up towards the hall. The surrounding trees arched over the narrow dingle, and it was cool in the shade, and quiet, with only the noise of tumbling stream to intrude on his thoughts.

He 'phoned Poppies from the kiosk on the Kings Road. Libby had not been at the agency, and he'd left a message with a girl he didn't know.

"We're very busy today," she said. "And I'm not really supposed to take personal messages."

"Really important," he stressed. "I've been called away to work, can she meet me at midday at Waterloo?"

"Alright, just this once. I'll let her know," said the bored voice. He could hear the receiver descending to the cradle.

"Midday!" he yelled. "Twelve today."

In the event he waited 'til one; ringing her office again and again until he ran out of change. But there was no answer, no answer at all. He'd almost missed the flight. In Gibraltar he'd been transferred to a waiting destroyer that sailed almost immediately, leaving no time for him to make a 'phone call or send any kind of letter.

The ship was at sea for less than 24 hours when it turned around and returned to Gibraltar. At first the below decks scuttle-butt put this volte-face down to some Admiralty cock-up, but an official explanation eventually surfaced. Britain and France were not, it seemed, quite ready to teach the gyppos a well deserved lesson over Suez. The liaison officer stressed that this change of plan had not been specifically organised to ruin his love life. And no, he could not use a Royal Navy signal to send his girlfriend a message.

A telegram greeted his return to Gibraltar. He was to travel to Nice and meet up with Alex Cross, the paper's southern Europe correspondent. He tried to contact Libby again from Gibraltar, then wrote to her at the model agency and to the bed-sit in Pimlico. Months later he was not particularly surprised when the letters were returned to him unopened, addressee unknown.

The dingle widened as he reached the hall, the track climbing steeply to a five bar gate that opened into the rear courtyard. The house looked forlorn, abandoned, with the interior shutters closed and a huge padlocked bar against the kitchen door. In the courtyard's lean-to garage an ancient Fordson tractor shared the space with a long sleek car partly hidden by a mildewed canvas cover. It was Rupert's Riley Kestrel, with its long running board and huge headlights. Neither vehicle looked as if it would be travelling anywhere in the near future.

In September 1944 James borrowed the Riley and scrounged enough petrol to take Michael for his first term at Blundells. There was hardly any traffic on the roads and the huge two and a half litre engine ate up the miles, with Michael hanging on to the leather straps as James flung the car round corners. They skidded to a halt on the school's gravel drive with Michael's eyes shining with excitement, all doubts about the new school forgotten.

Blundells had been Rupert's idea, he had been typically insistent that Michael should move to the school where he and James had been pupils. He found an unlikely ally in Edith, who did not share James' egalitarian inhibitions about a public school education. The decision was made when Rupert offered to pay the fees. But Michael did not welcome the idea of a boarding education, and the drive across the moors had been an attempt to sweeten the pill.

There was a crunch of shoes on gravel, and Michael walked around to the front of the house. It was James, as he thought it might be.

"Edith said you might be up here, memory lane?"

"Not really, just fancied the walk."

"It's still for sale. Frank says that there's been no interest at all. Not a jot."

James and Edith had been bitterly disappointed when the estate had been put up for sale, and the fact that Rupert had transferred the deeds for Overhill into James' name was minimal consolation for the loss of the hall and everything that went with it.

"Frank?"

"Frank Settle, the estate manager … or was … he's joined Temple and Jones, the estate agents. Most of the staff found something. I managed to swing Malcolm a job with the Council."

"Malcolm?" Michael tried to keep the irritation out of his voice. One of the trials of his visits home was the assumption by both his parents that he knew everyone in the valley.

"Malcolm Newbery, Graeme Newbery's boy."

Michael made a face that he hoped was interested and sympathetic and the same time. But in reality he entirely understood why Rupert had put the hall up for sale. The estate was loss making, and had been since the end of the war. This wasn't unusual, few families could afford the upkeep of a genteel estate in the austerity that followed the the victory in '45.

Rupert was a Brigadier at the War Office, heavily involved in some obscure inter-services department, and rarely came down to Totnes. Michael hadn't seen his honorary uncle since he had left Blundells to join the RAF. But he also knew that the real reason for James' displeasure was the fact that Rupert clearly assumed that James was not interested in running the estate, or worse, that James was incapable of so doing. Michael decided to change the subject.

"Sorry I was so bushed last night," he struggled with how to explain what needed to be said.

James pretended not to notice.

"Do you fancy the circuit walk back to Overhill? It's a cold lunch, so it won't matter if we are a little late."

Michael nodded. The circuit walk had been a favourite years ago, first as a great adventure, then later, in his teen years, as an opportunity for some photography. The walk took a wide loop away from the hall, following ancient bridleways up to a beech copse that commanded a fine view of the river valley. Then it was down to Overhill, along a little-used lane that led almost straight back to the house.

James set off for the gate. As Michael followed he thought back to the brief meeting in the paper's Holborn offices. Brian Oldfield, cigarette in hand, slouched in a swing chair behind a massively cluttered desk.

***

"Fifth floor are very pleased with you," said Oldfield, after waving Michael into a chair. "Especially after Suez, those pictures really put the cat amongst the pigeons. Webster … remember him?"

Michael nodded.

"He said that your pix were one of the factors that led to Eden's resignation."

"But Eden went in January!"

"Yes, but Webster says that your story revealed that the operation wasn't going as predicted. It showed the casualties, British casualties, and that gave ammunition to the Left here, and to the Americans … and to Macmillan, who wanted Eden out. The decision that Eden should go was taken in November. And Webster says that your story was part of that."

Michael looked across the desk. "What do you think?"

"I don't think. I leave that to the people who've been to university. But they were good pix, and your write-up was solid. You were lucky to get them out so quickly."

Oldfield searched his desk without success, then yelled for his secretary. An attractive woman in her thirties appeared wearing a tolerant smile.

"Where's that contract for Ratcliffe?"

"On your desk." She looked at the chaos and raised an eyebrow. "Try looking under the 'Standard'."

Oldfield moved the newspaper and found a folder marked 'Ratcliffe M'. He glanced up, but his secretary had already returned to her typewriter.

"As I said, fifth floor are pleased with you. Not just the Suez pix, your other work has been good. Better than I thought you would do. I liked those shots of Bardot at Cannes."

He opened the folder, checked the contents and flung it down.

"We'd like to keep you on … Alex would love to have you in Nice … but there's another possibility."

Oldfield explained that the agency had decided to put a correspondent into south east Asia, covering an arc from Singapore to Hong Kong. Michael's fluency in French would be useful in an area where several countries had been French colonies, and Michael's ability to write intelligent copy would allow the agency to kill two birds with one stone

"The offer's there," said Oldfield, pushing the folder across the desk. "You can work out of Nice with Alex Cross, covering the film festivals and the Monte Carlo rally and the local news stuff as you have done this past year. You might make correspondent at some point, because you can write copy. Or you can accept the other job, and fly out to Singapore next week … I know what I'd do."

***

Michael and James walked in comfortable silence up through the fields behind the hall, until they gained the slight ridge that led up to the beeches. They continued to the trees and paused in the shade to appreciate the river set out below.

"Remember that buzzard?" said James.

Michael laughed. He had been about eleven or twelve. They'd walked up in midwinter, after a week of frosted mornings, the air crisp with cold and the fallen leaves crunching beneath their feet. As they entered the beech hangar they surprised a buzzard tearing at a rabbit carcass. The startled bird screamed defiance, extending its wings and advancing down the track. An equally startled Michael stepped back, inadvertently pressing the shutter on his Christmas camera.

"Best picture I took that year," he said.

James pointed down the valley. "Look, there's a ship, coming upstream. Must be on a rising tide."

"Aiming for Baltic Wharf?"

"Yes, for the timber yard," James looked at his watch. "We'd better get back, Edith will be waiting."

Michael nodded, but the two men continued to watch the freighter's progress. And it was only when the ship slowed for the final approach to its berth that the pair turned as one towards the five bar gate beyond the beeches.

For most of the morning Michael had been contemplating the hurt he would cause if he accepted the foreign correspondent's job. It was not a simple decision. Oldfield's lack of confidence was not encouraging, and Michael knew virtually nothing about the countries he would presumably be reporting from. He had heard of Singapore, but he struggled to find Vietnam on the small globe atlas in his bedroom. And when he did the country looked tiny and insignificant. He turned to James.

"About the job ..."

James inclined his head and waited.

"I could stay in Nice as Alex's photographer, or take the other job as a correspondent. It's a difficult choice. I like working with Alex. The correspondent's job is something new, I'd be expected to write as well as supply pictures. That's not what normally happens; snappers do the pix, scribblers do the words."

James heard the anticipation in Michael's voice and knew the decision was taken. Michael was going through the motions of considering the choices, but by the middle of next week he would be flying to the other side of the world, where he might stay for the foreseeable future. James felt a numbing sadness that was close to grief; Edith was going to be devastated. He turned away for a moment, gathered his reserves, then faced Michael with a smile.

"That sounds exciting."

Michael offered his oh so familiar grin. "Yes … yes it is."

On the way back to London Michael suffered a crisis of confidence. He'd left Overhill after lunch, promising to let Edith and James know his decision as soon as it was made. Edith had been distraught, despite his reassurances that he was not about to disappear off the face of the earth.

The Devon landscape rolling past the carriage window offered a further reminder of what he was leaving behind. Whatever awaited him in Singapore, it would not be like this – different country, landscape, language and people. And he would know nobody, no-one at all.

By the time he reached Paddington he had recovered some of his composure, but the attractiveness of the familiar had been burnished by the visit home and, as he passed through the underground ticket barrier, he was genuinely undecided about which option to take.

Having arrived in London a good two hours before the appointment in Holborn, Michael decided to take the Bakerloo line and get off at Oxford Circus. He walked towards Soho and found himself turning right into Berwick Street and up the narrow stairs that led to Patten's reception.

"I hope you're not after a job," said Mrs Perceval as he walked through the door. Michael grinned.

"Hello Mrs Perceval, lovely to see you."

"Mr Patten is not here, which is probably as well. He was not over pleased by your sudden departure."

"Actually Mrs Perceval … it was your good self I came to see. And, in a way, it is about a job."

Mrs Perceval raised her eyebrows, then listened without interruption as Michael explained his dilemma.

"Thing is," he concluded. "I'm not sure what to do."

The woman looked at him steadily for a few moments, then closed her huge desk diary and pushed her chair away from the desk.

"Cup of tea? Milk with one sugar still?"

She busied herself with the kettle in the corner.

"We've kept an eye on you … saw the Bardot spread in Picture Post last month … and the Suez pictures last year of course. Mr Patten commented on those, said they were 'remarkable' – that was the word – 'remarkable'."

She handed Michael his tea and returned to her desk. For a while she contemplated her tea. The 'phone rang and she took a call about a booking, noting the details in her diary. Finally she looked across the desk.

"It seems you have a choice of suits, between hearts or diamonds, love or money."

"Do you play poker Mrs P?"

"Certainly not," she snapped. "I play contract Bridge. Are you still with that good looking girl, the booker from Poppies."

"No … we lost touch."

"Then it seems it must be diamonds," she looked at the clock. "You need to be away young man. I have work to do."

Michael finished his tea and made for the door.

"Thanks for the rosie lee, Mrs P. Wish me luck."

"We make our own luck, good or bad. Off with you … or you will late for your meeting."

She waited until his steps had reached the bottom of the stairs, then fed a sheet of paper into the Remington. "The queen of hearts would have been your strongest suit," she said quietly, before banging out a memo to Mr Patten with a little more than her usual force.

***

At the agency's Holborn offices Oldfield's secretary reported that her boss had been forced to cross town for another meeting.

"But I have everything you need – I'm to check it through with you."

She produced two manila folders and began to unpack the contents onto her desk, ticking each item against a checklist.

"BOAC ticket for Singapore, out from Heathrow, with a night stopover in Beirut. I've arranged visas for Thailand, Cambodia and Vietnam. This is the company's expenses policy, you have quite a generous expenses allowance, but we do need to see monthly accounts, and any item over five pounds must be listed."

She paused for a second, surprised by his silence and the blank expression on his face.

"We've opened accounts for you in Singapore and Bangkok, with the Hong Kong and Shanghai Bank. They cover most of the countries where you might be operating."

She reached for the second folder. Michael decided to interrupt.

"These are all for the Singapore job."

"Well, yes," she said. "Is there something wrong?"

"There's nothing for the Nice job?"

"No. Mr Oldfield told me to prepare paperwork for the Singapore posting. He didn't say anything about Nice."

"How did he know? … sorry, please ignore that … you were going to show me these next papers."

She looked at him oddly for a moment, then picked up a thick wad of paper.

"These are all the clippings I could find, I had them xeroxed from the files. They cover the main stories, mostly about the Malay emergency. I couldn't go further back than two years, didn't have time, sorry."

The next surprise was an envelope full of five pound notes.

"These are for initial expenses. It's a hundred pounds, so please be careful. It may have to last you for some time."

Two forms were added to the growing pile on the desk.

"I'll need a signature … here for the money, and another … here … for the tickets and contract information."

Michael stared down at the mass of papers, and at the typed 'Michael Ratcliffe' printed underneath the spaces he had been asked to sign. He reached for the pen and scrawled his name.

"Good, now we need to get you down to the telex room for a quick chat with our operator. You've not used a telex before? … no, Mr Oldfield didn't think you had. After that I'll see if I can find the deputy foreign editor. It's all a bit of a rush I'm afraid, but there's so much to do before your flight. Mr Oldfield will see you at nine tomorrow."

Michael had been too numbed by events to look at the tickets.

"When's the flight?"

Oldfield's secretary looked askance for a moment, then recovered.

"Tomorrow. You fly out tomorrow morning."

Lombroso

Libby walked through the swing doors with a few minutes to spare. Once inside the lobby she tried to calm down. As she crossed Shaftesbury Avenue she'd been assailed with a sense of being followed. Which was silly and schoolgirlish she told herself firmly; no-one was following her and nothing untoward could possibly happen in the lounge of a central London hotel.

Debbie had set up the meeting, dropping into the shop with a typed note that told Libby to present herself at the Mapleton Hotel near Piccadilly Circus at two pm the following Wednesday. She was instructed to bring any information that may be important, and to dress as for a business appointment.

"How will I know who to meet?" asked Libby, whose appetite for the venture had waned considerably over the past few days.

"He knows what you look like. Just be there on time, I had to pull a few strings to set this up."

"What do you think he will do? Will he …"

"Not in the Mapleton reception. That's for certain."
Debbie sighed and looked at Libby's anxious face. "I don't know, Libby. I don't think anything will happen at this meeting. He wants to look you over, he's curious. But he's different, not like the others. Just be sure, don't go any further unless you're certain you know what you are doing."

Libby thought of the grey future that awaited unless she did something to break away from the treadmill she felt her life had become.

"Don't worry. I'll be there, and I will be careful," she squeezed Debbie's hand and smiled. "Que sera, sera."

The meeting had been arranged for a Wednesday afternoon, when the shop was closed. She followed Debbie's instructions, dressing as for a business meeting in a pencil skirt and plain white blouse, and carrying the paperwork she had tried to present to the bank.

The man at the reception desk looked at her in a questioning way and she forestalled his attention by walking through the foyer as confidently as she could manage. In the lounge the red damask wallpaper and tired grey carpets sucked the light out of the air despite the large gilt mirrors and bright sunshine beyond the windows. Scattered Chesterfield sofas and single chairs were grouped around low tables. At one of these an elderly couple took tea; a pipe smoking businessman read The Times at another.

A barrel chested man with a broken nose and full, rubbery lips stood and walked towards her. Libby's heart leapt into her mouth, but he carried on past without giving her a second glance. Then a figure appeared from the gloom of one of the corner tables, cigar in hand and quite ridiculously attractive.

Tallish and lean, he had a shock of dark hair over a roman nose and goatee beard. He was dressed in a pale linen suit and cream silk shirt with no tie. Libby was struck by his eyes, deep-set and so dark as to be almost black. The overall impression was the casting director's idea of Lucifer taking a afternoon off, and Libby almost smiled at the thought, but then he was in front of her, presenting his hand.

"Libby? My name is Simon Lombroso, shall we sit down – coffee?"

The voice was almost accent-less, English with a trace of a warmer climate. He didn't wait for her answer, waving for a waiter and ordering another pot of coffee to join the one that was half empty on the small table. He lounged on the chesterfield, next to an astrakhan coat that looked far too warm for the day. Libby took the single leather chair, kept her knees together, and tried not to think about why she was there.

After a few seconds she realised that she was going to have to begin the conversation.

"Thank you for seeing me." There was a nod of acknowledgement. "I've been told that you may be able to offer some assistance to someone in my position."

The nod again, and the patient watching eyes.

The waiter arrived with the coffee. Lombroso poured for Libby, adding a dash of milk. Then he refilled his own cup with black coffee and leant back against the leather upholstery, dark eyes unwavering.

Libby explained about the shop, and her ambitions to run the business. She described the meeting with the bank, and her frustration with the manager's refusal to even look at her documents.

"You have brought them with you."

It wasn't a question; she handed the folder over and he began to sift through the pages.

"Please go on."

Libby talked about her meeting with Caroline, and the possibility of promoting her designs. Lombroso looked up:

"Tell me about the owner, Laura."

Libby described Laura's failure to make the shop thrive and her seeming inability to run any kind of business.

"I'm surprised more of our suppliers haven't followed Caroline's example and refused to supply."

Lombroso glanced at the papers.

"You have unpaids for Harrisons and for Lipmann. How much is the Harrison account?"

The figures were on the page that he was holding, but Libby reeled them off anyway.

"As of last Friday we owed them eighty pounds, seven shillings and fourpence. Lippman's is much less: nine pounds, four shillings."

He nodded. "Lippman wouldn't let an account go beyond ten pounds. Who is your landlord?"

The questioning continued. Lombroso would glance at a page of her notes, then quiz her about the detail. Libby began to feel a small surge of excitement. He was taking her seriously; did this mean that he would let her have the money she needed?

Lombroso turned the last page and closed the folder. He looked at her steadily. "So, what exactly are you looking for?"

Libby took a deep breath.

"I need three hundred and fifty pounds."

Lombroso's smile did not reach his eyes.

"That's a lot of money," he paused, his gaze travelling over her body. "You are very attractive, but three hundred and fifty? That is a small fortune, enough to buy a modest house … much too much."

Libby felt as if she had been slapped, she stood and made to leave.

"Then why did you agree to see me …"

"Sit down, girl," he said, with enough force to cause the the old couple to glance in their direction. Libby sat as if she had been pushed into the chair. Lombroso leant forward across the small table.

"I said 'No' to the money, but there is more than one way to skin a cat. Debbie said you had some money of your own. How much?"

"A hundred, perhaps a hundred and fifty. But I will need that to fit out the shop, pay the rent, buy stock …"

"One step at a time. First we need to deal with …" he looked at the papers and the cold smile reappeared. "Laura Mills-Johnson."

He stood and slung the coat over his shoulders.

"I will need some time to consider your problem. Meet me here at the same time next week."

Libby nodded, feeling absolutely naked as the eyes repeated their slow inspection of her body.

"One thing. If I do decide to help you there will be a payment due for my time and work. You are prepared for that?"

Libby did not have the strength to confront the steady gaze. She looked down and nodded.

"Good," he said. "Next time wear a summer skirt – and bring a cardigan."

Then he was gone.

***

A week later Libby once again walked through the hotel doors. It was another warm day and the cool of the lobby was welcome after the sticky heat of the Tube. As instructed she was wearing a simple summer skirt and carrying a cardigan. She'd made the journey via the shop, picking out a low cut blouse to accompany the skirt, underneath which, she had, after much deliberation, chosen a pair of tiny, silk briefs.

It had been an odd week at the shop. With a few weeks to go they had barely enough stock to half fill the rails and customers were few and far between.

Laura spent one uncomfortable afternoon going through the books. It was clear that there was, as Nicole would have said, 'too much month at the end of the money'. Laura was apparently relying on the sale of the remaining stock, but what was on the rails was either last season or in the wrong sizes.

On the Friday Libby came down from the storeroom to find Laura in conversation with the barrel chested man from the Mapleton. Laura looked up.

"This is Mr …"

"Jones," said the man, who looked through Libby as if she did not exist.

"He's come to look at the shop," said Laura. "His firm is thinking of taking it on."

The man turned to look at Libby.

"Jones and Jones, accountants and auditors. We have been looking for premises in the area for some time."

Libby thought that the man looked an unlikely accountant, and she watched with interest as he made a thorough inspection of the premises. After he left Laura confided that 'Mr Jones' had advised her to take professional advice about shutting down the business.

"He said it was important to leave a clean sheet, with the tax people and Companies House and so on. He said that his firm might do the work at a reduced rate, to help smooth the changeover. I'm not sure if I can afford it, after all, it can't be that complicated can it? But I've made an appointment. I can always cancel if I change may mind."

It was therefore not a complete surprise the following Wednesday for Libby to find the broken nose, barrel chest and rubbery lips waiting in the lobby of the hotel.

"Miss Young?" said the man, still giving no sign that he had seen her before. "Mr Lombroso would like you to join him in his car; it's just outside."

Libby hesitated, then followed him out onto the street, where Lombroso was leaning against the sleek coachwork of a dark green Daimler.

They must have watched me arrive.

The barrel chested man climbed into the driver's seat and Lombroso opened the rear door with a flourish. Libby stepped into the luxurious interior, pausing for only a moment when she realised that the side windows were screened by curtains. Lombroso followed her into the car, tapping on the glass dividing panel as he did so.

"Let's go George," he said, before turning to Libby. "You've met George of course."

"Mr Jones." said Libby.

"The very same. Versatile chap our George."

The car pulled out into the traffic. The drawn curtains and soft leather upholstery created a half-lit intimate space, invisible to the passing crowds. Libby felt a moment's foreboding that she pushed out of her mind. She had made her decision.

Lombroso turned to face her.

"I've looked into your problem, and I am prepared to help. You will get your wish, but you will need to play your part, there will be things to do at the shop. Necessary things … you understand."

"Will this be … legal?"

Lombroso laughed.

"A great many things are legal in business; you will be surprised." The dark eyes looked into hers. "And our agreement. You are certain you wish to proceed?"

Libby looked down and nodded quickly. Lombroso reached out and held her gently by the chin, tilting her face up to his.

"You will have to do exactly as I say … exactly. Are you sure you can do that?"

Libby made herself hold his eyes. "Yes, I am sure."

"We will see. Come here and put your head in my lap."

Libby had spent most of the previous week thinking about this moment, but she hadn't anticipated having to fulfil her part of the bargain in the back of a car. She hesitated, glancing beyond the partition, to the back of George's head.

"Exactly as I say," repeated Lombroso. "On your back, across the seat, with your knees up and your head on my lap."

Steeling herself to what might follow, Libby did as instructed, lying on her back across the bench seat. She kicked off her shoes and lifted her feet onto the leather. There was nowhere near enough room and the loose summer skirt fell away from her bare legs and crumpled around her waist.

"Raise your arms above your head."

Lombroso took her wrists in his right hand, pushing down and stretching her body until her back arched over his thighs. With his left hand he reached into a jacket pocket and produced a ivory handled flick-knife, holding it for a second in Libby's line of sight. A thin smile as he thumbed the catch. The narrow blade appeared. Libby froze.

"You will not be harmed," said Lombroso. "It's about submission … submission and control. Do not move, the blade is very sharp. Be still and listen carefully."

He began to explain the scheme that would allow her to take over Laura's business. Dates, times, documents … events to be arranged, a script to be committed to memory.

As the soft voice went through the details the knife slipped through the gap in her blouse, and, with a smallest of movements, cut the top button away. Then the next, and the next, until there were none left. He used the point to move the material to one side, exposing her bra. Libby could see nothing but the roof of the Daimler, but her senses followed every movement of the blade. She wondered how much George could see in his mirror.

She felt Lombroso's knuckles brush across her stomach, the blade slid over her breastbone and cut through the bridge of material between the bra cups. Then the point again, deftly dividing the severed pieces until her breasts were exposed.

She was acutely aware that her nipples were taut with … with what? Fear, tension, arousal?

Still the voice continued; there would be a new business, a company, shares divided between Lombroso and Libby. There would be no expense. Libby would keep her money to spend on the shop.

"I will have twenty per cent, you will have eighty. It will be hard work, but if you are as good as you think you are – then you should make some money for both of us."

Lombroso moved his hand over the crumpled skirt and pushed

her knees apart. His hand lingered between her legs, softly stroking to and fro across the narrow band of silk. Libby felt her body react, a fierce heat that spread across her loins, rising over her breasts to her face. Tiny sounds forced their way past her lips. She gritted her teeth and dug her nails into her palms, willing the gossamer touches to stop so that she could maintain some semblance of control. Finally Lombroso shifted his grip, sliding the cool blade across her thigh and under the briefs, cutting through the narrow hip-band. He did the same to the other leg, before closing the knife. Libby felt a swift tug as he pulled the remains away.

"Souvenir," he said, putting the scrap of material in his pocket along with the knife.

"Nearly there, boss,"

"Thank you George." Lombroso released Libby's wrists. "Sit up and put your cardigan on."

Libby quickly tied her blouse in a beach knot, retrieved her shoes and pulled on the cardigan. She tried to do up the buttons, but her hands were shaking. Lombroso pulled back the curtains to reveal the Kings Road; the car was parked outside the shop.

"Sublime," he read. "That's pretentious. You'll need a new name. You should use your own – Libby's perhaps, or even just 'Libby'."

He turned to face her. The smile appeared, this time with a trace of warmth.

"You did well, a good audition. Do you think you can remember the things that you have to do?"

Libby nodded, avoiding his eyes.

"Good. First thing next Friday then," he opened the door, and she stepped out onto the pavement. The car moved off immediately.

Libby clutched her cardigan to her body, imagining that everyone on the street could somehow see the mutilated bra and missing knickers. She fumbled for her keys, flung open the shop door and slammed it shut behind her, dashing upstairs to the safety of the tiny lavatory. Only when the door was closed and bolted did she allow herself the luxury of tears, and even then, she did not know why she was crying. Was it relief that the ordeal was over, shame at her body's reaction, or celebration that her wish was about to be fulfilled?

***

Over the next few days Libby attempted to maintain an appearance of normality. She went to work, dealt with customers, listened to Laura's meandering deliberations about the impending closure. But her mind was too often elsewhere, focused on the detailed instructions that had accompanied the trip in Lombroso's car, and the small movements of the stiletto that had punctuated his speech.

Laura failed to notice Libby's introspection, for the good reason that Laura had not really noticed Libby in the past six months. Nicole, however, did detect the change of mood, and Libby's reluctance to explain her preoccupation merely served to amplify her flatmate's concern. In the evenings on Moscow Road Nicole ran through a list of potential causes, ranging from some kind of mysterious illness to a natural depression at the prospect of the end of Libby's work at the shop.

Libby brushed the anxious questions aside, only losing her composure when Nicole hesitantly enquired whether Libby might be pregnant once more.

"No … good grief … No."

Nicole recoiled from the furious face. She attempted a contrite apology, but Libby cut her off.

"And what business of yours is it anyway? Who gave you the right to pry into my life? Pregnant! God almighty … do you really think I'm going to make that mistake again?"

Libby pushed past her flatmate and strode to her room, where she flung herself on the bed and glared at the ceiling, trying to avoid a side glance at the chest of drawers, where a newly acquired dutch cap nestled amongst her underwear.

***

On Thursday afternoon Laura disappeared for her regular appointment with her hairdresser. At four o'clock Libby saw the familiar and expected barrel chest and broken nose crossing the street.

"Hello George."

"These are the letters, sure you know what to do?"

"Yes, I know … do you think this will work?"

"With that selfish little madam? Hook, line and sinker, as long as you do your bit in the morning."

Then he was gone, as abruptly as he had arrived. Libby looked at the letters, which were addressed to Laura, and had the stamps and frank marks that anyone would expect of a letter that had been through the post.

The following morning Laura arrived at her normal time, taking off her coat and going upstairs to repair her face after the ravages of the journey from her flat in Hampstead. Libby made the usual cup of tea, and had it waiting on the counter next to the morning mail.

Laura opened a letter from the Council, and then another from a would-be supplier. Libby busied herself tidying the rails. She heard the rip of the paper and then a quiet: "What the …"

Another letter opened, then the third. After a few seconds of silence Libby risked a glance at the counter. Laura had spread all three letters across the polished mahogany and was gazing down in bewildered distress at the contents.

Libby saw Lombroso approaching the shop from across the road. He had abandoned the Astrakhan coat in favour of a black crombie and was wearing a bowler and carrying an umbrella.

"Laura, if it's alright with you I'll go up and pack those dresses for Mrs Crawford."

Laura nodded, her wide eyes still fixed on the letters. Libby heard the door-bell as she went up the stairs. She concentrated on squeezing two cocktail dresses into a box and tried not to listen for the voices downstairs. After fifteen minutes she returned to the shop, where Lombroso, minus the crombie and bowler, and with the letters in his hand, was deep in conversation with Laura.

"This is Mr Jones, from the accountants," explained Laura, who had recovered a little of her composure. Lombroso glanced at Libby and then back to Laura.

"These are confidential matters," he said, in a home counties voice that matched the pin stripe suit and oiled down hair. "Is there a place where we might discuss things in quiet?"

"Yes, of course," said Laura. "Libby, look after the shop, we'll be in the storeroom."

Customers arrived and left. Libby saw the sleek Daimler pull up on the far side of the road. She tidied drawers that were already tidied. She felt like a child at a birthday party, tense with anticipation, hoping for a present, but unsure whether the wrapped parcel was going to deliver exactly what had been promised.

Footsteps descending, then Lombroso appeared, striding through the shop without a sideways glance. After a few minutes Laura followed, clearly full of some great secret. Libby offered to make another cup of tea, and once the steaming liquid had been tasted Laura decided to confide.

"I'm so glad that has been arranged," she said mysteriously. When Libby failed to rise to the bait Laura was forced to offer the detail.

"Those horrid letters, and all on one day. Harrisons and Lippman – and the landlord."

She explained that the two suppliers had sent demand notices threatening imminent legal action unless the debts were paid in full.

"They were going to take me to court."

"And the landlord?" prompted Libby.

"Oh the same ... well, not the same really. He said I had to pay a refurbishment fee to make the shop ready for the next tenant ... or else he would take legal action as well. It was such a shock, being told that one might have to go to court – like a common thief."

Laura had forgotten Libby's status as a lowly employee. The relief had softened her defences and she was talking to Libby as she might to her friends.

"And then the man from the accountants explained ... I'm sure I would have sorted it all out for myself, but he came at just the right time ... like magic really."

"What did he say?"

"He said that the money is owed by the company, not by me ... the company that Archie set up at the beginning. You know Archie in a way, don't you – course you do. Archie set it all up for Caro and I. Anyway, it's the company that owns the stock and so on, and the accountant ... Mr ..."

"Jones."

"Yes, Jones. He said that all I have to do is close the company down ... go into liquidation ... voluntary liquidation. That was it. And that makes the bills disappear, just like that. I don't owe anything. And all because I made that appointment."

She paused for a second, amazed by her foresight and the serendipity of the whole affair.

"He will arrange everything. I had to sign a form and pay a small fee, but that was it. Whoosh, just like that. And then he said that one of his clients would almost certainly buy the stock. Not at full price obviously, but I haven't paid for it, have I, and I'm not going to, because the company is going into ..." she smiled in triumph.

"Voluntary liquidation," supplied Libby, understanding Lombroso's scheme at last.

"Yes…" a thought occurred to Laura. A detail from Lombroso's explanation bubbled its way to the surface of her thinking. Her face dropped its relaxed friendliness and she became cool and composed, Libby's employer once more.

"There is one minor point," she said. "He said that we must stop trading immediately, he's bought the stock after all, and apparently it's illegal to continue to trade whilst seeking liquidation. We must close the shop today … which means that I won't be able to pay you after this week. I know I said until the end of the month, but we must close today."

"But I will be be paid for this week," said Libby firmly.

"Oh yes," said Laura, as if paying Libby had always been at the uppermost of her thinking. "Let's see what's in the till."

***

Just over a week later Libby made her third visit to the Mapleton Hotel. She had spent the intervening days making plans to open her own business, paying a second visit to Caroline, where she spent a happy morning discussing designs and assembling a substantial order list. Other days were spent in the West End, visiting every clothes store she could, and making a close study of what shoppers were buying. She told Nicole that these expeditions were job hunts, and was just about able to tolerate the wave of sympathy that this information produced.

She was confident that Lombroso would follow through with the scheme. Her only doubts were about her side of the bargain, and she was nervous as she walked through the revolving doors into the hotel lobby. It was the last Friday in May and the streets were busy ahead of the weekend. She had followed Lombroso's instructions to the letter, wearing a camisole top and stockings under a pale blue summer dress.

George was waiting by the reception desk.

"Good afternoon Miss Young – would you care to follow me. Mr Lombroso has a suite."

He led the way to the stairs, ascending one flight, before turning off down a long corridor. He halted in front of room 106, knocked once, then opened the door for Libby, who was surprised to find a room furnished as an office, with Lombroso and another man waiting at a large desk.

"Libby, welcome, do come in, a seat?"

Lomboso seated Libby at the desk facing the window and then took the chair opposite, leaving the other man standing.

"This is Mr Tranter, my lawyer," said Lombroso. "I will let him explain."

"Good afternoon Miss Young," the man extended his hand. He was short, running to fat, with slicked down hair on a round head and thick pebble glasses. The hand was soft and damp. Libby could feel his eyes on her body.

"I've prepared some papers for you, and Mr Lombroso has asked me to run through them, and answer any questions." He waved a hand at the papers on the desk, and laid a podgy finger on the first.

"This is your company certificate, don't worry about the name, it's what they call an 'off the shelf' company. It's much faster to set up that way."

"And cheaper," said Lombroso.

"Just so."

The certificate announced the existence of Parona Holdings Ltd. and gave the directors as Elizabeth Young and Simon Lombroso, with Arnold Tranter as company secretary.

"Here are the share allocations. You have the controlling interest, with 800 shares. Mr Lombroso has 200. I am not a shareholder – sign here please."

Next came the stock list from the shop, and Libby was surprised to find that the listing included shopfittings like the display cabinets, till and the stock rails as well as the clothes. Laura had signed at the bottom, transferring all the items on the listing to the new company. Libby looked up at Lombroso.

"A lesson for you," he said. "Never sign anything without reading it first."

"Your lease for the shop as agreed with the landlord, Mr Brandon," said the lawyer. "We need a signature here, and here."

"It's a one year extendable lease at a very reasonable rent," said Lombroso. "Less than Laura was paying, and with no deposit."

Libby had met the landlord, who did not strike her as a generous man. She read the document, aware that the lawyer had positioned himself so that he could look down her blouse. She brought her shoulders forward to deepen the cleft between her breasts. There was a sudden stillness from the perspiring body alongside her. A glance at Lombroso, who raised an eyebrow and smiled. Libby nodded towards the lease.

"How did you …?"

"An exchange of favours. He had a problem and I had a solution."

Libby looked puzzled and the lawyer stepped forward.

"Mr Brandon had a problem with some tenants, blacks, causing trouble, the usual thing, no-one wants to live next to them."

The smile became sly.

"Mr Lombroso was able to re-locate them to one of his own properties."

There was no answering smile from across the desk and the lawyer quickly picked up an envelope.

"The locks at the shop have been changed. Here are the new keys, two sets. You have access as from this morning," the oily smile broadened. "You could pop in on your way home."

Libby wondered how much the man knew about her arrangement with Lombroso, quickly concluding that the answer was probably everything. She closed her mind to him, picked up the keys and put them in her handbag.

Lombroso stood. He was wearing a silk gown with a dragon design that Libby later discovered was a Japanese kimono. It was the first one she had ever seen and she resolved immediately to find the supplier.

"Are we done, Tranter? Yes? Off you go then."

Libby ignored the proffered hand and the man retreated towards the door. As he left Libby could see George waiting in the corridor.

"It's time," said Lombroso, opening a connecting door into the neighbouring room. He stood on the threshold, indicating that Libby should step through.

She had anticipated this moment from the first conversation with Debbie. Her emotions had run from fear to disgust, to humiliation and disbelief that she was even contemplating selling her body. She had considered and reconsidered, going over the issue time and time again. She had thought about the future regrets, the sense impressions and images that might come back to haunt her in the years ahead, but the conclusion was always the same. She would not be condemned by circumstance to a life as a drudge.

And was this so very unusual, she asked herself. Models took their clothes off, tableaux girls like Debbie posed in the nude, wives stayed married to men they despised. This would be an afternoon, a moment in time, by five o'clock it would be over and done with.

In her first thoughts she had pictured a fat balding businessman, much like the lawyer so recently despatched. She had prepared herself to be co-operative, agreeable even, but, when the moment came her imagined strategy was to hold her face away and concentrate on anything but the body pressing down on her own.

What she had not foreseen was the current situation. She had not imagined Lombroso, or the anticipation she was feeling, the heat on her face and tremors up and down her spine. There was no self deception; this was not love, or even affection. She faced the reality that she was entirely comfortable in giving up her body to this man, to do with as he pleased.

Libby walked into the room, which had blinds drawn against the afternoon sun. There was none of the furniture usually found in hotels, but for the large bed stripped of its covers, with three red pillows in the centre of a black sheet.

A small vaulting box waited at the foot of the bed, of the kind that Libby had used for gymnastics at school. Its padded surface laid out with with a number of silk scarves, short lengths of soft braided cord, and four leather straps with buckles. The centrepiece of this display was a carved ivory phallus, decorated in red Japanese characters.

Libby gave barely a glance to this discomforting detail, because her eyes were drawn to the framed picture behind the bed. It was a poster sized enlargement, reaching from the bedhead to the ceiling: three nude figures, entwined in devotion. Libby looked up at her counterpart, the modest face turned away from the room, one hand cupping Debbie's breast. It was the 'Three Graces' picture that Robbie had taken whilst she was at college: Libby, Debbie and Nicole.

"It's a commission," Robbie had said. "Could be my big break."

Libby turned to the door, where Lombroso watched her reaction with an amused smile.

"You see, Libby, I feel I have known you for some time," he picked up a silk scarf from the vaulting box. "Shall we begin?"

Parona

Nicole had spent weeks on the accounts, chasing down discrepancies, matching payments to invoices, reconciling the figures – so it was irritating to be telephoned by the new accountants, who had 'just a few queries' about the books.

The timing was poor. Libby was busy preparing for the coming trip to America. Her days were filled with last minute meetings with the designers and workshops, whilst her nights were interrupted by long distance calls to the States.

"It's about the disbursement of profits," said the serious looking young man at the accountant's office the next day. "The dividends paid to shareholders."

He opened a box file and extracted a sheaf of papers.

"Miss Young is the sole shareholder in her company."

Nicole nodded; this she knew already.

"The company – EYECO – owns the Covent Garden and Tottenham Court Road shops," the young man continued.

"The Kings Road shop is owned by a separate company – Parona Holdings. Miss Young is the main shareholder with 80% of the shares; the other twenty per cent are held by a … Mr Simon Lombroso. Miss Young draws no salary, but received £1600 pounds in dividends last year from both companies, whilst … "

The finger slid down the page …

"Mr Lombroso received £2000."

The accountant looked up at Nicole.

"The sums paid are all covered with the necessary payment chits, but …"

"The payments don't match," said Nicole.

"No," said the earnest face across the desk. "Strictly speaking, Mr Lombroso should have been paid £200 in dividends, probably less, given that his shares are only for the Kings Road business."

He glanced up at Nicole.

"This is not an an Inland Revenue audit. If the company wishes to make additional payments to Mr Lombroso, then it is of course able to do so, but …"

"Not as a dividend," said Nicole.

"Indeed."

"So we should investigate another way to make these payments?"

"That would be wise."

***

The accounts had been Nicole's responsibility since the early days, almost since the first shop had opened. Her relationship with Libby was rekindled in '56, after years when they had barely been acquaintances, never mind friends. Nicole had just begun a new job, working for a travel business near Marble Arch. Alongside the job came a new-ish flat in Bayswater, and it was on the doorstep on Moscow Road that Nicole found Libby one October evening. Libby was desperate and needed sanctuary, support and a new beginning. Nicole, as ever, provided the refuge that Libby required.

There was never any question of Libby keeping the baby. After the emotionally draining months of isolation in Norfolk, the birth and subsequent adoption, Libby returned to Moscow Road and the new beginning gradually took shape. The job, at a shop on Chelsea's Kings Road, then the new business, which in the first year Libby had virtually run on her own, often sleeping in the cramped storeroom above the premises. On the occasional nights spent at Nicole's flat she was too exhausted to do anything other than have a bath and go to bed. Nicole would enter the bathroom to find her flatmate asleep in the tepid water.

In that hectic first year Libby's Mondays were spent down in Limehouse, consulting with Caroline Quinn about the designs that seemed to fly off the rails almost before they were made. Sundays found Libby at the Moscow Road flat, poring over accounts and appealing to Nicole's arithmetical skills in a attempt to make sense of the figures. After one long afternoon of bills and accounts Libby marvelled at Nicole's apparently magical ability to introduce some order to the rows of numbers.

"I should be paying you to do this," she said, half seriously. And then she hesitated. "Why don't I do just that … Nicole, please, would you?"

"Would I what?"

"Work for me, for the business."

"But Libby, I have a job, and it pays quite well."

"Part time then, name your price. I'm serious, Nicole. I can choose designs and spot a winner. But you're a wizard with figures."

At first it was just a weekly few hours, but the work expanded as the business grew. Nicole dealt with the staff paperwork, navigated the Inland Revenue minefields, chased bad debts, kept an eye on the flow of cash through the business. This freed Libby to seek out new lines, spot interesting designers and charm the well-heeled women who were increasingly opting to buy her clothes. When the Covent Garden shop was added to the group Nicole threw in her job and joined Libby full time.

Nicole first met Lombroso in '61, after the opening of that third shop in Covent Garden. He strolled through the door in a cream suit and fedora. Nicole thought he looked ridiculous, foreign and dubious – in that order.

"Libby here?" he said.

"She's busy at the moment."

"In the storeroom?" he said, making for the stairs.

"That's for staff," said Nicole, attempting to block his way.

Libby appeared at that moment, with a handful of dresses.

"Oh it's you," she said. "Nicole – this is Simon Lombroso. Simon, this is Nicole, she handles our accounts."

"The efficient and reliable Nicole," said Lombroso, standing back and appraising her. "I imagined someone less …"

"Imposing?" said Libby, with a smile.

"Attractive." said Lombroso firmly, with a theatrical bow. "Why haven't I met this lady before?"

That was when Nicole realised they were lovers, she could feel the electricity between them, enough to boil a kettle.

What Nicole could not understand was how Libby found the time to have a relationship with anyone when she worked 12 hours a day six days a week and spent each Sunday at Nicole's Moscow Road flat. But then it clicked.

She sees the banker every month, but Lombroso? A banker?

Nicole knew nothing of how Libby had financed her business. One minute her flatmate was deep in the dumps about her failure to raise any funds, then suddenly she was signing leases and buying stock. At first Nicole imagined that Libby's father had provided the money, but that theory was ditched when Libby gave instructions for regular payments to be made to Cattanea: a company with an address off the Tottenham Court Road.

Lombroso equalled Cattanea, a fact confirmed when Nicole made a visit to Companies House and paid a small fee to search the files. Questions to Libby about Lombroso were not so easily answered. Her first response was to assert that the matter was none of Nicole's business.

"It's about the accounts. Which you asked me to do."

"He's a shareholder," said Libby eventually. "Put the payments down as a dividend."

And that had been the solution, until Libby decided to move the annual audit to a more prestigious firm.

***

Over the next month Nicole was kept too busy to raise the issue. Libby was away, Nicole had to fill the gap. There was a new manageress to be interviewed, and the spring stock take to complete. Then the day after Libby returned from the States there was a break-in at Kings Road. The burglary provided the opportunity; Libby dropped into the shop to check whether any of the new designs had been taken.

"No, just the float from the till," reported the shop manageress. "And a warm coat from the display. He doesn't seem to have gone upstairs at all. The police think it was a vagrant."

"Libby – whilst you are here," said Nicole.

"Change the locks anyway," said Libby. "And double check the new stock."

The manageress nodded and Libby pulled on a coat and scarf as she turned to Nicole.

"What now?"

"The new accountants have raised some issues about the accounts; especially about the payments to Lombroso."

'What issues?" Libby snapped.

"It's about the payments as a dividend. They've advised that we should make the payment in another format, and that we should be …"

"Get it sorted, Nicole, that's what we pay you for."

"It would help if I knew what the payments are about. Is it a loan repayment or …"

Libby made for the door.

"Get it paid. I don't care how. Just get it paid."

The door slammed shut; the manageress ceased her pretence of checking a catalogue and offered Nicole a complicit smile.

"I had the locks changed yesterday."

Nicole returned the smile and made for the stairs.

"Yes, I'd noticed. I'll be upstairs; I've some telephone calls to make."

In the cluttered office cum storeroom Nicole cleared some boxes from the desk, consulted the Roladex, then dialled carefully.

"Mabledon Hotel"

Nicole paused in surprise.

"Can I help you, caller?"

"Mr Lombroso?" said Nicole .

"He is not in his room," said the voice. "Can I take a message?"

Nicole thought for a moment.

"Yes. It's about Parona Holdings. Shall I spell that? Oh good. Could he contact me at the Kings Road address. No … no name. He'll know who is calling."

***

At eleven the following day a dark green Daimler pulled up outside the Kings Road shop. From the upstairs window Nicole watched Lombroso stride across the pavement. She'd already briefed the manageress.

Footsteps sounded up the stairs. Lombroso's head appeared and glanced around the room.

"Where's Libby?"

"Actually it was me. I left the message; I wanted to talk to you about our accounts."

Lombroso threw hat and coat onto a pile of boxes and sat at the desk. The deep set eyes drilled into her own.

"What would you like to know?"

Nicole gave a quick resume of the conversation with the accountant.

"We can't carry on with this payment as a dividend. We just need to know what …"

"Does Libby know about this … the accountant, your call, this meeting?"

"Yes," said Nicole, as convincingly as she could. "I saw her yesterday. If the payments are to continue we need to make them in a different way. The accountant suggested …"

Lombroso stood and gathered his coat and hat.

"Not now. I need to be somewhere else. Come and see me … at the Hotel. You know where it is? Good, Friday at 11."

He started down the stairs, then paused to look back. Nicole was wearing one of the new spring collection, a two tone mini-dress modelled on a Mary Quant design. Lombroso's head was level with her feet. Nicole felt his eyes travel up and over her body.

"That dress suits you," he smiled. "Don't worry, I'm sure we'll find a solution."

Over the next three days Nicole tried without success to have a conversation with Libby, who was flying back to New York the following week. On the appointed day Nicole wore the most conservative dress she could find, gathered her accounts files, and took the Tube from Notting Hill.

In the hotel lobby a vaguely familiar man waited by the desk. A penny dropped.

"It's George, isn't it? George Evans?" said Nicole smiling.

The man looked confused.

"You gave me a lift home once. It was a party at Poppies, you're Debbie's father."

The man nodded slowly, the battered face easing into a half smile.

"Moscow Road, just past the telephone box. Nicole. You left early."

Nicole nodded, and the two smiled at each other for a second before George looked around the lobby.

"So what brings you here?"

"Oh, I've a business appointment."

George's smile disappeared.

"With Mr Lombroso? You're Miss Pattison?"

No-one could have missed the shock and surprise in his voice.

Nicole nodded. George paused, as if he were re-appraising, reconfiguring his reactions.

"Best come this way then. Mr Lombroso has an office upstairs."

It was indeed an office, with a military style desk, leather backed chair on castors, filing cabinets and a long table laid with manila folders.

"Nicole … sit, sit," said Lombroso. "Yes, in the swivel chair. George, still here? That will do, you can wait downstairs."

Lombroso was dressed in close fitting dove grey trousers with a matching double breasted pinstripe waistcoat, black silk shirt and cream tie. He stood by the long table, arranging the files.

"You've brought your accounts … good, good."

"It's as we discussed the other day," began Nicole.

"The dividends – yes, I have had the same conversation with Libby. We need to find an alternative way to make the payments – that's correct, is it not?"

Nicole nodded.

"It would help if I knew what the payments were for," she said.

Lombroso smiled broadly, genuinely amused.

"Yes … I expect it would."

Suddenly he stood, and in a smooth fluid movement stepped behind Nicole's chair and pulled it across the room to the table.

"I helped Libby set up the business, she and I have a special arrangement."

He reached into one of the folders and extracted a set of

photographs, arranging the pictures across the table, like a dealer distributing cards.

Nicole had seen the main picture before; it was the 'three graces' commission, taken by Robbie all those years ago. The others were a portfolio study on the same theme.

Lombroso pulled her out of the chair.

"Come, come."

He led her to the adjoining room, where a poster sized version of the picture overlooked a large double bed.

"Libby, Debbie … and yourself of course," said Lombroso. "You know Debbie of course, and George?"

Nicole nodded, trying to avoid being drawn into the room. Lombroso drew her back to the table, pushed her into the chair and selected another folder, another set of pictures.

'It started with Michelle."

Nicole stared in shock at the tableau being laid before her. A naked body, fourteen or fifteen at most, barely more than a child, tied and bound, sometimes to a bed, sometimes to a small vaulting box. Lombroso picked up the third folder.

"Michelle was a rewarding subject at first, willing to learn … but then came Libby."

Another row of pictures, just as revolting. Libby's oddly contorted face in the foreground, but this time with Lombroso in the frame. Lombroso in a Venetian carnival mask, but definitely Lombroso. In some pictures he was using a whip, and in others something else – a large ivory phallus. Nicole looked away.

Lombroso moved behind the chair, pushing it hard against the desk so that Nicole was unable to move. He put both hands on her head and turned her face towards the images.

"Do not be squeamish," said the soft voice in her ear. "These are beautiful, worth a great deal of money in the right quarters. And there was no coercion. Libby was a willing participant. Perhaps too willing."

Nicole's hands gripped the arms of the chair. She began to have an inkling as to why she had been summoned; her mind recoiled from the thought.

"Libby has tired of these games. She thinks that money can fill the void. And it is true, the pictures are worth a great deal, even more so now that her name is known. But I have enough money."

His hand stroked her face, she jerked her head away, staring resolutely at the wall as the fingers traveled to her neck and on to her breasts.

"She has told me about your history together. About your nature … and the feelings that you try so hard to conceal."

Nicole glanced at the door, seemingly miles away. Lombroso released his grip and stepped back, gathering the pictures, sliding the images back into their folders.

"These can be yours, to keep if you wish, or to give to Libby, though my guess is that you will burn them. That would be a waste, but no matter."

He pulled the chair away from the table, swivelling it round to that they faced each other. A cold smile as he leant forward and put his hands on the chair's armrests.

"Otherwise … there are people who would buy these pictures … and then there would be copies, magazines, stories in the newspapers. You can prevent that; you can make all that go away. Libby will be safe. Money cannot buy these pictures, but they do have a price. My demand is for a few moments of your time. You understand what I am saying?"

He looked into her eyes, the dark gaze holding her own. Nicole forced herself to nod.

"Good – a week today then. Here, at eleven. Wear that dress from the shop."

He turned away.

"George will take you home."

A week later Nicole stepped out of the hotel. She fought the urge to look back, and forced a slow stroll. She caught a 94 at the lights near Piccadilly, but it was an age before she got to Moscow Road. Once inside the flat she ripped off the tainted clothes and ran a hot bath, scrubbing with the pumice stone until her skin was raw.

The echoes of the morning's events filled her head. She had been resolute, determined, and she told herself over and over again that she had no choice, no alternative. But the touch of Lombroso's body had burned itself into her mind. The memory lay on her skin like a tattoo.

At least I have the pictures.

She dressed quickly, gathered the discarded clothes and put them with the rubbish. She looked at the plain manila folders, then at the larger print of the 'three graces' picture. A quick visit to Libby's room revealed one of the long cardboard tubes that her flatmate used for designs. Nicole put the rolled up print inside. With the kitchen scissors she cut the other photographs into tiny pieces.

Resisting the urge to return again to the bathroom and scrub her skin, Nicole faced her reflection in the mirror, there were no marks, no outward signs of the violation her body had undergone.

'I will get through this," she told her reflection.

She decided to visit the three shops, collect the staff timesheets, do some work, anything to avoid being alone with the memory. Gathering her bag and coat and bag she left the flat and made the short journey to Kings Road.

"Oh hullo," said Paula the manageress. "I hoped you'd call in. You have a visitor."

She inclined her head to indicate the stairs that led to the upstairs room.

"I wasn't sure whether you would be here this afternoon, but they said they would wait … I say, are you alright? You don't look well."

Nicole, suddenly nauseous and faint, clung to the doorframe for support. She glanced at the stairs, fearful of what she might see.

"I'm fine … really, but …"

"Nicole!" said a familiar voice from the stairwell. Debbie appeared wearing hipster slacks and a sweater.

"Nicole," repeated Debbie. "I thought I'd drop in, need to see you … come up to the office."

She hesitated and smiled.

"Shouldn't say that should I? It's your place not mine. Couldn't make us a cuppa, could you love? Think Nicole here might need one."

Paula offered a small tight smile and stepped into the alcove to make the tea.

Debbie escorted Nicole to the upstairs office, took her coat and bag then pushed her gently into a chair.

"I'm too late," she said. "You've seen him haven't you?"

Nicole nodded, too overwhelmed to enquire how Debbie knew what had happened.

"Shit," said Debbie with feeling.

Paula appeared with the tea.

Debbie waited until Paula was safely back in the shop. They heard a customer arrive.

"George told me," she began. "He had a row with Sly, walked out. About you as it happens. 'A step too far' he called it. Then he had a row with me. Asking all kinds of questions that he had no right to ask, even if he is me dad."

She took a slow sip of her tea.

"He knows what kind of man Lombroso can be … George knew about Libby, and I think he must have known about Michelle, though he won't say. When was that? When Robbie took the pictures. I was nineteen. Can you believe that?"

Nicole nodded. It did indeed seem a very long time ago.

"Michelle killed herself. About a year later. I think Sly was making her … anyway, she walked into the river after taking a bottle of pills."

"Did you … did he …" Nicole struggled to find the correct word.

"Did Sly try it on with me? Oh yes, and not just once or twice. But I've never been into that, not then, not now. Men who like that kind of thing are dangerous."

"How did Libby …?"

The shop door jangled, and Debbie put her finger to her lips and waited until she was sure that there was another customer downstairs.

"That was me, my fault. I should never have sent her anywhere near him …but she was desperate for the money. She got what she wanted .. but Sly doesn't like to let go, not once he's got his hooks in."

"She's been paying him off," said Nicole. "Thousands of pounds. He's got pictures … they're disgusting, awful."

She paused, hands clasped together in her lap, avoiding Debbie's calm gaze, as the morning's events resurfaced in her mind.

"That's why I went to see him … why I let him … well, you know … to get the pictures. So that he can't threaten Libby anymore."

"Oh, Nicole."

Debbie seemed to visibly deflate. She stared at Nicole, her expression a mixture of frustration and pity. She took a deep breath, gathering herself to say what had to be said.

"That's not how it works; it's not a one off. He likes to keep it going. George says that the girls are expected to come back. It's all about making you do what you don't want to do. I don't know how Libby lasted for as long a she did … perhaps she enjoyed it at first, some girls do."

"But I got the pictures, I don't have to go back."

Debbie threw her hands in the air.

"For Christ's sake, Nicole. I know it was a long time ago, but you worked in the agency, you should know something about photography … there will be copies, negatives … and there are secret cameras in that room. So he now has pictures of …"

Nicole dashed for the wastepaper bin and was noisily sick.

Paula appeared at the top of the stairs.

"I knew she wasn't well," she said.

"Probably something she ate," said Debbie. "Call us a taxi, there's a love. I'll take her home."

Once she was safely installed in the taxi Nicole allowed herself to cry. Softly at first, but then with huge chest heaving waves of tears. Debbie held her tight until they reached Moscow Road. In the flat she made another cup of tea.

"Drink that," she said. "Get the taste out of your mouth."

Nicole drank the tea obediently.

"What can I do? I can't go back, I just can't … can't do that again."

Debbie knelt down and took Nicole's hands in her own.

"You are not going back, I promise. We can fix this if we are strong enough."

PART TWO

Rupert

As he walked through the Paddington ticket barrier Rupert attempted to put the committee meeting and its aftermath out of his mind. It was a long overdue visit to Overhill and he was wearing his weekend clothes: hacking jacket, soft cotton shirt, wool tie, cord trousers and a pair of Church's brogues. He found an empty carriage in first class, placed his small suitcase on the rack and settled down to complete the Telegraph crossword.

'Lose status as a union member' was 'bachelor', and 'arrive at a straight stretch of river' was 'reach'. Ten down was 'French journey for working girl' (5, 2, 4). Rupert wrote 'belle de nuit', then recalled a recent film review and changed the answer to 'Belle de Jour'. That meant fourteen across could be 'jaywalker'; he was really getting it now.

The sliding door slammed open. A youngish man looked into the compartment. His shoulder length hair spilled over the collar of an army greatcoat, worn over a striped green shirt with a wide collar.

"This'll do," he said, laying a guitar case carefully on the window seat before throwing a battered leather holdall onto the luggage rack. A tall, slim girl followed, about 25 and blonde, carrying a green Harrods bag and wearing a mini-skirt and a roll neck sweater. She glanced at Rupert and sat down. The man put his hand on her thigh and sprawled out with his battered tennis shoes on the opposite seat.

"This is a first class compartment," said Rupert.

The man grinned at the girl and made a great show of scrutinising the blue first class sign on the door.

"You don't say."

The girl rolled her eyes. She stood and reached for the bag on the rack and retrieved a paperback. With some surprise Rupert recognised the book's bold cover design. It was the Penguin edition of Solzhenitsyn's 'Ivan Denisovitch'. The girl dropped the book on the seat and reached up to the rack again, causing her skirt to ride up and revealing tiny white briefs. The man caught Rupert's stare and winked.

"We're going all the way."

Rupert looked away, embarrassed at having been caught out.

"Skip it, Andy," said the girl, dropping a crumpled copy of the New Musical Express into his lap.

"All the way," the man repeated, putting his hand back on her thigh, only to have it promptly removed.

Rupert buried his nose in the Telegraph, and tried without success to concentrate on the crossword. The guitar case was covered in stickers that were clearly souvenirs from concerts and events rather than luggage labels. One read 'Blonde on Blonde' and Rupert wondered if this was some obscure reference to the girl in the compartment.

As the train approached Reading the conductor appeared, giving the tennis shoes a pointed look as he slid back the door. The young man grinned and returned his feet to the floor. Rupert presented his ticket as his fellow traveller checked pockets.

"I'm sure they're somewhere," he said. The girl fixed her gaze on the paperback.

"There is a penalty for travelling without a ticket," said the conductor, adopting the expression of patient fortitude that had recently replaced bureaucratic indifference as the convention for public service employees.

"Golly, Kaz. We might be arrested, or something," said the young man in mock terror. "Oh look, here they are, in my pocket all the time."

The conductor punched the ticket without a change of expression and moved on to the next compartment.

"You are a child, Andy," said the girl, who spent the rest of the journey buried in the tribulations of the Soviet gulag. Her companion flicked through the NME for a while, before returning his feet to the opposing seat and falling asleep.

Rupert tried to picture himself at the same age, but the memories of his childhood and adolescence were like the sepia snapshots of the period, artificial and lifeless. Rupert's childhood self had been erased on the first of July 1917, on the road between the French villages of Albert and Bapaume.

Out of a company of 205 men, there were 19 survivors. Rupert was the only officer to return from the battlefield, having been knocked unconscious by a bullet striking his helmet in the first attack. The men he had lived alongside for over a year were dead; their bodies strewn across a battlefield blasted by artillery and raked by machine guns.

All consuming guilt is a common reaction to senseless death and perplexing survival, but Rupert did not suffer the mental agonies experienced by many who survived the war. There was no shellshock, no descent into depression. Survival created a new Rupert, dedicated to the men he led into battle. One of his first actions was to find and frame a regimental photograph, to ensure that their faces would never fade from his mind. The decorated hero who resumed the war shunned personal relationships in favour of an ongoing bond with the dead; a contract with the fallen, fulfilled by duty and honour.

There had been no backsliding. Rupert's sense of obligation was as strong in 1968 as it had been in 1918. The focus had widened over the years, and family and heritage were today almost as important as the unformed faces of the dead. But he was increasingly visited by a sense of futility; an awareness that the years of duty had been laid at the altar of a creed destined for oblivion. He glanced across the carriage at the sleeping youth, who had begun to snore gently. The girl intercepted his look, her half smile of amusement quickly erased by the cold dislike she read on Rupert's face.

Did they really die for this?

***

The pair left the train at Exeter, to be met on the platform by an anxious looking man in a business suit, who picked up their luggage and hurried them towards the stairs. Rupert watched the trio depart then crossed the platform for his connection. The Totnes train was dirty, with discarded newspapers on the floor, chocolate wrappers and crisp packets on the seats, and a slimy banana skin on the luggage rack. The train spent an inordinate amount of time waiting at a red signal and arrived over half an hour late. Rupert caught a taxi for the short journey to the hotel, and requested an evening meal in his room.

"Dunno 'bout that," said the receptionist. "We might not be able to spare a waitress."

The room was in dire need of a lick of paint. A television balanced on the desk, removing any function it may have had as a place for writing or reading. Rupert's window overlooked the river, but scruffy lace curtains and grime streaked glass meant it was almost impossible to see out, with the added side effect that the room was gloomy.

Rupert transferred his clothes to the wardrobe, took off his tie, shoes and jacket and lay back on the bed. He was tired and out of sorts. The journey from London had crystallised a sense of disconnectedness that he had felt all too often recently. There was a word for this: anomie, a feeling of isolation and exclusion. As if he had been transported to a parallel universe, superficially similar, but with different protocols and conventions.

An hour later a waitress arrived to take his order for dinner. After knocking softly the teenager opened the door to find an elderly man sound asleep on the bed. She smiled and looked at her watch. It was eight fifteen and the kitchen shut down at nine. The girl crept into the room, took a pen from the desk and underlined the section on the room service menu that said sandwiches and snacks were available until midnight. She left the menu on the bedside table and padded to the door, closing it softly behind her.

After breakfast the next morning Rupert walked up Fore Street past the solid collection of grocers, butchers, banks and offices that identify Totnes as a prosperous market town. A line of shoppers outside Luscombe's prompted a memory of standing in just such a queue before the first world war, having gone into town with the cook to collect the weekly meat order.

The clock over the Eastgate read nine fifteen. Rupert walked under the arch to the old town, where the street narrowed to the extent that pedestrians had to squeeze past a delivery van waiting outside the ironmongers. A patient tailback of traffic led up to the parish church, where two funeral cars created another bottleneck.

Haslam's occupied a imposing building with a Georgian frontage and decorative ironwork on either side of the entrance. The receptionist established that Rupert was expected and escorted him up to Gordon Haslam's office on the first floor. Rupert had known his father, and Haslam's had been the family solicitors since well before the first world war. At one time this kind of business would have been done at the house, but it had been some time since the family's affairs had demanded a private call.

And besides, we haven't got a house. At least not one in a fit condition to receive a guest.

"Good morning Mr Threwe, I'm Gordon Haslam, we've corresponded about the sale. May we offer you a cup of something? No? I expect you know Peter Goodridge, from Temple and Jones."

A tall man in a crisp blue suit rose from his seat near the window and offered his hand.

"We've met I think, haven't we Mr Threwe? Year before last, shortly after I joined the agency. I was just watching the funeral procession. It's Frank Settle, an ex-employee of ours, and your old estate manager I think."

Rupert was shocked. Frank Settle had worked for the family for nearly thirty years.

Frank. How old would he be, 70? 80? Why wasn't I told? James could – should – have let me know.

The man was still talking. "Our senior partner is attending, and I think I saw your brother going into church just now."

Goodridge turned to the large table spread with a map of the property.

"The buyer's agent will be here shortly, I thought it would be a good idea to consider their revised offer."

"Revised offer?" said Rupert.

"Yes," said Goodridge, the two men exchanged a glance.

"The buyer would like to include this land and these woods in the sale."

Goodridge gestured at the map, where a L-shaped piece of land and a narrow stretch of woodland had been outlined in red and green.

Rupert glanced at the schematic, hesitated, then studied the proposed boundaries carefully.

"This is the land that I have earmarked for Overhill," he gestured at the red marked area. "This is occupied by my brother's horticulture business, and the woodland is used for coppicing. There's a well used bridleway that allows access from Overhill down to the river."

"Yes," said Haslam slowly. The two men exchanged another glance and Rupert guessed that the 'revised offer' had already been agreed.

Well ... I haven't agreed it.

"It's a very generous offer," Goodridge again, with a winning smile. "It brings the sale price up to 300K – sorry, three hundred thousand pounds"

"We thought that you might welcome the additional funds," said Haslam, and Rupert realised that Haslam's, as his solicitors, probably knew the exact state of the mortgages. Three hundred thousand would clear all the debt attached to the Hall. He wondered whether the solicitor had shared the information with the agent.

Or even with the buyer? That would be outrageous ... but possible.

"The client has indicated to us that he is quite happy to allow your brother to continue his existing usage of the land."

Haslam again. Rupert was now convinced that a deal had been done.

These two are working for the other side, but the offer is tempting.

There was a twenty five thousand pound shortfall in the mortgage, and Rupert would have to sacrifice a large proportion of his pension fund to fill the gap. This deal would make that problem disappear, but at what price for James and Edith?

The receptionist re-appeared and introduced a ruddy faced man in tweeds as Charles Farrand, the London property agent representing the buyer. Farrand shook hands with Rupert with the air of a man being introduced to the village idiot.

"Terrible journey down, terrible," he said.

Haslam and Goodridge offered bright smiles of sympathy.

"The A4 was chock-a-block and, as for the A38, less said the better. You people don't know how lucky you are, out here in the sticks, where the only traffic is a horse and cart."

"Shall we get straight into the work," said Haslam. "We don't want to detain Mr Threwc for too long."

***

Two hours later Rupert left Haslam's offices and climbed into the taxi their receptionist had ordered. He felt exhausted. There had been an interminable discussion about the terms of sale, with at least twenty minutes spent discussing the contents of the garages at the Hall, which apparently still housed the old Riley.

At the end of the meeting he came under pressure to agree the inclusion of the land that he had reserved for Overhill. He held out, even after the obnoxious London agent raised the offer by a further ten thousand pounds. Haslam and Goodridge clearly thought he was making a grave error of judgement, but he would not put James and Edith's retirement in the hands of a man like Charles Farrand.

Rupert sat back in the taxi and closed his eyes. The prospect of an afternoon at Overhill should have been pleasurable, but Edith would not welcome the news about Michael's new job in Vietnam and the blame would be laid at Rupert's door. They both believed that Rupert had over-meddled in Michael's life, from the decision to pay his school fees through to the liaison job in Paris.

Rupert had been stationed in Berlin when Michael was offered the RAF courier role. James knew that Rupert's FO job was connected to intelligence and the coincidence seemed too much to believe. James said as much on his last visit.

"You were there, in Berlin, doing your mysterious whatever, and then suddenly Michael has an offer of a too good to be true job carrying I don't know what kind of secrets. Then he leaves the RAF, Edith and I heave a sigh of relief, but less than a year later he gets another mystery offer and ends up flying into Suez with 40 Commando."

"James, you know I can't discuss my work," said Rupert, much to his brother's disgust.

And now this latest news about Frank, coming right on top of the decision to sell the Hall. James will want to rake it all over. As the elder brother I have to take responsibility for these things, but James has never accepted that ... and he should have told me about Frank.

It never occurred to Rupert that he might detail how he had, just that morning, saved the land at Overhill. Just as he never made it clear that the transfer of Overhill House to James and Edith after the war had been his decision alone, and not a codicil arising from their father's will as James had assumed.

In the event the afternoon visit was not the trial that Rupert had feared, though the walls did occasionally resound with the echo of matters left unsaid. The news of Michael's posting to Vietnam had already reached Overhill, and James was contrite about the funeral.

"I wrote," he said. "But I know you're always travelling around. I should have 'phoned your office and asked them to pass on the message."

Rupert turned down the offer of a bed for the night and returned to the hotel. Noise from the bar below his room made it impossible to get to sleep and he lay awake in bed going back over the day. The sale of the house ought to have been a relief, but signing the contract had been one of the hardest things he had ever done.

Ma and Pa struggled to keep the estate going. I could have stayed, made a go of the estate – that's what Pa expected, but duty called. I thought I had a career in London. An important job. And how has that ended?

Finally, after avoiding the issue all day, Rupert returned to the committee meeting and its awful aftermath. Giles Mayburn's presentation had been as stuffed with Americanese as Rupert had expected. Fitzgerald's report was a damp squib, and Giles's suggestion that it should be re-drafted and brought back to the committee in three month's time was seconded and approved before Fitzgerald caught his breath. Sir Neil Franklin dropped into the room just before lunch.

"I won't stay long," he said, settling himself into a chair that Mayburn vacated. "Just wanted to thank you all for the excellent work that you have done."

Rupert felt a rising sense of foreboding.

"I've been reviewing that progress with the Minister and we have agreed that we need to build on your good work by giving the group a clear goal."

Robertson smiled around the room. Rupert followed his gaze and realised with shock that the others knew what was about to happen. Mayburn was wearing the mask of smug superiority that he fondly imagined conveyed an impression of inscrutability.

"You know that the lack of an adequate headquarters for our foreign intelligence services has long been a matter of disquiet," Franklin waited for the nods of agreement. "Well … the Minister has accepted our case … and we have been given Cabinet approval to acquire a site, and begin long term planning."

"There's a possible site on the south bank, next to Vauxhall Bridge," said Mayburn.

"Yes," said Franklin. "Perhaps a little premature to think of actual locations … anyway, it has been decided that this committee …" he glanced around the room, "… with its wide experience of estate matters."

"Indeed so," said Mayburn.

"This committee," continued Franklin, in his 'I am making an announcement' voice, "will have oversight of the medium term planning. Giles here will lead on that …"

Franklin turned to Rupert.

"None of this would be possible without your work, Rupert, and the savings this group has identified over the years. We especially appreciate the fact that you stayed on to look after this project. And after such a distinguished career that deserved a better reward than a dusty committee room, what?"

"Quite so, Sir." said Mayburn.

And that was it. Goodbye Rupert. Sign here, hand over your security pass. Mind the step on the way out. And I didn't see it coming. Not at all.

Rupert squirmed in the bed, vainly seeking a comfortable position.

Touch of heartburn. All that travelling can't have helped. Should have accepted James' offer of a bed. Might have had decent pillows. Not these too soft marshmallows. It was good to see James, he's really made something of Overhill.

James and Edith! Who would have thought that? A maid marrying into the family. But she's been good for him, they have made a success of their lives – a real success. And they made a decent job of the boy. Something to be proud of.

In the morning the cleaner waited until after ten and then knocked several times before entering the room. The curtains were drawn and it took a second or so for her eyes to adjust to the light. She saw the grey face and open eyes, and fled back down to the safety of the lobby.

Kontum Hills

They had been on the move since daybreak, first on the hot and steamy valley floor, then up into the hills, following faint paths that continually branched and divided. As they gained the ridge they found a broader and obviously well used trail, and Hopwood sent scouts to reconnoitre ahead.

It was cool beneath the trees. High above their heads the sunlight dappled across the forest canopy. Lianas snaked upwards, coiling around thin trunks then leaping sideways to ensnare new victims, building a tangled stockade. A huge fir had fallen, bringing other trees down and creating the clearing where the platoon had halted. On the green filtered gloom of the jungle floor ferns, banana plants and bamboo had already begun the task of filling the open space, and most of the patrol were hidden in the undergrowth.

Michael opened his pack, extracted his notebook and wrote: 'recce halt, clearing, lianas – tangled stockade'.

The previous entries read:

January 29th 1968

7am – helidrop with paratroopers from the 226th, Kontum Hills, west of Dat To,'

13.00 – no action so far, beginning the climb into the hills.'

He checked his watch, it was 5.15pm.

***

"You can write stories without going to the front, the trouble is, they wouldn't be very good stories."

The speaker was Bob Oakley, universally called 'Woody', a staff reporter who had been in the country since '61. It was a late night at Jerome's bar on the eighth floor of Saigon's Caravelle Hotel. This followed a long evening waiting around for a 'critical' press briefing that was postponed, rescheduled and finally cancelled, after which a massively disgruntled press corps decamped to the rooftop terrace for a collective bitch about the new liaison guy who had wasted their time.

Michael had long ago about worked out that there wasn't a front, at least not as such. The entire country was a war zone, and it was unsafe to drive almost anywhere out of Saigon. The city was not immune from the war. The tamarind trees on the once elegant boulevards had been cut down to widen the roads for military traffic, and the pavement cafes were fitted with high wire screens to deter grenade attacks by vietcong guerilas who by-passed the roadside checks with impunity.

Woody lit a cigarette and sipped his rum and coke. He had adopted the new English reporter as a protege after their first meeting, a few days after Michael's transfer from Singapore. At his first daily briefing Michael found an empty chair next to a heavy set bespectacled man who said "Hell no, take a seat," when asked if the place was taken. Michael assumed that the quiet American was a fellow newcomer, only to discover that Woody was a Rhodes Scholar, and one of the most experienced correspondents in Saigon.

"It is a war, after all," Woody continued. "The five o'clock briefing can give you the numbers. It can't show you the way the battle actually went. It's when you look at this plot of land and add up our dead and their dead – and you ask yourself, what did that mean? You can't do that without being there."

Michael was tempted to say that he knew about reporting a war. He'd seen fighting at Suez and Malaya, and he'd been alongside Ghurkas fighting Sukarno's incursions in Borneo. But he was realistic enough to know that the Americans would not be impressed by what they saw as minor police actions, not when there was a real war involving the US of A. And besides, Michael liked Woody, and valued his considerable experience.

"So – the contact you mentioned. The colonel in special forces?"

"Yeah, Ericson. Reckons that there will be some action out of Dat To tomorrow. I can't cover it, and the bureau are letting it go. It would be a feature and they are up to their neck in features. But your guys might like it. Interested?"

"Very. How do I get there."

Woody looked doubtful for a moment.

"You sure about this, you have a field pack, Halizone tabs, a camo net?"

Michael nodded. "Woody, I'll be fine. Stop fussing."

"OK. Be on the flight line tomorrow morning at six. There'll be a Buffalo or a C-130 going in that direction.

***

A shout, then a burst of machine gun fire, up ahead, along the ridge.

"Sheee-it."

A deep soft voice, Sergeant Knox. There was a concerted round of metallic clicks as the troopers readied their weapons. Captain Hopwood started talking urgently into the radio. Two men appeared, found Hopwood and made a rapid fire report. They had surprised a North Vietnamese soldier in a larger clearing, about 200 yards down the trail. Hopwood stood and raised his left hand, palm up. Forty troopers got to their feet. Hopwood made a flat, curving arc with his left hand, then pointed up the trail. The troopers spread out and began to move along the ridge.

The Vietnamese had been shot in the chest. There was a ragged bandage around his head and another on his leg. Hopwood decided that the man had been on his way back to camp for medical attention. Next to the body lay the standard weapon of the North Vietnamese Army: a battered AK-47; Soviet-designed and manufactured in China. The new clearing was man-made, with neat piles of felled trees, a perimeter of two-man trenches and a central hut large enough to accommodate about thirty. There was no sign of any recent occupation, but the Americans knew that the NV were tidy soldiers. They rarely left anything behind, including their dead.

The clearing offered Michael an opportunity to take stock of his companions. On the trail so far the platoon had been so spread out that Michael had only spoken to Captain Hopwood the CO, his radio operator Bobby, and Sgt. Knox, the huge negro he had met that morning at the staging base. The patrol was an unrepresentative mix of downtown America, more than half were black. The M16s were ubiquitous, but uniform and personal kit had been freely adapted to personal preference. Knox had told Michael that the Captain was the only college graduate.

Hopwood used the radio again.

"Contact made at .."

He looked at the map and gave the co-ordinates.

Twenty five miles away at the Dat To forward command a freshly showered intelligence officer (G2) leant back in his swivel chair, took a bite out of a waffle and a sip of coffee. He checked Hopwood's new position again the midday survey reports and flicked the radio mike to transmit.

"Understood. Air reconnaissance suggests a build up of NV forces in that area ... maybe a battalion."

"A battalion – fucking Jesus," said a trooper behind Michael.

The light was fading almost visibly, as lights dim in a theatre, and Hopwood decided to stay where he was for the night. He called in the two sergeants, Knox and Rivera.

"We're stayin' here. Establish a perimeter, make sure the guys eat. We lose the light in about twenty minutes."

The jungle in Kontum goes dark before seven, and except for the chattering of the small birds and animals it is silent. After a while the bird and animal sounds become part of the silence. Other senses came into play, and Michael's head was full of the smell of the jungle: sweet, earthy and heavy with moisture. The rotting vegetation is high in phosphorous, and glows with enough light to see the lines on your hand or read the dial on a wrist watch, but not enough to see the approaching Charlie intent on cutting your throat.

Michael had a small flask of Scotch, which he passed to Hopwood and Knox and the radio operator, Bobby Viroe. Then he did his best to get some sleep.

***

A soft jab in the ribs, then another, until the discomfort dragged Michael out of his sleep cocoon and back to the jungle floor. It was still dark, and he could barely make out the figure above until a wide grin identified Sgt. Knox.

"You'm bin snorin' man," the black face whispered. "Gonna wake up Charlie an' have him come an' complain."

"Sorry …" Michael struggled for a second, then pulled the Sergeant's first name out of his memory. "Sorry, Sam …"

He was about to say more, but the big man put his fingers to his lips and stepped back into the undergrowth. Michael attempted to return to sleep without success.

The plea to Woody for the opportunity to cover a real story stemmed from the sense that the posting to Vietnam had not been the success that Michael had expected.

After nearly two years in the country Michael had still not seen any action. He felt as if he were treading water, marking time, which was all the more frustrating as he seemed to be surrounded by journalists whose reports were hitting headlines all over the world. His reporting had largely consisted of recycled US releases leavened with the occasional colourful feature: Nightlife in Saigon, or a Mekong River Patrol. The plum assignments were usually snapped up by the Americans, or by the TV reporters whose reports would be aired a full 24 hours ahead of anything Michael could deliver.

He told himself that it wasn't a gung-ho hunger for front line action that motivated his request to Woody, but an honest desire to function as a genuine reporter.

And then there was the guilt. Michael had been overseas for four years. The weekly despatch from Overhill made it plain how difficult this was for James and Edith. The plea for a clue as to when he might be able to return had become a regular postscript to the letters. Michael was acutely aware that his one trip back to Europe had not been to Overhill, but to Nice, for the wedding of his ex-colleague Alex Cross to a beautiful and very French bride.

Michael shifted position on the warm damp hollow and tried to put the guilt and frustration out of his mind. He recalled a line from a World War Two correspondent who'd written that when he was in an uncomfortable spot, and trying to sleep, he thought about women.

Michael thought about the German girl who had taken his virginity in a ravaged apartment building off the Kufurstendamm, and the French liaison girl at the Nato base near Versailles, and their assignations in the Malmaison Forest that had tested the back seat of her Deux Chevaux to destruction. He thought about Libby, and wondered what might have happened if she had been able to meet him at Waterloo. Finally he thought about Ngoc, waiting back at the apartment in Saigon: petite and enchanting, unknowable and opaque. Clouded, like a beautiful negative exposed to the light.

An hour later he was still awake as the first troopers emerged from the undergrowth and began to stretch the sleep out of their bodies. In the dawn half light men cleaned their weapons and dug into their C rations labeled: MEAL, COMBAT, INDIVIDUAL. Each carton contained a day's rations: two sandwich meals, salt, pepper, sugar, powdered cream, coffee, gum, toilet paper, matches, and a pack of five cigarettes.

Shots fired, two singles then a long burst from a machine gun.

A sheepish soldier arrived and halted before Hopwood. The disturbance had been a small group of armed Vietnamese, uniformed and not alert, who had stumbled into camp, seen the Americans and fled. The GIs, equally startled, had time for only a few rounds, before Sgt. Rivera opened up with the machine gun. Two of the Vietnamese were dead, The three survivors scampered across a small stream and disappeared into the bush. Hopwood shook his head, and smiled.

"Oh hell, I'll bet they spent the night with us," he said. "They probably thought we were the 226th North Vietnamese Regiment, for crissakes."

He reported the incident to G-2, who received the information without comment. Michael thought about the implications. A long-range reconnaissance patrol cannot operate once its presence is known to the enemy. Twice the Americans had been forced to fire, and now three Vietnamese were heading for their headquarters to raise the alarm.

A few minutes later the squad on 'point' found a small arrow-shaped sign with the words 'đi thẳng'. During his service in the Mekong Delta Hopwood acquired a passable knowledge of Vietnamese. The words, translated, meant 'friends go straight'.

In the next hour of slow progress up the trail the troopers discovered more small clearings, more huts, more prepared defences, all deserted.

Wrong word, thought Michael. *Not 'deserted' – waiting.*

Hopwood decided that his band had uncovered a staging

area capable of accommodating a regiment of 1,000 men. The knowledge was not comforting.

"I don't like any part of it," he said.

Suddenly there was gunfire all down the line. Michael flung himself on the jungle floor. Sgt. Knox opened fire with his M16 and began heaving grenades. The firing continued for five minutes then died abruptly as the Vietnamese melted into the bush. A black trooper flopped down beside Michael.

"You the English reporter?"

Michael admitted that he was.

"You picked a great patrol. Y'ain't got no wars of your own to go to?"

Michael explained that he had got bored with the English wars and had come to Vietnam to check on the American version. The trooper doubled up with laughter and turned to his friends.

"Sheee-it. D'ya hear that – doncha wish you talked like that?"

The big man turned back to Michael with a broad grin.

"Hey, Mr. Reporter. How much you get paid for this?"

"Not enough."

Hopwood appeared to brief Michael on the situation and the troopers quickly found other things to do.

"We've found what we came to find," said the tall lean captain. "The problem now is how to get home. That last attack was to test our strength. We can expect them to come back in numbers. We need to get back down the trail to that big clearing. It's the only place the choppers can land."

Hopwood pulled a holstered handgun from his pack.

"Take this, it's a .45, you might need it."

Michael nodded, unwilling to admit that his sole experience with firearms was an afternoon on the rifle range during his RAF basic training. He took the huge gun and packed it away.

Slowly, in fits and starts, the Americans worked their way back down the trail. As he waited for the inevitable attack Michael worked at disbelief and distraction. Put a film in the camera, focus the lens, take pictures, transcribe dialogue:

"Sheet, I wrote her back, she do anything she want."

"Aint nuthin' you can do, we over here and they over there."

"Yeah."

"You hear Thomas get killed?"

"Yeah?"

"Sheet, a mine blew him up and there was nuthin' left – but nuthin'."

"Sheet."

"I tell you, Man, this is some kind of war."

"Sumthin' else!"

"Crise, I was in a platoon and there's nuthin' left of that platoon now. I'm the only one left."

"Gimme some fruit."

"Tray-ja fruit for some butts."

"Fuck you."

"Three butts."

"Whyn't you pick up the butts back there, when we got the C packs?"

"'Cause I was on point, savin' your ass in case old Charlie come along."

"Gimme the fuckin' fruit."

"Three butts."

"Sheet, man, I ain't got but half a pack."

"Goddam I got to get this weapon fixed."

"Hey, Mr. Reporter. What the fuck you doing here?"

At two-thirty in the afternoon the first grenade crashed down the ridge line. It went wide with a thump. Again, another, closer. Thump! Thump, Thump, followed by a savage storm of fire that shredded the surrounding vegetation into a green mist. Three troopers were down and others were screaming for the medic.

Hopwood radioed forward command and requested artillery

and air support. In the next three hours, 120 rounds of 105mm and 90 rounds of 155mm artillery dropped into the surrounding jungle. In addition to the artillery barrage there were air strikes. Hunkered down in a shallow trench surrounded by dense cover, Michael felt as if the world was coming apart.

The Vietnamese were a half seen presence. No one knew how many there were. They were no mortars, so the unit was probably company-sized or smaller. But they had grenades and small arms and automatic weapons. They fought from concealed positions and they had the element of surprise and knowledge of the terrain. It was, after all, their base camp.

In the next trench Hopwood spoke quietly and easily into the radio which was the only link with safety. As long as the artillery held out Charlie could not advance; that was the theory.

The sniper fire came closer, nipping the tops of the bushes. The artillery seemed to be hitting indiscriminately, as Hopwood called it closer to the American lines. But in reality there were no lines. There was only a group of men huddled on a trail that did not even show on the map.

Michael lay on his stomach in the trench with his face pressed into the sodden ground. He reached into his pack for the .45 and took it out of its holster. A wounded trooper, his voice loud as a bullhorn, called from the right flank. "Get me out of here!" The same phrase, over and over again, the voice cracked with agony and pain. Then a scream followed by silence. Michael dismissed the tortured voice from his mind. It was easier to focus on the 45.

In Malaya and Borneo Michael had come under fire, but that had been flying in a helicopter, or riding a troop carrier on a public relations jaunt surrounded by cheerfully competent Ghurkas. The enemy had been distant, unseen; the risk impersonal and easily dismissed. This was different; dozens, perhaps hundreds of Vietnamese were trying to kill him in an area no bigger than a football field.

He could hear the individual shards of shrapnel tearing through the bushes, and feel the bullets zipping overheard. He gripped the gun and tried to get his pounding heart and rapid breathing under control.

It's adrenaline, he told himself. The phrase 'fight or flight' popped into his head. As if there was a choice.

His muscles were taut, ready … for what? Pain, unimaginable violence, death? Michael had seen dead and injured men, and he had no desire to join their ranks, but in the jungle that day he discovered that his real fear was that he might give in to the desire to close his eyes and hunker down, allow his trembling body to abandon control, or run screaming towards the inevitable.

Slowly he returned the revolver to its holster. He was not a soldier; he had a different job to perform. He reached for his camera, set the shutter speed to 125 and the F stop to 5.6. He raised his head a fraction.

"I'm a reporter" he whispered, then he raised the camera and began taking pictures.

Grenades again, and the troopers returning fire. Bobby Viroe the radio operator stood up to fire his M16 and took a burst in the chest that threw him into the trench alongside Michael. Sgt Knox pushed the body out of the way and fired his gun into the undergrowth, killing a Vietnamese soldier less than three yards away.

The choppers arrived, the downdraught flattening the vegetation, crew gunners spraying the departing Vietnamese with machine gun fire. Wild eyed GIs jumped from the still hovering machines with banshee whoops and screams.

The black humorist re-appeared.

"Where's that newspaper fella?"

"He got hurt."

"Hurt? Sonovabitch."

Michael had been caught in a grenade blast, and had been peppered with shrapnel down his right side.

"You're OK," Hopwood had said.

"The hell I am, I'm hit."

"I mean it, you're OK, no real damage."

"Christ almighty, there's blood everywhere."

"You're all right."

Michael's arms and legs shook uncontrollably. A medic scrambled up and used a morphine ampoule, punching the needle into Michael's arm. Slowly the shaking died away, to be replaced by an overwhelming feeling of fatigue.

"You're all right," said Hopwood.

"I'm not all right."

They were both laughing, Michael from shock and relief, Hopwood from the fact that the attack had been thrown back by the cavalry, just like in the movies.

***

FROM: NIGHTED-SENTINEL-LONDON
TO: RATCLIFFE C/O 2258882 AP SAIGON

++CONFIRM RECEIPT OF COPY. WHERE WAS THIS?++

Michael sat at the Telex machine in the Associated Press office in Saigon. He had filed his copy at 3pm then stayed by the machine to answer any questions from the night editor in London. His right arm and leg were bandaged and he still felt dozy from the morphine. He had been hel-evaced out with the wounded, and treated by hard pressed medics at the Dat To casualty station, before being flown back to Saigon early that morning. Bob Oakley picked him up at the Tan Son Nhut air base and drove him to the AP press centre.

On the drive back Bob explained how there had been firefights across the country over the past two days, with American and

South Vietnamese units engaging opposition forces at battalion strength and above.

"They've never attacked in strength like this." he said. "It's completely new. They've come out into the open, our boys are cock-a-hoop. I spoke to a marine pilot last night, he said it was a 'target rich environment'."

Once at the press centre Michael had written a 1200 word feature that Bob had pronounced 'good – really good', and Michael had glowed with the warmth of the compliment. He tore London's message off the Telex, then typed:

KONTUM HILLS WEST OF DAT TO

A short wait, then the machine clattered a reply.

++IS THAT IN THE DELTA?++

Michael looked up in disbelief at Oakley, who rolled his eyes.

Bob looked thoughtful. He paused, unsure of how to deliver the bad news.

"A lot of the action we saw yesterday was in the Delta. The networks were all over it, blanket coverage. I expect your guys will have already seen the TV stuff."

Michael nodded grimly and returned to the machine.

NO. NOT THE DELTA

Minutes passed, until the machine chattered again.

++NO INTEREST FROM NEWSDESK. WILL PASS TO FEATURES TOMORROW. DO NOT SEND PIX UNLESS INSTRUCTED.
 ENDS++

Michael decided to pass on a late night at Jerome's bar and took a tuk-tuk to the apartment on the wrong side of the river. His mood was not improved when he found the place in darkness. Ngoc must be at home with her mother; a reminder that the girl's primary loyalty was to her family, not to the tall westerner who at some point would disappear from her life.

Leaving his cameras and equipment in the lobby Michael headed for the kitchen and a much needed coffee, only to see a yellow telegram waiting on the kitchen table. It was from Overhill, as he knew it must be.

Edith in hospital after fall. Could you come?

Michael stared at the words, his mind flying across the world to the couple who had given him a home. For a moment he was overwhelmed with self loathing, crushed by the burden of the years lost to an apparently vain ambition. Then he dragged the big suitcase out from under the bed, and began to pack.

PART THREE

Marcus

From the corner of newsroom David Lewis could just about see the doors that led out to the lifts and stairs. The intervening space was crammed with desks arranged in pairs, enough to accommodate fifty journalists and their accumulated clutter.

A blue haze of tobacco smoke diffused the white fluorescent light flooding the room. It was quiet, with a few muffled telephone conversations against a background of intermittent typewriter stutter.

David had reported on business news since joining the paper. Business lacked the drama of crime or the fury of politics, and David's copy rarely hit the front page, but it was steady and predictable, with an annual round of conferences that offered an opportunity to escape from the office.

He worked opposite Bryan Lambert, the Shield's City correspondent, who preferred to face the window and east London skyline. The adjoining desk accommodated the svelte and meticulous Sylvia Newsome, the paper's fashion correspondent. Sylvia had to endure the chaos generated by Peter Thornleigh, who no-one had ever accused of being either svelte or fashionable. Thornleigh wrote the racing pages, but sat nowhere near the other sports reporters. This was not an accidental pairing, the two chose to share desk space in what some assumed to be a bizarre sexual coupling. David had a simpler explanation; when specialities are worlds apart there is less chance of one's desk partner stealing a story.

David spied the gangling frame of Marcus Phillips navigating his way through the maze of desks. Marcus had just left Dulwich and was indulging the new fashion to take a year out, with six months at the Shield, to be followed by an equal time travelling the world before going up to read PPE at Oxford. His aim, apparently, was to get a First, then join the paper as a political correspondent. David thought this a perfectly reasonable ambition, despite Marcus' conspicuous lack of talent, and the fact that political correspondents were usually recruited from the ranks of the paper's most experienced journalists. Being the nephew of the Chairman would probably help.

Most of the Shield's reporters viewed the boy as a dangerous liability. Helping him out might elicit some short term brownie points with the management, but Marcus was so useless that he was likely to cock something up, and the resultant shrapnel would rebound on the unfortunate hack. Bryan Lambert was firmly in the 'keep well clear' faction, but David felt sorry for the boy and had given him some simple jobs in the library.

David broke off from trying to beat some news value into the latest CBI whinge about the education system and threw a paper clip onto Lambert's desk. Bryan looked up in surprise.

"Marcus is on his way over," said David.

Lambert groaned and spread the Telegraph's business pages over his sandwiches. As Marcus arrived Lambert abandoned his typewriter and offered his chair.

"Need to nip out and check a story," he explained, rolling his eyes at David as he made for the door.

Marcus took the vacated chair and passed a thick manila folder across the desk.

"These are the clippings on the people you asked me to look up."

This was Marcus's second attempt at library research. The

previous week he had taken the original clippings out of the library, instead of making copies and returning the originals to the file. The librarian had blown a fuse. Irene was a short, fat, formidable woman with a rat-trap mouth and a voice like a rusty hinge. Her tirade of abuse had reduced Marcus to tears.

David walked into the aftermath of this episode. He sent Marcus up to the canteen to recover, then mentioned that the boy was the nephew of Ramsey McKay.

"You know, the Ramsay McKay who owns the paper, the one who doesn't have any children of his own."

"Couldn't give a stuff," said Irene.

Whatever the short term scars left by Irene's brutal introduction to library research, Marcus appeared to have absorbed the lesson, because the current crop of clips were all photocopies. David opened one file to find a sheaf of crime stories. Puzzled, he glanced across the desk. Marcus was reading Lambert's Telegraph, and had leant on the paper only to find his elbows sinking into something soft and yielding. He was gingerly lifting the corner of the news-sheet in an attempt to discover what had been squashed.

"Marcus," said David, trying not to smile.

"Who were these clips for? The ones about …"

David glanced down.

"Simon Lombroso … I didn't order them."

"Oh, yes, sorry," said Marcus. "They are for Mr Fielding, must have got them mixed up with yours."

David glanced through the clippings, which seemed to relate to a London gangster who had been murdered in 1962.

"These are crime, Marcus. Fielding is our medical correspondent."

"Yes, I thought it was odd," said Marcus, surreptitiously smoothing out Lambert's newspaper.

"Funny thing though, one of your subjects is mentioned in his file. That's a co-incidence isn't it?"

David stopped still for a moment as his news radar went into overdrive. He recovered quickly and closed the file.

"It is a co-incidence, yes. But these things happen don't they? Thanks Marcus, great job. Don't worry about the Lombroso file, I'll drop it along to Fielding. I need to see him this morning anyway."

David waited until Marcus was safely through the news room door, then re-opened the Lombroso file. It contained news clippings going back to the war, culminating in the murder story in the spring of '62. There was a sheaf of Companies House reports, showing directorships in the name of Simon Lombroso over the same period. Several were cross-referenced, mostly to a lawyer called Arnold Tranter, who had been struck off by the Law Society in 1969. Finally there were half a dozen company reports dating from 1957 to '62; these were cross-referenced to one Elizabeth Young.

"Irene, you gorgeous creature," said David under his breath. He had to wait a frustrating few hours for Fielding to get back from some BMA briefing. Then a few minutes more until he could see Fielding begin to type up his notes. David picked up the Lombroso file and made his way across the room.

"I think these are yours," he said.

"What?" barked Fielding, who was notoriously irritable when writing copy.

"Notes on Lombroso. Crime files, Marcus dropped them off by mistake."

"Crime files?" Fielding took one look at the contents and snorted in anger.

"Jesus Christ that boy is a cretin. He can't be trusted with anything."

"Wrong man?" said David.

"Wrong man? Wrong bloody century. I'm doing a piece on Victorian medicine. Cesare Lombroso was an Italian doctor who believed in phrenology. That's …"

"Bumps on heads – yes, I know. Look, I can see you're busy, do you want me to ask Marcus to get you the right clips?"

"For god's sake, no. I'll finish this and 'phone Irene later."

***

David spent the next three hours in the basement chasing down every last reference he could find to either Lombroso or Young. In the Lombroso file he found some photographs that Marcus had missed: a pornographic picture of a very young girl and nude study of three girls.

In pencil on the back of the nude trio were the words:

'this is the one: D, N and L'

Underneath there was a signature, R. O'Neill. In the bottom left hand corner was the letter 'P' and a reference code in Irene's tiny writing.

David walked into Irene's office and waved the photograph.

"Any provenance on this?"

With great reluctance Irene planted her cigarette in the ashtray, broke away from the mountain of clippings on her desk, reached over and took the picture. She turned it over.

"Lombroso. The boy wonder had clips from this file this morning."

"Well, yes, but background? history? It's not a clip so it can't have been published."

"It's the 'Three Graces', or at least a study based on the sculpture. But then a well educated young man like yourself knew that already."

Irene enjoyed her own wit for a few seconds then returned to the picture.

"These photos are from Lombroso's effects, from the Met's evidence file. See – there's a P for 'Plod' on the back. And we certainly wouldn't have published this one, not in '62, or even now come to think of it. This girl looks about fifteen."

"And O'Neill? Any ideas who that might be? Or DNL?"

Irene sighed heavily.

"Do you lot upstairs expect me to do all the bloody work? There's no cross-reference to anyone, so that means No, I don't know who O'Neill is. If we had a reporter present he might suggest the photographer as a possibility. Unfortunately there don't appear to be any reporters in the building."

"I suppose D, N and L might be the girls' names," mused David, but Irene had picked up the cigarette and returned to her filing.

Back in the newsroom he dashed off four hundred words on the retail prospects for Christmas, followed by a call to the picture desk to order a recent photo of Elizabeth Young. After leaving work he took the tube to Leicester Square and the Mableton Hotel. By-passing the reception desk for the bar he enquired about long serving staff.

"Someone who was here for the Lombroso murder in the sixties, there's money in it, for both of you."

The barman looked sceptical until David slid a ten pound note under a beermat promoting Watney's Red Barrel. The note disappeared and the barman called to his colleague.

"I'm out the back for a mo"

Five minutes later he reappeared followed by an elderly man in a porter's uniform.

"This is Jim," said the barman. "He was here in '66."

"Come round the back," said the man. "We're not supposed to meet customers out here."

David followed the porter through double doors to a dingy corridor, past kitchens and storerooms to a tiny room lined with lockers and sheets of shift rotas pinned to a noticeboard.

"Jake said a tenner," said the man.

"Depends," said David. "The right date would be good for starters."

"It was '62, April, just after the Grand National. I remember cos I backed the winner, Team Spirit, made a few quid."

David produced a ten pound note.

"And"

"He was shot twice, nobody heard a thing. He had a visitor that day, picked her up in the foyer. That's how the posh ones arrived, for the others he used the rear stairs."

"He saw a lot of girls then." David handed over the note, which was tucked away in a waistcoat pocket.

"Not half, all kinds. Dolly birds, older women, young girls, barely out of school some of them, all kinds. He was into rough stuff; leather, whips an' that. Takes all sorts."

"And the visitor?"

"Tall for a woman, wearing a headscarf and a raincoat, so nobody saw her face. Eddie – on reception – swore it was a bloke in a wig, reckoned she didn't walk like a woman. The filth said it was George – who did it like – cos they'd had a row the previous week, him an' Sly, that's what they called Lombroso. It wasn't George in the raincoat, that's for certain; George was built like a brick shithouse."

"What was the room like, any chance of seeing inside?"

"Nah, they split it up, it's two singles now. He didn't like people going in, not even the cleaners. But people did, obviously. It was a suite, with an office and a bedroom. That was something else, a real horror show."

"The police report says that a picture was taken."

"Yeah, not the whole thing though, they left the frame, cut the picture out. Only thing they took, so they said, plod that is. Look, squire, are we done? I'm supposed to be on duty."

"One more thing, the picture, did you ever see it?"

"Just the once, it was in the bedroom, above the bed. Nudes, a couple of dykes."

David reached into his jacket.

"Like this one?"

The man found a pair of glasses and studied the photograph from the Shield's files.

"Yeah. That's it. I'd forgotten there were three. Classy though ain't it? Not your usual tits and bums."

***

David took the tube back to Walthamstow, standing most of the way, lost in what his first editor on the Walthamstow Gazette had called the '3Ps' – potentials, pitfalls and possibilities. On the short walk from the station back to his flat he bought a bottle of wine to celebrate.

The next morning he rose early in order to get into work before nine. He made a trip to the picture library to pick up the colour print ordered the day before. Then he waited in the news editor's office. Tony Baldwin appeared at 9.15.

"Lewis," he said without enthusiasm. "What brings you to my frosted splendour? Another IoD exclusive?"

David smiled wearily. A few weeks after he began work at the Shield he had rushed into Baldwin's office enthusing about a 'leak' from a contact at the Institute of Directors. Baldwin had sent him down to the basement to examine the IoD file, where David had found similar exclusive 'leaks' appearing on an annual basis for the last twenty years.

"No, it's not IoD."

David explained the link that Marcus had discovered between the 1960's murder and his planned profile on Elizabeth Young.

As Baldwin listened to the story he leant back in his chair, put his fingers together in a steeple shape and focused on the ceiling.

"Corroboration?" he said eventually.

David placed two pictures on the desk, one from the Lombroso file and the other delivered by the picture library that morning.

Baldwin leant forward and studied the two photographs, one in colour, the other in black and white.

"Well, fuck me sideways," he said. "Right. Bring this to conference. We'll go in together. Discussed this with anyone? No? Good, didn't really think you would. No-one, no-one at all knows about this. Total schtum. Kapish?"

David returned to his desk and tried to concentrate on a press release that claimed that Felixstowe was the UK's largest container port. David thought this unlikely and booked a call with the port press office to nail down some of their less than credible statistics, then another to the Port of London in the hope that he might generate some kind of row. He took a call from Chrysler who wanted to take issue with a recent 600 worder describing their UK business as in its death throes. He looked at his watch. It was 10.35. He went to the lavatory and sat in one of the cubicles staring into space until his watch read 10.55. Then he joined Tony Baldwin at the lift.

The Shield's morning editorial meeting was held in the conference room next to Paul Hectre's office on the fourth floor. Hectre had been the editor of the Shield for eleven years and had driven circulation to make it one of the most successful papers on Fleet Street. He was a tall man with a dome forehead and a rugby player's physique. Enemies and rivals said that he had a soft centre of reinforced concrete and the manners of a neanderthal. His morning conferences could be brutal affairs and David was nervous about the prospect.

In theory any reporter on the paper could drop into the meeting. The weekly memo from the editor's secretary issued regular reminders on the subject. In reality the meeting was reserved for heads of department and a few insiders, so there were raised eyebrows when Tony Baldwin escorted his protege into the room.

Most of the spaces were already taken. The deputy editor sat to Hectre's left, with the chief sub on his right. Then came Sport, Foreign, Features, Pictures and Production, with an empty chair waiting for Baldwin. The only woman in the room was Penny

Carter, the vitriolic columnist whose acidic observations about modern Britain were partly responsible for the paper's success. David took up a position by the door and tried to look unobtrusive.

The meeting began, as it always did, with a post mortem on that morning's edition. Hectre wanted to know why the Sports desk hadn't got the Viv Anderson story run by the Telegraph.

"Cos Cloughie says it's bollocks."

Hectre held the sports editor's gaze for a moment, then moved on.

"Home news. Good story about that bloody lunatic in the midlands. Five dead – Jesus! Nice pix though. I bet they were shitting themselves in West Bromwich. Pity he didn't start shooting at the Hawthorns, they could do with a new centre forward. What have you got for us today?"

Hectre directed a meaningful glance at David, which Tony Baldwin ignored.

"We are going to lead with a new poll showing that the Conservatives have edged ahead. We've got comment from Keith Joseph and Roy Hattersley, and we're getting street reaction from the vox-pop team. Second lead might be a picture led piece about Moonraker, the next Bond film. Roger Moore in space apparently. Inside pages have a spread on strike-hit Britain. More problems at Ford and Chrysler. Bus drivers and bakery workers threatening to come out. Prince Andrew might be joining the Navy – so they could be next."

There were thin smiles around the room.

"Can we find a real victim of these fucking strikes?" demanded Hectre. "Find me a old lady who's died because the local council hasn't delivered her meals on wheels, or a young mum run over cos the Tube drivers were out. Get your team off their idle backsides and out on the streets. We need to show the damage these fucking unions are causing. Find me a real case study and we'll run it as the lead. Hold the political stuff for the home pages."

Hectre turned to his deputy. "And Brian, the leader will focus on the strikes. Whose country is this? That sort of thing."

The meeting continued with each department head reporting on the planned copy, with the final exchange reserved for Production, who tried to explain why the presses had rolled nearly an hour late the previous evening.

"The printers walked off the job just as we were ready to roll."

Hectre rolled his eyes and growled.

"It's that cunt Manton, trying for another bloody bonus. We lost the overseas, Scottish and western editions. It's going to cost a fortune. I want rid of the bastard."

"We can't sack the father of the print chapel," said Production. "We'd have the whole building out."

"Well poison him then," Hectre glared round the room. "I know, I know … but you need to do something. Right, meeting over, go and do some bloody work."

As the room cleared Hectre's gaze switched to David, and then to Tony Baldwin.

"It had better be good, Tony."

Ten minutes later Hectre leaned back in the huge leather chair.

"So what you are saying is that we have this Eytie lowlife Lombroso, who was a kind of cross between Paul Raymond and Rachman – blackmailer, pornographer, slum landlord?"

David nodded. Hectre made a note on the pad on his desk.

"And he was murdered in 1962, by person or persons unknown. Plod arrested the wrong guy."

"George Evans – cleared in '64, after doing two years in Wandsworth," said Baldwin.

Hectre's eyes returned to the single sheet of paper on his desk.

"And … Lombroso, was involved with this woman Elizabeth Young, who is the young lady with the nice tits in this picture."

Hectre waved the black and white print.

"That's what we think, Chief." said Baldwin.

"Who are the other two?"

"We don't know, Chief."

"And who the fuck is Elizabeth Young? Should the name ring a bell with me? Because I hear no chimes."

David placed the colour picture on Hectre's desk. Hectre studied the print, then turned to its black and white companion.

"Fuckin' hell."

"My words exactly, Chief," said Baldwin. "Libby the fashion queen, aka Dame Elisabeth Young, entrepreneur, smasher of glass ceilings, multi-millionairess, relentlessly single, very private."

"And Lombroso died a mysterious death in 1962," said David. "Just as Libby was expanding her business."

Hectre leaned forward and jabbed a finger at Baldwin.

"We'll go with this. Tony, make this a Spotlight investigation, brief the newsroom; no snooping no leaks. Find an office and take David off the business desk. Give him – who can we spare?"

"Helen Jackson is a capable journalist, and she's currently working the fashion pages."

"OK, Jackson it is. And Marcus. He can be your footsoldier."

Hectre ignored the horrified expressions.

"Yes, give the boy a real taste of the job." He jabbed a finger at David. "You'll report to Tony about everything you find, and I mean everything. And no cock ups, if we get this wrong she'll sue us to the skies. Make sure the story stands up. Clear?"

"Clear, Chief," said Tony.

***

The day after being given the green light on the story David briefed his small team, beginning with a blood curdling warning to Marcus about what would happen if so much as a hint about their work leaked out of the building.

"Got that?"

"Yes, David. Scouts' honour."

"Good, now go and rustle up some coffee."

They had gathered in the tiny first floor office that Tony Baldwin had somehow managed to find for them. When Marcus returned David despatched him to the comparative safety of Companies House to do some extensive research into Lombroso's network of companies.

"Are you coming with me?" said a forlorn voice.

"No"

"But how will I manage? I don't even know where it is."

"There are telephone directories in the news room, look it up. Now buzz off, because Helen and I have work to do."

Helen Jackson watched this performance with a carefully blank expression. She waited until the door closed behind Marcus, then turned to David.

"I don't suppose there's any chance of sending him back upstairs?"

"None. Orders from high. He's our good soldier Schweik."

"Wasn't the point about Schweik that he only pretended to be an idiot?"

"We can only hope."

David was impressed with Jackson. She was a vivacious brunette, with wayward curls and a penchant for undersized sweaters. He had never worked with a female hack and didn't know what to expect, but she came over as smart and capable, and had great legs, which gave her several advantages over most of the journos in the newsroom.

"You know, this could be a huge story," she said. "Do you really think she killed him?"

"We don't know do we? And we may never find out. But they were involved, he was linked to her business for years, and someone shot him – very conveniently. And then there's the photograph."

"I'd like to start with that," she looked across the desk for a reaction. David nodded.

"OK. You chase the photographer down, try and get idents for the other two girls in the picture. At the same time do some work on Libby's contemporaries from the fifties. According to her biography she worked closely at the outset with a designer called Caroline Quinn."

"I don't think she's in the industry now, I don't know the name."

She looked up from her notebook.

"What will you be doing?"

"I'm going to have a chat with our friends in the Met, try and find out what happened with the murder investigation, which seems to have been a balls-up from start to finish."

David Lewis

Once the Christmas break was over David began his research with a list of contacts provided by Tony Baldwin.

"You should be able to get the crime reports from Smithy," he'd said, ticking a name on the list.

"Pete Burrows is good for Fraud, but I'd start with Mick Cobham. He was working Vice when all this happened. Runs a pub somewhere in Greenwich."

The up market restaurant was not what David expected, but the man who appeared at his request to see the owner could not have been anything other than a policeman. Large, solid, cynical – laid against a background of latent violence.

"Press card?" he'd demanded, before ringing the paper to check. "Says he's David Lewis: fair haired, five eight, medium build, smarmy, posh accent."

David underwent a close examination as the paper verified the description.

"They say you are you," said Cobham eventually. "I owe Baldwin a favour, otherwise I wouldn't give you the time of day. I'll be another twenty minutes or so. Sit yourself down and enjoy the ambience."

He waved for a waiter.

"Table 14, get him a drink, nothing too expensive."

David ordered a Pinot Grigio alongside tagliatelle with bacon and mushrooms. The food arrived quickly and David was mopping the remains of the sauce as his host reappeared.

"Good?"

David nodded, his mouth full of warm ciabatta.

"Not my doing. I run the business end and the bar. Cristina runs the kitchen."

"Your wife?"

"Daughter. Now, what do you want to know?"

David produced the picture of the young girl from the paper's files.

"Simon Lombroso and Michelle Allenby – you were on the case. It would be 1948 or '49."

"Thirty years ago. Jesus. Not askin' much are you."

"You were on the case though."

Cobham looked the picture.

"Yeah, this is Michelle. I was on the case. Just been transferred out of uniform. Thought I knew it all. Just like you."

He turned to the bar and mimed pouring a beer.

"Kenny – Peroni."

Once the beer had arrived Cobham contemplated the slender glass for a while as he marshalled his memories.

"Michelle Allenby, from Dudley – no, Bromsgrove. Solid middle class family, she was seventeen when she died. Michelle was a classic runaway, left home after a row with her father, turned up in London. Down to the bright lights with a boyfriend, who soon has her doing tricks for his mates. So she runs away from him, and gets picked up by Lombroso, who instals her in one of his flats. But she still has to do what he says, which means funny games with leather and ropes – and lots and lots of pictures."

"Like this one," David produced the 'three graces' picture of Libby, Debbie and Nicole.

Cobham picked it up and studied the faces.

"Nah – this is a class above."

"So what kind of pix?"

"Porn – pure and simple. We picked up the thread when the pictures started appearing in Soho. Lombroso's name came up, we knew him from his other activities, but he used a mask, so we couldn't get a firm ID."

Cobham sipped his beer

"Then the girl died, June or July '51, found on the foreshore near Tower Bridge. We quickly identified her as one of the girls in the porno pix. The PM report said that she had rough sex, possibly rape, in the hours before her death. She had been living in one of Lombroso's properties, but we couldn't establish a link beyond that. We pulled him in, searched his house and office – nothing."

"Was he tipped off."

Cobham sighed.

"Probably – I mean, we found nothing, nothing at all. And we never made a link to a photographer or a photo lab."

"But you're sure that Lombroso was in the business?"

"Oh yeah. And he killed that girl. No doubt in my mind, him or his minder. Poetic justice there, pity we couldn't make it stick."

David looked up from his notebook.

"What? The charge against George Evans."

"Yeah. Not my case, I was with the Flying Squad by then. But yeah, George was the man."

A group of businessmen piled through the door. Cobham drained his glass, and stood away from the table.

"Tell you what though …"

David retrieved the notebook which had been on its way to his bag.

"You could try Lenny Roberts; he's still in the business."

"Soho?" asked David

"Nah. That's mags, videos and rip off merchants. Lenny has a camera shop in Paddington with a sideline in kiddy porn. He's more your specialist supplier. If you go and see him, be sure to wear the rubber gloves."

The businessmen formed a noisy scrum by the bar, waving ten pound notes and demanding champagne. The barman looked in their direction, and Cobham nodded an acknowledgement.

"Now bugger off, I've got work to do."

Heathrow

The driver was late. Nicole waited in the chrome, steel and carpeted splendour of the office reception and watched the rain beating against the wall of sheet glass. Grey faced pedestrians hurried by, heads down against the wind. On the far side of the street a rat scurried along the gutter before disappearing into a pile of rubbish bags.

Nicole looked at her watch. The duty receptionist approached nervously.

"Miss Pattison?"

Nicole glanced sideways and nodded.

"Just to say that I have rung the agency and they confirm that the driver is on the way."

"Good," said Nicole.

"It's all these strikes."

Nicole looked at the girl with amusement.

"Don't tell me we've booked with an agency where the drivers are on strike."

"No, well, I don't think so. But the streets are all jammed because of the Tube strike. You can hardly squeeze through on the pavements, what with the dustbin men out. The rubbish keeps piling up, it's terrible …"

Nicole saw a limousine pull up outside.

"It's here now. Make yourself useful and get an umbrella, there's usually one behind the desk."

The girl hurried away and returned with one of the the office umbrellas; golf course sized and emblazoned with the company logo – Libby's – in flowing gold letters.

"And make sure that there are several umbrellas available for Libby and the team – in case it's raining when we get back."

"Oh yes, of course."

"Well, come on girl, snap to it."

The girl opened the huge umbrella and escorted Nicole out to the pavement, where the driver waited by the open door. Nicole eased herself onto the rear seat.

"Heathrow, ma'am?" said the driver as he climbed behind the wheel. "She's comin' in on Concorde ain't she? Lands at eight thirty. We'll have you there in plenty of time."

He pulled the oversized Mercedes out into the traffic, looked in the mirror and decided his passenger didn't want to chat. The woman fell into his 'older totty' category. About fifty, but still worth a second look. Bit like that Bond girl, he thought. The one in Goldfinger – Britt Ekland was it? No, course not. Honor Blackman. Nice legs, pity we can't see more of 'em.

Nicole settled into the seat and unbuttoned her coat. It had been a foul cold day, but it was warm in the car, and she relaxed against the leather. Ninety minutes later the car pulled into Heathrow's arrivals area. The driver jumped out and opened the door.

"I can't park here, ma'am, But don't you worry, I'll just circuit round 'til she arrives."

It had stopped raining, but a chill wind swept the approach to the terminal building. Nicole pulled her coat tight and dashed for the warmth of the arrivals hall. She checked her watch: seven forty-five. The plane was due at eight thirty and it would take at least another half hour to pass through the layers of bureaucracy that welcomed visitors to the country. She looked in vain for anywhere that might offer a cup of coffee, but the small cafe was closed and the machines were out-of-order. The only place to sit was a hard plastic bench. Nicole picked up two used coffee cups and a discarded copy of 'The Sun', with a front page picture of the prime minister under the headline: 'Crisis – What Crisis?' She put the lot in a nearby waste-bin, wiping the bench with a tissue before sitting down to wait.

It will be tonight, she thought. She was going to do it before she flew out. My spell in hospital scuppered that. And she likes to do these things face to face. So it will be tonight.

***

"What's my job title?" Nicole had asked, on her first full day, all those years ago.

"I've thought about that. You're our purser."

This began a trend of using naval ranks as job titles at Libby's. The shop staff were ratings, shop managers were commanders, delivery men were stokers, and Libby was the skipper.

There was a sudden commotion at the gate, and a rush of passengers flowed through, tired and tanned, wearing sombreros and carrying bags full of duty-free. Nicole scanned the crowd, but this was obviously a holiday flight and she quickly returned to her thoughts.

She had been so pleased about the job, thinking it would mean working together with Libby again. Things might even go back to how they had been, in Camberwell.

Coming out to Heathrow was probably an over-reaction, but Libby needed to be told what had happened that morning, when a ghost from the past had made an unwanted reappearance in their lives.

Claire Wellings had delivered the news; she'd requested an urgent appointment about a 'serious matter'. Nicole sighed when she saw the message. Claire was a nineteen year old trainee, her boss was known for having wandering hands. He'd been warned before about his behaviour and faced instant dismissal if the allegation held any substance.

"My boyfriend works for one of the nationals: 'The Shield'."

Nicole looked at her watch. This wasn't what she expected, she had appointments, a full diary. The girl paused, nervous about being in the big office, unsure as to whether to continue. Nicole knew that she had a certain reputation amongst the junior staff. Anything to do with the press was handled by the media team, whereas Claire worked in the design section. But she was a capable girl; not the type to raise a fuss about nothing. Nicole tried without success to look less severe.

"Go on."

"He's not a reporter or anything, it's a temporary job in their library, that's where they keep copies of all the old papers, they take clippings and file them away. It's just that yesterday he had to clear up after one of the reporters. Put the files back, that kind of thing."

"What did your boyfriend discover?"

"It was the files," said the girl. "They were nearly all about Libby, going back years and years.

***

Nicole's thoughts were interrupted by a new group coming through the arrivals gate, including Libby, who looked shrunken, stressed and tired, flanked by new assistant Pippa, and Andrew, who handled contracts for the group. Pippa was dressed in her usual stylish punk: leather jacket, 'Fuck You' T-shirt , tartan micro-skirt, fishnet tights, and patent leather ankle boots. She'd had her hair done in New York, and was now a Debbie Harry style two-tone bleached blonde.

"Nicole," said Libby. "You didn't need to come out to meet us – is the car outside?"

Nicole explained about the driver circuiting the terminal.

"Andrew," said Libby. "Go outside and see if he is there … Pippa, why don't you go as well."

Libby waited until the pair were out of hearing.

"You shouldn't be here, Nicole. There was no need, and it … it complicates things."

"I thought you might need some help with bags," said Nicole. Libby gave a sour smile. They both knew the bags were following by crate, along with the clothes from the exhibition.

"Well, that was good of you, but no."

Andrew re-appeared, waving from the terminal's sliding doors. Nicole saw her private moment slip away.

"There's something I need to tell you."

Libby's face hardened.

"Once we were back at the office," Nicole added quickly. "I never see you properly."

Libby took a breath, Nicole could almost hear her counting to ten. Andrew gesticulated from the door. Libby nodded towards him and raised a hand, palm outwards, followed by a single finger. She turned to Nicole.

"Not now, I'm tired. And I'm not going back to the office tonight. Get a taxi home, and I'll see you in the morning."

"But you'll be so busy in the morning, you always are. And you've been away for a week. There will be morning conference, and the exhibition follow up …"

"I will make the time," said Libby firmly, already walking towards the exit. "Eight thirty, in my office."

***

At eight twenty in the morning Nicole left her office and took the lift up to the fifth floor. The company's headquarters was just off Oxford Street, occupying the same building as the flagship store.

Libby's still used naval rankings, but Nicole had long ceased to be the 'purser'. An accounts section to deal with the franchised shops and worldwide trade occupied an entire floor of the building. For ten years Nicole had been Libby's executive assistant, a position she held until displaced by a series of assertive young women, whose average period of tenure was about a year. Pippa was the latest incumbent and Nicole thought she was probably good for another three months.

Nicole's role was store liaison, acting as a conduit between the various store managers – the commanders – and Libby. Nicole also acted as a buffer between Libby and the many people determined to snatch a portion of her time. She had a media assistant to handle the press, and two cadets to deal with correspondence.

At first this sentry role had involved an early morning diary meeting with Libby, but in the last few years this precious time alone had been delegated more and more often to Libby's PA. It had become a source of bitter amusement to Nicole that the gatekeeper no longer had the keys to the gate.

When Nicole arrived at Libby's outer office Pippa offered a cheery 'Good Morning', followed by:

"Libby says she'll be with you in a few minutes."

Pippa had stuck with the Debbie Harry look, with the red tights, white mini-skirt and a denim waistcoat over a red plunge bra. She didn't appear to be wearing a shirt or blouse.

"It's cold today innit," she said.

Nicole nodded, resisting the temptation to point out that the girl would be warmer if she actually wore some clothes. The door opened and Terry Walker appeared, beckoning Nicole into Libby's office. Terry was the company lawyer, and the only person in the building wearing a suit. He looked uncomfortable, but not because of his clothes. Nicole guessed that Libby had asked him to be present because today was going to be the long awaited 'goodbye Nicole' day.

Libby's office didn't have a desk. Instead there were easy chairs arranged around a huge low table. One wall was full of pictures from the last big exhibition, another had a massively enlarged copy of a 'Madness' album cover, alongside a slightly smaller copy of the cover for latest album by 'The Slits'. Rumour had it that Libby had slept with Palmolive, the band's lead singer, but if the rumours were to be believed then Libby slept with any warm body that came within a hundred yards.

Except me that is. No rumours about me.

Libby sat at the huge table with her back to the door. She wore her standard office dress of sneakers, jeans and plain white T-shirt. She glanced up at Nicole and dropped some stills from the New York exhibition onto the table. She arranged the photos and stood up to greet her visitor.

She looks better this morning. More relaxed, that's because she's made her decision.

"Nicole, I hope you don't mind, but I've asked Terry to drop in. Would you like a seat? No? Look, I'm not going to beat about the bush. This isn't an easy thing to say. We've decided to let you go. There have been a lot of changes over the last few years and your role has become a little detached from the rest of the organisation."

Nicole suppressed a smile, the last bit was true enough.

"We've looked at how we might deal with the responsibilities you currently manage and we think that some can be better provided externally and others by dedicated staff within the office."

Libby looked directly at Nicole for the first time.

"We'll give you a really generous package, more shares and a lump sum. Terry has prepared a summary."

Nicole looked at Terry and raised an eyebrow.

"We'd like you to sign a non-disclosure agreement," he said. "It really is a very generous offer."

"And if I don't want to go," said Nicole, looking at Terry, but the words were addressed to Libby.

"Oh, come on, Nicole. It's not working, it hasn't worked for years, you don't fit in, you're just not ..." Libby turned away.

I can finish that sentence: not glamorous, not in tune, not a party girl, not fashionable, not young ...

"I'm sure it's a generous package Libby. And I'll give it serious thought. But that isn't why I wanted to see you today. Perhaps it would be best if you and I talked through this together – alone."

Libby looked back to Terry and made a: 'Now do you see?' face.

"I'm sure whatever it is can be said in front of Terry."

"As you wish. When you were in New York I was approached by a reporter for an interview, from the 'Shield'."

For the first time Libby showed a loss of composure.

"For God's sake, Nicole. You should know how to deal with stuff like this. Who was it? Sylvia Newsome? Or their new girl, what's she called? Stephanie something or other?"

"No. It wasn't from their fashion or society pages. The reporter's called David Lewis; he's with their Spotlight team."

"Spotlight? Are you sure?" said Terry, puzzled. He turned to Libby. "They do investigations, exposures – that kind of thing."

"I do read the papers, Terry."

"He didn't say he was from Spotlight," said Nicole. "He said the interview was for a business profile, but it isn't."

"What do you mean?"

Nicole explained about Claire's boyfriend and the research files in the Shield's library.

"And it's not just you. They are also investigating Simon Lombroso."

Two minutes later, after a perplexed Terry had been ushered out of the office, Libby sat in one of the huge chairs and faced Nicole over the low table.

"What the fuck is going on? What questions about Lombroso? He's been dead for ..."

"Seventeen years," said Nicole.

Hectre

David's small team filed into the Shield's fourth floor conference room, where Tony Baldwin waited alongside deputy editor Brian Delaney and Graham Formby the company lawyer.

Delaney and Formby shared a mutual respect for demonstrable competence alongside an ability to ignore their boss's explosions of rage.

Formby was one of the few men in the building who replied to Hectre's bullying in kind. In clipped Eton tones he would trade insult for insult, expletive for expletive. Formby was also almost alone in defying Hectre's instructions on staff dress. His standard workwear of jeans, check shirt and leather waistcoat led most people to assume that he was a country and western singer who'd come to the paper's offices for an interview.

The contrast between Delaney and Formby was stark. The deputy editor was a full foot shorter than Formby and wore expensive three piece suits, with gold tie clips and cufflinks. Delaney had joined the Barnsley Chronicle at 16, working his way through the provincial press until he made the nationals. He was contemptuous of the university students who had taken the 'fast lane' to the top floor.

"Hectre's the boss," he would say to anyone stupid enough to whinge. "If you don't like him go and start your own fucking newspaper."

Tony Baldwin waved at the coffee and sandwiches laid out on a side table and then waited with thinly concealed impatience as David and his team spread themselves around the room.

"OK? For Christ's sake Marcus, go find a chair."

Baldwin drummed his fingers noisily until Marcus returned.

"All here, Brian."

Delaney laid yesterday's Telegraph to one side and turned to David.

"The Boss is taking a call from the Chairman; he'll join us when he can. Right, Lewis, shoot, from the top, the works."

David inclined his head towards Helen Jackson, who opened a folder and passed a black and white picture around the room.

"The picture is based on the "Three Graces" by Antonio Canova. The snapper was a rising photographer called Robbie O'Neill. As we know one of the three girls is Libby Young, aka Dame Elizabeth Young, the other two …"

"We have corroboration of that do we?" said Formby. "That this is Libby Young."

Helen looked up and met his eyes.

"Yes … as you'll see shortly … when she left school after the war Libby took an art course at Camberwell before going on to Goldsmiths to do a degree. That's when this pic was taken, in the summer of '49. For a while Libby lived with the photographer – Robbie O'Neill. We're not certain about the central figure, but the other girl is Debbie Evans, aka Debbie Turner aka Debby Delores."

Brian Delaney looked up in surprise.

"What, the Putney Madam? The one who ran that brothel busted by the News of the Screws?"

"The very same," said David. "Sorry Helen, your show, do go on."

"We've talked to Debbie. She'd be about 19 when this was taken. These days she owns a nightclub in Majorca, but at this time of year she's in London. She confirmed the snapper's name and the fact that Libby – who was just 17 – is one of the other girls..

Debbie also said that the picture was a commission – for Simon Lombroso, who was murdered in 1962."

Helen looked over to David. They had agreed on how to present the research.

"Debbie is the daughter of George Evans," said David. "Lombroso's driver and gopher, who did time on remand for the Lombroso murder before being cleared in 1964. I expect that's how the original connection was made."

Helen handed round a second set of pictures.

"These are a few years later. It's a feature piece by the Express. It's on Kings Road. Pix are by Michael Ratcliffe and …"

Brian Delaney leaned forward.

"Ratcliffe? From the Sentinel?"

Helen nodded.

"He's out in Hong Kong at the moment, working the far east beat," said Delaney. "He's a good bloke, not involved in this is he?"

Helen shook her head.

"You were with him at the Sentinel, weren't you? No, Ratcliffe's not involved, as far as we can tell he just did the pix for this shoot. But you can see Debbie and Libby are the models."

"Who's the third model on Kings Road?" asked the lawyer. He waved the 'Three Graces' black and white.

"That's Annabel Sullivan, now Annabel Santori, wife of …"

"Marco Santori, the boss of the F1 racing team," grinned Tony Baldwin. "Oh boy, this gets better and better."

Helen handed round another photo and a news clipping.

"This photo is also connected to Lombroso. It's a teenager called Michelle Allenby, whose body was found in the Thames in July '51."

She paused for a moment, enjoying the startled look on their faces.

"Lombroso was questioned about her death. She had been living in one of his bed sits."

"But no charges," said Formby.

"No," said Helen. "No charges. Coroner's verdict was misadventure."

"No shit, Sherlock," said Baldwin.

Helen smiled carefully.

"The Kings Road pix were taken in 1956. Then there's a gap, Libby disappears for a year."

"O'Neill?" asked Delaney.

"His motorbike hit a lorry on the North Circular in 1954."

"So, she disappears," said Baldwin. "But not with O'Neill."

Helen continued as if she hadn't heard the interruption.

"Her stepmother thinks Libby had a baby, but she's a miserable cow and I don't believe a word she said. Debbie claims they lost touch for a while, thinks Libby was temping, says the baby story is ridiculous."

Baldwin pointedly looked at his watch.

"Move on, we haven't got all day for this. Conference starts in half an hour."

Helen shuffled papers.

"Libby next appears in late '57. She opens a shop on the Kings Road, takes a three year lease, refurbs the shop, and restocks with designs by Caroline Quinn, who moved to do haute couture in Paris a few years later. After that Libby recruited her own designers.

"Lombroso appears to have supplied the money for the shop," interjected David. "Marcus – tell us about Lombroso, and make it snappy."

Marcus made as if to stand, then sat down as he saw the look on Tony Baldwin's face.

"Simon Lombroso, Italian, from a village in the Parona region, near Milan. Came over in '36, initially to Glasgow to work in a chip shop."

"You're making this up," said Formby.

"No sir, really, he was …"

"It's in the police report," said David. "Go on, Marcus."

"Lombroso was interned in 1940, and released for war work in 1942. This included some bomb site clearance in London. In 1944 he set up as a landlord with three properties. Apparently he just took control of bomb damaged houses where the owners had been killed. By 1946 he owned more than a dozen …"

"It was easy to do," interjected Formby to general surprise. "Owners often kept the deeds at home, or in some cases there was no proper documentation. If no close relative stepped forward someone like Lombroso could step in and make a convincing claim for the property. We dealt with a few cases like that in the '60s when I was a junior."

Marcus beamed gratefully before returning to his notes.

"Lombroso set up a network of companies, all named after villages in Italy. One of these, Parona Holdings, was set up for Elizabeth Young at about the time she opened her first shop. Lombroso had a twenty per cent stake, but appears to have been paid a substantial dividend, even in the first three years when the shop was not declaring a profit."

Helen Jackson selected a paperback book from her folder.

"Libby's authorised biography makes no mention of Lombroso. But it stresses how little profit those early shops made, and how Libby was almost on the breadline."

She replaced the paperback in her folder, and crossed her legs, largely for the benefit of Tony Baldwin, who was the only man in the room giving her body any attention. Marcus looked up from his notes, and cleared his throat.

"By 1962 Lombroso had largely stopped being a slum landlord. His money came from property development: shopping centres, holiday parks, that kind of thing. The week after his death Parona Holdings was wound up, and the Kings Road shop became part of EyeCo – where Elizabeth Young is the sole shareholder."

"A week after his death?" asked Formby. "Before the police investigation had concluded?"

"The paperwork was filed two days before he died," said David. "Apparently by the company secretary, someone called Patterson or Pattison, difficult to tell. Lombroso's shares were transferred to Libby, in return for £2,000 – which he never received."

"And the police didn't pick this up?" asked Delaney.

"The police didn't pick anything up." said David.

"The investigation was a joke. Lombroso was shot with his own gun: a Beretta. The police arrested his driver – George Evans. Lombroso and Evans had a very public row in the hotel foyer the week before, something about a woman. George had a chequered past: assault, threatening behaviour, car theft. He'd been Lombroso's driver for years, so presumably knew where to find the gun. The Plod saw him as the number one suspect; he was charged the next day, went down for ten years."

Delaney jabbed a finger towards David.

"And the problem with that is?"

"Everything. The case was destroyed at the appeal. No-one saw George anywhere near the hotel on the day of the shooting, but he was seen that afternoon at Walthamstow dog track. He even had betting slips, but the Plod convinced the jury that he had accomplices and that they had made the bets."

"He was convicted because he offered no real defence," said Formby. "It was his daughter who assembled the case for the appeal. Debbie did the spadework, I checked with her brief."

Delaney laughed.

"We should have Graham on the news team. So, who did shoot the bastard?"

"We don't know. There were unidentified fingerprints on the gun. The apartment had been searched by someone, but the only item the police know was taken was a framed copy of the 'Three Graces' picture we have here. Lombroso had a visit from a woman the week before, and that may have been the cause of the row with George Evans. The receptionist at the hotel thinks the same woman saw Lombroso on the day he was shot: a tall blonde."

Baldwin made a sour face, and turned to David.

"Fifteen minutes to conference. Is there anything to connect Libby Young to the murder?"

"Not directly; she was in New York at a fashion show …"

"Which makes for a pretty good alibi," said Delaney.

"But she's got motive," said David. "Lombroso had history with vulnerable women. The Met's vice division had kept an eye on him for years. There's was case of the Michelle girl, then they had a statement from one victim, but she wouldn't follow through. She lived in one of his flats, got into debt, Lombroso bailed her out. But the price involved playing his games, bondage, that sort of thing. And he took photographs. This girl said that Lombroso always took photographs. Which means that he took photographs of Libby"

David reached into his folder and paused, relishing the moment, before distributing a handful of black and white prints.

"Pictures like these."

"Fuckin' ell," said Delaney.

"We can't print these," said Formby.

"Suitably censored, blacked out bits?" asked Delaney.

"Possibly, but there wouldn't be much of the picture left."

Formby studied the picture, turning it round to show the unmarked rear view.

'What's the source? It's not the Met evidence file, no stamp."

"It's a porn dealer, not Soho, specialist. He says the man is Lombroso … he didn't know who the woman was."

Formby found a magnifying glass on Hectre's desk.

"OK," he said. "I can see the resemblance – it does look like Miss Young, but the man could be anybody. I don't see how we can run these pix without some kind of additional corroboration."

"We're not running them," said Paul Hectre, who had slipped into the room as the group focused on the pictures.

"We're not running the story, full stop. Firstly the woman was in New York, which sounds like a good alibi to me, second we don't have a clear ident on these pix, third Libby gives a fortune to fucking charity … including half a million quid last year to the Rowan Foundation."

Delaney glanced at Formby, who shrugged; the party was over. Hectre continued, counting the points down on his hand..

"Fourth, and most important, it's not what we should be running. We need to get rid of this fucking government. Find me some pics of Callaghan being shafted by an eytie pimp and I'll print them."

Hectre picked up the Lombroso picture.

"And this goes nowhere – got that?" He glared round the room. "If I hear so much as a whisper outside this office, I'll have the cunt's balls on toast."

Hectre tore the picture into pieces and turned to the two reporters.

"Now fuck off whilst we get on with some real news."

***

Back in the first floor office David threw the research folder onto the crowded desk.

"That's that then. No Pulitzer this year."

"All that work," sighed Helen, carefully retrieving the folder.

"And no follow up? Not even trying to ID the woman who visited Lombroso on the day he was shot?

"We got no-where on that," said David. "The hotel staff had no idea who it was; 'tall blonde' said the receptionist, but one of the others thought it was a bloke in a wig, something about the shoes and the way he or she walked."

Helen frowned, leafing through the papers in the folder before looking up again.

"There's a rear entrance to that hotel, and Debbie was working at the Blue Lagoon in Soho – two streets away."

David retrieved the folder.

"Off limits remember. 'Cease and desist' said the Boss. Besides – what's her motive?"

Helen's frown deepened.

"And what's the Rowan Foundation anyway?"

"It's a charity, big one, arts and education. EyeCo are a leading contributor … it's how Libby got her gong."

"It's aunt Rebecca's charity," said Marcus brightly. "She's the president."

His smile dimmed as Helen and David turned to stare.

"That would be," said Helen. "The aunt Rebecca who is married to Ramsay McKay, Chairman and owner of the paper. The Ramsay McKay who was just on the 'phone to our editor?"

"Yes," said Marcus.

PART FOUR

Paul

Barrow and Fisk is the oldest solicitors' partnership in Woodbridge. Not that the casual observer would discern this fact from the entrance, which is a simple doorway off the High Street. The upstairs offices are a better clue, offering a panoramic view of the river, encompassing the tide-mill, shipyards and moorings that provided the original partners with much of their trade.

Contracts, bills of lading, salvage, navigation rights, these were the firm's day-to-day business in 1790, when the brass plate was firmly affixed to the east Anglian brickwork. And smuggling, because the original Mr Barrow occupied a double role; first as the local magistrate charged with enforcing the law, but also as the principal buyer of the black goods brought ashore after dark. In contrast Mr Fisk's expertise lay in marine contracts, the local shipwrights and agents appreciating his skill in creating intricate clauses and covenants that led would-be plaintiffs to retreat in dismay.

Seven generations later the Barrows had long departed for the more lucrative delights of the City. The town's bustling shipyards and slipways had been replaced by a cram packed marina, and the high street's no nonsense shops had given way to establishments that catered for what the chamber of commerce called the visitor economy.

The current Mr Fisk was, if truth be told, slightly embarrassed by the extra-curricular exploits of his predecessors, but he could be relied upon to tell a suitably bowdlerised history of the firm to the occasional distinguished gathering, adding with a rueful smile that such excitement rarely intruded upon the humdrum modern day routine of conveyancing and wills.

'Except today', he thought, frowning at the manila folder on his desk.

The intercom buzzed.

"Your 10:30 is here."

"Thanks, Olivia, one moment."

Graeme Fisk sighed and picked up the thick folder, marked in blue to donate a will, and with the name Nicole Pattison handwritten in Olivia's neat script. He glanced at the clock, which revealed that his visitor was ten minutes early, then at the large, expensively framed picture, leaning against his bookcase. Tasteful it might be, but the triple nude study had been the subject of inappropriate humour amongst the office staff, Graeme couldn't wait to get rid of it.

"Offer Mr Stannard a drink, Fiona, I'll be a few minutes."

He flicked the intercom switch without waiting for his secretary's reply, opened the folder and spread the papers across his desk.

The Pattison file had been started in the 1950s at a time when Graeme's father was the senior partner. The first document set out the terms of a money transfer, thirty shillings a week, from Ms Pattison to a local family, the Stannards. The amounts remained modest for several years, until 1965 when the figures began to climb. They reached a peak in the early seventies, when the sums amounted to several thousand pounds a year. The last payment to the Stannards had been in 1992, to cover Rosemary Stannard's funeral expenses.

'So far, so simple,' said Fisk to himself. The complications followed that death, and coincided with the retirement of the elder Mr Fisk.

The file followed Paul Stannard's career, from school to a foundation art course at the local college, where Nicole's instructions paid for art materials and the 'bus fares to Ipswich. Then onto art college proper, where an obscure arts trust called the Rowan Foundation arranged for a student group to attend a summer school in Florence.

Paul Stannard became a teacher, married, divorced and, in a mid life change of direction, moved to Wales to start a new life as an artist. At each stage in this journey he was shadowed by Nicole, who used her chequebook to smooth his progress.

The senior Mr Fisk's role was to protect the anonymity of these arrangements, which was easy whilst Rosie Stannard was alive, but became increasingly complex after her death.

One of Graeme's first tasks as the new senior partner was a transfer of five thousand pounds to Paul Stannard, with the instruction that it should be channelled through the Stannard estate, as if it were a bequest from Rosie's will. This was followed by occasional instructions to transfer monies and make purchases, none of which, in Graeme's view, lay within the proper practice of a family solicitor.

Graeme Fisk's options to back out of the obligation were constrained by a strong sense of duty to his father. There was also the fact of Ms Pattison. Graeme met his client rarely, most recently in London, in connection with a bizarre request to anonymously purchase paintings from a gallery in Pembrokeshire. That had created some challenges, but Nicole Pattison was clearly a formidable woman with significant funds at her disposal, and not, in Graeme's view, someone whose wishes it would be wise to ignore.

The recipient of most of these bequests waited in the adjoining office, and the fact that this morning's business would fulfil Ms

Pattison's last instructions offered a slim silver lining to the day. Graeme glanced at the picture again, allowing himself a grim smile. He would be able to close the file, and breathe a huge sigh of relief.

***

On the long drive back to Pembrokeshire Paul Stannard had abundant time to absorb the multiple shocks delivered during his short interview with the solicitor.

Paul had been eleven when his parents told him about the adoption. It was his first day at the high school, when Frank said that he was old enough to know the real story.

Until that day the cottage in Woodbridge had been the entirety of Paul's world. Frank was a shipwright at Everson's and Rosie a cook at Paul's primary school. Paul was a cosseted only child, and his life revolved around boats, fishing and the river.

The disclosure was an unlooked for disturbance to that placid pool. At exactly the age when most children begin to develop a sense of identity he found himself at the centre of a masquerade; part of a narrative where the central characters were offstage and unknown.

"So where's my mother, what's she called? Why did she give me up? And my dad. Who's he?"

Frank's answers to these questions offered no satisfaction.

"Your mum couldn't look after you, she was called Elizabeth … we don't know much else about her, except that she came from London …"

Paul's pride in his new school uniform melted away. Frank and Rosie made vain attempts to reassure. From that day they acquired new identities, their status as parents irretrievably eroded. Paul began to refer to his 'real' mum and 'real' dad, causing tangible hurt to the couple who, until that day, he had loved without question.

When Paul received Graeme Fisk's summons to Woodbridge

he imagined that he might finally receive some answers; a narrative to attach to the shadowy figure who had haunted his life.

"I thought you might think that," the lawyer had said. "But no, this is not about your mother, at least not directly. I cannot reveal anything that might identify your mother without her authority. And I have strong reasons to believe that such consent would not be forthcoming."

Paul was instead introduced to Nicole.

"Nicole Pattison died last month, February 14th. Barrow and Fisk have acted for her for the last 40 years. She lived in London, and seems to have been a well paid executive in a corporate role. She was not your birth mother, or even a relative. She was, I think, connected to your mother ... a friend perhaps, or a close colleague."

Fisk explained the long history of interventions. Paul already knew about the monthly allowances that had secured a more comfortable childhood than Frank and Jessie might have been able to provide. That conversation had occurred years ago, along with the assumption that the funds originated from his mother. But the revelation that Nicole had been the source was a complete surprise – and the detail was staggering.

"The summer school? She paid for that?"

"Arranged would be more accurate – but yes."

Paul remembered his first professional exhibition, a year after the divorce, and the glow of astonished pleasure when he found that every one of his paintings boasted a red spot in the corner.

"You're saying that she bought them – all of them?"

Fisk nodded.

"I knew they were good," the gallery owner had said. "Had full confidence you'd do well. It's a London buyer. My guess is that they'll grace the walls of some very posh offices."

Paul's recollection was that the gallery had been reluctant to commit to the exhibition, opining that the landscapes might struggle to find buyers. The swarm of red dots transformed

Paul's fortunes. The gallery ditched its scepticism and became an enthusiastic supporter; prices doubled as a result.

A horrifying possibility crossed Paul's mind.

"Did she carry on …" he struggled to articulate the thought. "Has she been buying all my paintings?"

"No," said the lawyer, much to Paul's relief. "I'm not sure we would have been able to do that, even if she'd asked us to."

"And this money? It comes from my mother? This Nicole person is – was – an intermediary of some kind? I've no idea who she is, I've never met her."

Graeme Fisk paused to consider his answer.

"That the money originated with your mother is what we have always assumed. It's what Mr and Mrs Stannard believed …"

He paused again.

"And you have met Nicole. The Stannards clearly knew her well, they told me that she visited quite often when you were a child."

"But …"

Graeme put up a hand to forestall the question.

"There are things I cannot say, my instructions are quite clear … I suggest we move to the main business of the meeting. There is a modest bequest, and some personal effects."

He gestured to the corner of the room and Paul swivelled round in the chair to be confronted by the triple nude picture in the corner.

"She wanted you to have this, her instructions are very specific on the matter."

***

It was late evening by the time Paul arrived back in St David's. He unloaded the Volvo and went to bed, leaving the picture and the small suitcase in the lobby.

The next day he took his usual early morning walk down to the harbour at Port Clais. Paul worked in watercolours and acrylics and his paintings sold well beyond the confines of Pembrokeshire's galleries. This daily stroll on the coast path was the creative heart of his painting, offering an endless range of subjects and challenges. There were seals at the foot of the sea cliffs, the ever changing seascapes, even the strolling holidaymakers on the high street.

As he reached the small harbour there was a flash of movement; a sand martin skimming the surface of the water. The first he'd seen that year. Paul reached for his camera, but the bird was away, over to the far side of the valley. Still, the image remained in his head. He didn't need a photograph; he'd always been able to paint from memory.

He smiled ruefully at the momentary loss of confidence that had accompanied yesterday's revelations. His thoughts were more sanguine today. Success might have taken a little longer without Nicole's support. But it would have come, because he knew how to paint.

Returning inland he squeezed past the early visitors on Nun Street's narrow pavement, before spending the rest of the morning making the most of the light to work on his latest commission. At midday the clouds rolled in from the west and he abandoned the painting to deal with correspondence and lunch.

It was mid afternoon before he felt able to deal with the aftermath of the previous day's events. In the lobby he moved the expensively framed print into the light and gave it a professional appraisal. It was a black and white study based on Canova's 'Three Graces'. Reasonably faithful to the sculpture, the picture was a studio portrait taken by a professional. From the style Paul guessed that it dated from the early fifties. The three girls looked very young, but standards were different then.

It was heavy, he'd struggled to bring it in from the car. He wondered where to put it, or even whether he would keep it at all.

Returning to the studio with the suitcase he cleared a space on his work table and opened the lid.

Laid on top was a blue and white cotton minidress: reminiscent of Mary Quant's early work. He checked the label: Libbys – Kings Road.

Next came a folder of pictures, each in an individual plastic sheaf; a photogenic child with chestnut brown hair and sparkling eyes. In the first picture wearing school uniform, then the same girl on a beach that looked like Brighton, then as a long haired teenager on the back of a motorbike. Some showed a young man, a James Dean lookalike with the same bike. There were family pictures, almost sepia with age; dressed up in a garden, with an older man that Paul guessed was her father, and a woman in a pure white blouse and severe skirt that reached almost to her ankles.

He checked the folder again. In the top corner a title had been written in small neat handwriting: 'Libby – pictures'.

Slowly a thought crystallised. Paul seized the motorbike picture and skipped downstairs to the hall. It was the same girl, on the left of the trio ... the same girl.

Paul rocked on his heels, suddenly faint. Tears pricked his eyes as he stared at the picture. This was his mother – this girl – in the painting and pictures. He leaned against the wall and slid down until he was sat on the floor. It was as if the world had shifted, realigned, refocused. The sense of instability that had been ever present since that first day of school suddenly dispelled.

For a long time he stayed there, immersed in the images, absorbing the detail. What had she been like, this girl from the past whose genes he bore? A free spirit obviously, but what else? It took some time for Paul to realise that the answers to these questions might be found upstairs. He dashed back up to the studio.

Paul examined the collection laid out on the desk; more folders, some rough sketches of the three girls in the Canova picture, an expensive looking hardback of wildlife photographs, and a small package with the single word 'Paul' written in the same neat handwriting. He was intrigued by the package and decided to leave it 'til last.

A blue folder contained press clippings. An article from the Totnes Gazette dated September 1940 described a bomb attack on a village school; a 1956 Daily Express article enthused about an event on the Kings Road: three girls outside a cafe. Paul studied the faces – a statuesque brunette at the cafe table bore a strong resemblance to one of the girls in the picture downstairs. The girl sat on the table was his mother – but with shorter hair. He smiled to himself; she was undeniably pretty – like that actress from the film – 'Breakfast at Tiffany's' – Audrey Hepburn?

Then came coverage of a fashion show in New York in 1964. None of the models resembled the previous pictures and Paul laid the folder to one side. The next folder was another puzzle. It was newspaper clippings again, but an eclectic mix, from the Suez war to Brigitte Bardot at the Cannes Film Festival, then to Vietnam and Cambodia. Paul skimmed the text of the stories, but couldn't see a link; the bylines simply read 'from our correspondent'.

Paul reached for the package.

Now then, what's in here?

He cut the top off the padded envelope, spilling a paperback and a sealed letter onto the desk.

The book title was 'Libby' – styled in flowing gold letters above a photograph of a slim woman dressed in white T-shirt and jeans. This was an older version of the other pictures: more life experience in the face and shorter hair, but the same bold eyes. The rubric on the rear cover declared the book to be the authorised biography of Dame Elizabeth Young: designer, entrepreneur, sixties icon and twentieth century phenomenon.

Paul stared in astonishment. He knew Libby; everyone of his age knew Libby. She'd been splashed across the newspapers, featured in TV documentaries, interviewed on 'Parkinson' with Mick Jagger. His wife had shopped at the store.

"Hello, Mum"

***

Flat 4
21 Moscow Road
London
W2
October 1996

Paul,

I am writing this in 1996 because time is limited and I believe there are some things that you should know.

My name is Nicole. Your mother and I have been friends and colleagues since we were teenagers, so I have known you since before you were born.

First things first. Please do not blame your mother for the decisions she was forced to make.

You were the result of a brief relationship she had with man called Michael Ratcliffe. It seems that Michael was called away to work abroad, and it's possible that he was never informed about Libby's pregnancy.

Whatever the facts of the matter Libby found herself expecting a child in 1956 – very different times to today. The options at the time were limited. Abortion was illegal and life for an unmarried mother would have been difficult. There would have been no possibility of a career, and Libby was such a talented person, as anyone can see from her subsequent success.

Libby chose adoption, with Frank and Rosie, who desperately wanted a child. You will probably not remember, but I visited quite often when you were a small child, and I know that Frank and

Rosie loved you as much as any child could expect – whether adopted or not.

I know that things were difficult for a time after Frank and Rosie broke the news. Perhaps it would have been better had they told you earlier. In any case I'm pleased that you forgave that lapse in judgement. You gave a lovely address at Frank's funeral – I'm sorry that I was unable to attend Rosie's service, but I was in hospital.

I am enclosing a biography and other material about Libby; she is currently in a nursing home in Berkshire. She had a stroke a few years ago and developed a form of early dementia as a result. On the reverse of this letter are the contact details of a mutual friend, who will be able to arrange contact if that is what you decide. I hope you will go; Libby does not get many visitors, but enjoys the company.

Your father had a successful career as a photographer. I enclose one of his books, and a folder with some of his other work. He spent a lot of time in the far east, but returned to the UK a few years ago. I don't have an address, but his publisher is Darwen House, who ought to be able to help if you want to make contact. Do bear in mind that he may be unaware of your existence. It might come as a shock.

I never had children of my own, but I have kept a close eye on your progress. You have done well – Libby would be proud of your success.

Nicole Pattison
October 20th 1996

Claire

Wednesday evenings were usually spent with Claire. After an inauspicious start their relationship had settled into a comfortable routine of alternate dinners, weekend walks and occasional overnight stays. These were usually at Paul's's apartment, ostensibly because he possessed a bigger bed, but actually because Claire was disinclined to cycle home in the dark.

It was Claire's turn to cook and Paul picked a Chardonnay off the rack before driving over to Solva. Claire's flat was above a shop just outside the town, where property was marginally less expensive. The kitchen was the usual chaos.

"No witnesses," shouted Claire as he let himself in. "Make me a Kir."

Paul made a show of covering his eyes as he swapped the Chardonnay for an opened bottle of Sauvignon Blanc in the fridge. He poured two glasses and added the cassis.

"In the kitchen?"

"Yes, please."

Paul delivered the Kir and planted a kiss on the nape of Claire's neck.

"What are we having?"

"I'm doing a Delia, Crab cakes, fresh off the quay, with Fennel Nicoise. Take your hands off my bum and go and read the paper."

Paul retreated to the tiny living room and re-assembled the gutted remains of the Sunday Times.

"The Sun is backing Labour to win the election."

"Everybody thinks that Blair will win – he's been handed the result on a platter. Now let me cook, I'm doing the dressing."

Paul placed himself so that he could watch Claire working. He picked up the Times magazine and tried to concentrate on an article predicting that global warming would soon replace the ozone layer as the main focus for environmentalists.

Bit late there, mate. Claire has been banging on about global warming for the entire time I've known her.

Paul glanced over to the kitchen, remembering their first meeting, when she had tried to persuade him to allow a Greenpeace poster at the gallery. He'd enjoyed the heated discussion that followed, and had been pleasantly surprised when she accepted his invitation to continue the argument over dinner.

On the opposite wall a pinboard detailed the progress of their relationship: event tickets, restaurant bills, daft pictures – a 'before and after' of Claire.

The 'before' was three years ago, before the accident, and the long stay in hospital that turned her life around. The 'after' matched the Claire in the kitchen, wearing her habitual combination of leggings and sweater, the tawny blonde curls in rebellious disarray. It was nearly a year since the argument at the gallery, and Paul was still surprised that this wonderful creature was willing to share his life.

Claire brought the plates to the tiny table, along with the Chardonnay from the fridge.

"Morrison's finest," she said. "You spoil me."

Over supper she took him through her day, beginning with the swim.

"The tide was right so we could swim here off the beach. Anna of course – Jill and Mike were there as well. Then work – I've three arrivals for the weekend, and the gas certs for the Mathry farm cottages."

"Did you bike it? It's a long way out."

"Yes, the engineer was a bit surprised."

Claire ran a fledgling business supporting the area's many second home owners. In the winter months this meant keeping an eye on the property; in season the work focused on getting the homes ready for the owners, or for holidaymakers renting the property. For ten years Claire had done similar work for another company, before striking out on her own after her accident. Her other job was as the relief head waitress at one of St David's busy restaurants. She looked up at Paul.

"And I've been asked to do a shift at the Mariner on Saturday – that's OK isn't it?"

"Fine – back to mine afterwards?"

"It's 11 til 9, I'll be knackered."

Paul grinned. "You'll just have to fuck me on Sunday morning."

Claire grinned back whilst delivering a sharp kick under the table.

"Your studio, your bed, you do the fucking. If you're lucky I might wake up."

"That's a date then."

For those who make their living by the sea weekends are for work. Paul's busiest days were Friday to Sunday, and Claire was usually working either Friday or Saturday, and sometimes both. It was how their Wednesday nights had begun: a midweek opportunity.

"Oh," said Claire. "I forgot to ask. How was your trip over to Suffolk, anything exciting?"

Paul had given the barest details of the visit to Woodbridge, partly because he had been given so little information in advance. He reached into his bag and put Libby's paperback biography on the table.

Claire raised an eyebrow.

"Bit of a long drive to pick up a book."

"There were some documents and a framed picture as well, it wasn't just the book."

"That's a pity," said Claire. "All that way and it was nothing to do with your mum at all."

Paul held her eyes for a moment and smiled.

"Ah but it was."

He reached across the table and removed her plate, replacing it with the paperback.

Claire looked at the book, back to Paul, then again at the book, turning it round so that she could read the rear cover.

"This is your Mum?"

Paul nodded. Claire's face shrieked confusion.

"But she's famous … We would have heard, surely, that she'd died I mean."

"Ah well," said Paul. "She's not dead, as least I don't think so."

He explained about the mystery Nicole and the way that she had shadowed his life.

"Like a fairy bloody godmother," said Claire, laughing. She held up the book.

"Have you read it?"

"Yes – it's a bit rose tinted in places – and it doesn't mention me at all."

"But this Nicole person – her letter – she says that you should go and see her."

"Yes," said Paul.

"So, will you?"

Paul hesitated, that very question had kept him awake for most of the previous night.

"I'm not sure yet. She's what – 65? And with dementia … how much would the meeting mean to her? And she's presumably very well off … I wouldn't want anyone to think that I was chasing her money. The book's not recent, it was published years ago, in '81, after she got her gong. There's a lot I don't know, about Nicole for example. But … yes, I think I'd like to see Libby if I can. She's my mother after all."

"Good for you."

***

Later that night Claire contemplated the sleeping face of the man in her bed. He was eight years older with a completely crap taste in music and no dress sense. But he was her man. He listened when she spoke, and took her opinions seriously. That had been the attraction at the very first meeting – that he argued against her view without taking the piss. And that easy smile, all the way up to the eyes. Claire could easily lose herself in those eyes.

As a child Claire had been the third in a family of five, without the responsibility of her elder sisters, and lost in the shadow of the attention paid to the youngest boy. She felt unloved, a feeling exacerbated by her parents' unnecessarily acrimonious divorce when she was in her last year of primary. At secondary school she retreated into herself, taking refuge in chocolates and books. Her weight ballooned as her confidence plummeted. From school she moved on to the local further education college where she trained as a cook, before dropping out at eighteen to begin a series of dead end jobs and forgettable relationships.

By her thirtieth birthday she had achieved something of an even keel, working for the lettings agency and at the Mariner, being appreciated because she was diligent and capable. But she felt that life had passed her by, that she was living in a scenic cul-de-sac enjoyed by other people.

Then came the accident. A fall downstairs that broke her back in two places.

"The spinal cord is undamaged we think," the surgeon had told her. "But we need to repair the damaged vertebrae and we cannot operate until the swelling has completely reduced."

The upshot was eight weeks of immobilisation, on her back, neck bolted to a frame, fed liquid goop by the nurses.

Eight weeks is a long time to contemplate a life full of wasted opportunities, and Claire made a number of resolutions. She would ditch Paddy, the useless boyfriend who had visited the hospital a grand total of three times during her stay. She would stay at the Mariner, because she liked the owners, but the lettings job would go, because she could do a much better job by herself. And by the Spring she would be a size 10.

The operation arrived eventually to be followed by three months of physiotherapy with Anna, who first restored Claire's fitness in the hospital gym, and then her confidence.

"Your back will always be a weak point, so you need to develop your core strength and keep the weight down. Running is out – too much impact. So it's cycling and swimming."

"In the sea?" said a horrified Claire. "It's November!"

Anna grinned.

"As it happens I help run an open water swimming group. Water temps in November are quite good after the summer, it's in the late spring that it's really cold. And even then you wont really notice in a wet suit."

By the end of March Claire was hooked, with or without a wet suit. And she was a size 10.

As she lay awake Claire contemplated the news that Paul had been given. It was such a bitter sweet surprise. To discover that someone who had watched over him for his entire life was gone, and that the woman who had given him away was alive but in no condition to receive any kind of meaningful contact. And what did this mean for Claire, their relationship; their life in the back of beyond? Would it whisk him away, this man she had found, her diamond on a muddy shore?

Against the background of Paul's soft breathing Claire contemplated these questions, eventually deciding that worrying about the issue would provide no answers. But there was one thing she could do. In her considerable extended family she had an uncle Steve, who worked, if she recalled correctly, for the Libby's department store in Bristol.

It turned out that uncle Steve had no connection with Libby's, being the regional transport manager for M&S, but the phone call wasn't a complete waste of time.

"Because I know someone who should be able to help."

Two days later Steve rang back.

"Found him at last. He's living on his boat. His name's Frank, he says ring when you like, cos he's got one of those new mobile phones."

***

A week later Claire appeared at Paul's flat, after a long days spent spring cleaning her holiday lets. She disappeared into Paul's bathroom, emerging after twenty minutes, glowing from the shower and wearing his favourite black dress.

"Gosh," he said. "What are we celebrating?"

"Us, me and you, you and me."

Paul looked suitably puzzled and she waited for a few moments before coming to his rescue.

"Our first anniversary, it's been a year."

"I thought that was next week … April 1st … the date stuck in my mind for some reason."

"No, our first date was at the gallery, when we had that lovely row. That's when I decided to go out with you."

"But, I asked you," protested Paul with a grin.

"A minor detail," she said, steeping forward into his arms. "Anyway, that's why I wore the dress. So that you could take it off."

An hour later Claire raised her head from Paul's shoulder, and poked him gently in the ribs.

"No way," he said. "Not yet. Not even for your lovely self."

"Not that," she giggled. "At least not yet. I have some news for you."

Claire explained about her uncle, and his retired friend Frank, who had been Logistics Manager at Libby's, before he retired to a narrow boat on the Grand Union canal.

"Nicole Pattison was a senior exec at Libby's, he had quite a bit of contact with her. She was very practical apparently, and the others weren't. At least that's what he thought. So Nicole had a lot to do with the contracts and delivery schedules. He says that she was good looking in a serious kind of way: tall and slim – with nice tits."

"He really said she had 'nice tits'?" asked Paul in surprise.

"Well, not exactly, but that's what he meant. He thinks she had cancer, something long term, hospital appointments going back years. Apparently her and Libby went back all the way to the start of the company."

Paul sat up in bed, the better to concentrate on Claire's story.

"Go on."

"He said Libby was a 'different kettle of fish',"

Paul laughed.

"That's what he said," she said indignantly.

"It was, really – 'different kettle of fish' – I've never heard anyone say that, why would you put fish in a kettle? Anyway, he said she was distant, cold. Not just his opinion, other people said so as well, at least the ones he knew. And then she had a stroke, about three years ago. Middle of a fashion show – went out like a light. Come to think about it I seem to remember something in the papers. Anyway, it was off to hospital and she never came back. Company has been going downhill ever since."

"My mum the cold fish," said Paul.

"Sorry, love."

"It's alright, if I'm going to meet her then the more I know the better."

He ran his fingers down her naked back.

"You don't appear to have any clothes on."

She sat up and looked down in feigned surprise. He reached for her, but she rolled out of range,

"You said 'No' … not even for my lovely self … 'exhausted', you said."

"I'm not sure I actually said 'exhausted'."

Debbie

The contact details in Nicole's letter were for an address in London. A carefully crafted letter produced no response for a month and Paul began to suspect that the information was out of date. Then a reply arrived, suggesting a meeting at the retirement home.

Greenlands was in Teddington, next to a big secondary school about half a mile from the Thames. The taxi dropped Paul at the end of the drive, It was a beautiful morning and he stopped to admire a row of apple trees coming into blossom. A green BMW roadster pulled up and a tanned face appeared at the window.

"You must be Paul, be a love and move that cone out of the way."

The woman pointed to a parking bay blocked by a large yellow cone marked 'reserved'. Paul picked up the cone and hesitated, as the BMW slid into the space.

"In the boot," said the driver, as she activated the boot mechanism. "Fret not, we'll put in back."

The woman who climbed out of the sports car would have won a glamorous granny contest hands down. Pure white hair cut close to a tanned face that had enough lines to indicate maturity, but not enough to offer any tangible clues as to exactly how mature. Dressed in designer jeans and a sweater top, she moved with a dancer's grace, but shook his hand like a boxer.

"I'm Debbie, and you are most definitely Paul – you're the spit of Michael – to a T."

She took his arm and led the way up the drive to the door.

"I'll do the talking," she said, leaning on the intercom call button.

Greenlands was a newish building, carefully landscaped with an exterior that could have belonged to a mid market hotel. A buzzer sounded and Debbie pushed Paul through to the lobby. This was more institutional, with a visitors' book, notice board and antiseptic dispenser.

A solidly built woman in pastel blue coveralls appeared and gave Debbie a warm embrace.

"Where you been, somewhere nice? She's missed you, so have I – and who's this, your toyboy?"

"Lena, lovely to see you you again. I've been working; this is Paul, he's not a toyboy, much too old."

Lena appraised Paul and laughed.

"'Listen to her … 'working' she says!"

Lena laughed again as Debbie completed the visitors' book entry.

"Look at that tan, I should have such a tan."

"How is she?" asked Debbie.

"She's fine, no real change …" Lena turned to Paul. "She has good days and bad days."

"And the lawyers? Everything OK?" asked Debbie.

"Is fine, don't worry, everything is up to date."

An elderly woman appeared with a walking frame, shuffling barefoot towards the front door, wearing nothing but a dressing gown over a vest.

Lena took the woman by the arm.

"Joyce, shall we go and find your slippers? And we need to get you dressed I think. Otherwise this young man will be whisking you away," she paused and looked back.

"Can you find your way down?"

Debbie nodded. The lobby opened out into a long wide corridor that had been transformed to resemble a street scene, with a red telephone box, benches, large potted plants and reproduction railway posters depicting seaside resorts. Debbie gave a cheery 'good morning' to an elderly man sat at one of the benches.

"It's Terry isn't it," she said, taking his hand. The man looked nonplussed for a moment, then smiled and nodded.

On either side of the corridor large shop front style windows revealed individual lounges furnished with oversized easy chairs, occupied by residents gazing listlessly into the middle distance. A smaller room was equipped as a hair salon, another as a shop, complete with a stock of books, cards, magazines and sweets.

"It's purpose built," explained Debbie. "Each unit can take eight residents, and has its own staff. Libby's in Nightingale, that's this one."

She led the way into a large room, where three women in crumpled mismatched clothes sat in front of the large TV screen paying scant attention to the new Prime Minister being interviewed by Eamonn Holmes. Across the room a young woman in a blue coverall was helping a man with a children's jigsaw puzzle.

"Look," she said. "This is a ship. Do you think it goes here, in the corner?"

The elderly resident looked at the jigsaw piece, then at the care assistant, then down at the bright colours of the almost completed puzzle, apparently seeing all of these things for the first time.

"I'm not sure," he said. "What do you think?"

Two staff sat at a large table writing up notes in ring bound folders. One looked up and acknowledged Debbie.

"Oh, hello. She's in her room, with Sheila, being dressed. Make sure you knock."

Double doors led to a corridor where each door had a name and a picture. The first celebrated 'Alec', with a photograph of a confident middle-aged man at the wheel of an E-type Jaguar.

"That was Alec, doing the jigsaw," said Debbie.

Paul stared at the image, trying in vain to connect the confident, almost arrogant figure with the jigsaw-puzzled man in the next room.

"Life in the waiting room," said Debbie. "Ain't it grand. Best get used to it, because this is where we're all going. Start makin' ready now … this is Libby's room."

The picture on this door was an older version of the jacket photo for Libby's biography. David steeled himself for the reality, then the door opened, as Libby stepped out into the corridor.

For a second or two she didn't seem to realise they were there. Paul was relieved to find that she looked reassuring normal. Her right arm was in a black sling, and she was dressed in a long flowing open jacket over a white T-shirt and tracksuit bottoms.

She looked up and saw Debbie.

"Oh it's you, how lovely."

The two women embraced. Libby's hug fierce and prolonged. Eventually Debbie pulled herself away.

"I've brought someone to see you …" she began.

But Libby had already spotted Paul.

"Michael … Oh, Michael."

Libby collapsed into Paul's arms.

"Where did you go?" She began to cry softly into his shoulder. "I've missed you so much …"

Paul stood helplessly, his eyes a frantic appeal for help.

"Sorry, Libby," said the care assistant. "It's not Michael, not this time. It's Debbie's friend, come to see you."

This precipitated more tears. Carefully Sheila peeled Libby's arms away and led to her to a chair. Debbie motioned Paul to stand where he could not be seen.

"Look," said Debbie, seating herself next to Libby. "I've brought you the latest show catalogue."

Debbie spread a large fashion catalogue across Libby's lap.

"What do you think of this?" asked Debbie. "I'm not sure."

Libby sat tense in the chair, disorientated by the apparent return of a figure from her past. Debbie continued to turn the pages and comment on the designs. Eventually Libby looked down and focused on the pictures.

"That jacket's nice," she said. "But these, what's the word …"

She jabbed at the page in annoyance.

"Culottes," said Debbie.

"Yes, yes, I know, I know – culottes – they're all too long, no-one wears this kind of thing."

Paul watched as Debbie led the conversation, touching on the weather, shopping expeditions, a stubborn stain on Libby's jacket. Their conversation seemed normal, even animated. After half an hour the care staff began to lay the big central table for lunch.

"Time for us to go," said Debbie.

"It's alright for you," said Libby. "I'm stuck in here."

"But you were very ill, you need more time to recover," said Debbie. "Can Paul give you a kiss goodbye."

She took Libby's hand and nodded to Paul.

"Remember now," said Debbie. "This is Paul, not Michael."

Libby looked at Paul, apparently without recognition and without any of the distress from a few minutes before.

"One of Debbie's many young men," she said, allowing Paul to kiss her cheek in farewell. "Everyone here thinks I'm doo-lally."

Once they were out of the room Debbie turned to Paul.

"The last stroke was two months ago. That's why her arm's in a sling; she can't move it properly. They say that the next one could kill her, or she might live for years. But it's the other thing, the dementia, that's the real problem for me. Each setback damages her a little more; as if she's was being salami sliced away from the person she used to be. She was fine today, but it can be quite difficult. It's OK as long as you keep to the here and now."

Back at the BMW Debbie replaced the no parking cone.

"Where's your car?"

"I came on the train, via Reading, then a taxi from Richmond"

Debbie raised an eyebrow, and indicated the passenger door.

"Well, that was noble. Jump in, I'll treat you to lunch," she smiled at his obvious hesitation. "It's alright, I won't eat you, and it's just round the corner from the station."

On the short journey from the residential home Debbie demonstrated a combination of driving skill and impatience with other road users alongside a flexible interpretation of the highway code. Paul had never been a passenger in a sports car, or as a driver for that matter. The low level view was disconcerting, and he wondered whether the impression of breakneck speed was real, or simply a result of sitting so close to the tarmac.

"So, the divorce, from what's her name – Angela." asked Debbie , whilst undercutting a slow moving delivery van. "Whose fault was that?"

"No-one's really. We just drifted apart."

"Hmm – and you moved out?"

"Yes, I moved out."

"And you hadn't met your latest – the lovely Claire."

Paul was unsure about the implications of 'latest'.

"No, I hadn't met Claire at that time."

"You broke up, moved to Wales, set up as a painter. Something you'd always wanted to do?"

"Yes"

"So why didn't you do that whilst you were with Angela?"

Paul considered his answer as Debbie dropped into the left hand lane to move past a line of traffic, before turning right into Twickenham high street, to a chorus of outraged car horns and flashing lights.

Why hadn't he? He'd thought about it on lots of occasions, discussed it with Angela several times, but never taken the plunge. His growing dissatisfaction with teaching, the unfulfilled ambition. But there had always been lots of sensible reasons to stay as they were. The real answer ... there was a screech of brakes as Debbie reluctantly gave way to an Evening Standard delivery van.

"The real answer, I suppose ..."

"Is that she didn't want you to. Had no confidence in you. Thought you couldn't hack it."

Debbie swung into an empty parking bay and turned towards him.

"It was her fault," she said bluntly. "She was holding you back. We're here."

Debbie's geography proved to be not entirely accurate. The delicatessen cum restaurant was in fact 'just round the corner' from Debbie's flat, off Richmond Green. The deli was authentic Sicilian, down to the black spaghetti with garlic prawns, served by the proprietor's daughter.

"How long have you known her, Libby, I mean?" asked Paul as the plates were cleared away. "And what was Libby like? As a person, before the illness. And Nicole. I know so little about them."

"Now there's a question," said Debbie, pouring herself another glass of wine.

"We were both teenagers, Libby and I. We worked for a model agency, Poppy's near Tower Hill. I was an occasional model, and Libby was a temp in the office, though she did some modelling later on. Nicole never did that, although she could have. She was tall enough, with a good figure. She had an accounts job somewhere, I forget where."

Debbie took a sip from her glass, considering what to say.

"There are givers and takers in the world. Nicole was a giver, always willing to help out, run the errands, clear up after a party. Libby was a taker."

She caught the expression on Paul's face.

"Don't get me wrong. She could be lovely, attractive, great company ... and she was good at her job. But we were all extras in Libby's movie. The spotlight always had to focus on the star."

Paul absorbed the information quietly for a moment, before asking the question that had nagged at the back of his mind since the visit to the solicitor.

"How did Nicole end up being the one to keep an eye on me? Did Libby ask her to … pay her even."

Debbie reached across the table and took his hand.

"Libby let you go. She knows nothing about you because she never asked. She certainly didn't provide the money."

She contemplated his puzzled expression and laughed.

"You've still not realised have you? Nicole was in love with Libby, hopelessly and stupidly in love. With no prospect of it ever being returned, because Libby was not capable of that degree of affection. Whenever Libby was in trouble she would go to Nicole – and good old Nicole would pull the rabbit out of the hat."

She met his eyes, her tough expression softening in response to the emotions crossing his face..

"And you … you were a part of Libby. So Nicole loved you as well."

"What about you?" said Paul eventually. "Where do you fit into all of this?"

"Me? I'm just chasing the money."

It was Paul's turn to laugh. Debbie had already explained that Libby's wealth was tied up in a trust fund administered by lawyers whose fees seemed designed to leave nothing left for the taxman.

"OK," said Debbie. "There won't be any money. Nothing that will come to me any rate, or to you come to think of it. As to where I fit in … "

She leant back in her chair, and finished her wine.

"The simple answer is that Nicole asked me to do it – to look after Libby, because no-one else was stepping forward. A visit once a month, it's no big deal,. And anyway, we have a bit of a bond Nicole and I."

She caught the quizzical look in his eye.

"Not like that, although I wouldn't have said 'no' if she had asked," she laughed. "Anything for a friend."

Debbie gathered her things together and stood back from the table.

"And there's another thing you should know ... there's been a reporter ... Helen Jackson, a freelance for the red tops. She's been digging around, trying to dish the dirt on how Libby started her business. Not that there is anything to find."

There were out in the street. Debbie pointed out a direction sign to the railway station,

"It's that-a-way. About five minutes. Safe trip back to sunny Wales. It was nice to meet you, I must get down some day. Meet your sexy girlfriend."

She kissed him gently on the cheek.

"This Jackson woman. I don't see how she could find out who you are, but if she does, be careful. She's poison."

***

Two months earlier Debbie walked into a London bar ostensibly to meet a London lawyer representing a Spanish consortium interested in investing in her Mallorcan club. A woman met her in the foyer and led the way to a corner table before introducing herself as Helen Jackson.

"I'm here because I'm curious, " said Debbie. "Because the Spanish say they have never heard of you."

"I'm an investigative reporter," said Jackson. "This is about Simon Lombroso. And before you decide to do anything silly the guy over there is one of our snappers and he just loves to take pictures of people assaulting reporters."

She had positioned Debbie in the corner, taking the next seat so that Debbie would have to clamber over the table or push past the smiling reporter in order to escape. Debbie looked across the room at the photographer, who was ostentatiously laying his camera out on his table.

"What about Simon Lombroso?"

Jackson laid a photograph on the table, a poor quality reproduction of the Three Graces picture taken all those years ago.

"This is you, on the right."

"If you say so."

"The girl on the left is Libby Young, but then you know that. Perhaps you even asked her to do the session, despite the fact that she was underage."

Debbie made no reply. She suspected that Jackson had a tape recorder running. She shrugged, raising her eyebrows and leaning back against the leather of the banquette.

"No comment?" said Jackson. "Lombroso was a pornographer and blackmailer. He liked to blackmail girls into posing for pictures, then he would up the stakes and expect them to have BDSM sex, with even more pictures. You'd know about that kind of thing of course, having run that brothel in Putney – when was that – '70, '71?"

"1971," said Debbie. "And it was a gentlemen's club; we were set up."

"I'm sure. Anyway I think he was blackmailing Libby, with pictures like this."

She pushed another photograph across the table; a naked woman tied to a chair, being forced to fellate a masked man wearing a red kimono."

Debbie glanced at the pic and looked away. The pictures had been destroyed, burnt, negatives and all, or so she had hoped. She had always suspected that others might exist, but to see the proof was a shock. Acutely aware of being watched, Debbie composed herself and looked back at the photograph, which was recognisably Libby, at least to anyone who knew her well.

Helen Jackson leant forward to press her advantage.

"We know all about the company and how he helped her start

her business. But it all got too much didn't it, especially when she began to be successful, when she had too much to lose. So she arranged to have him killed, whilst she was in the States, when she would have a cast iron alibi. That was clever wasn't it?"

Debbie picked up the two photographs.

"Are you finished with this fairy tale?"

She put the 'Three Graces' picture on the table

"You'll get nowhere with this. It's from a high quality photo session by a well known photographer. Libby was a model before she started her business. It's in her biography for fuck's sake … and as for this."

She pushed the second picture back towards the journalist.

"This could be any whore from Soho. No one has ever linked Lombroso's murder to Libby, because if they tried they would face a libel case that they would lose. There was a trial, and a retrial. The police went through it all at the time, and my dad was cleared. I'm sure that's all in your notebook somewhere, so what's this really about?"

Helen Jackson smiled, glanced over to the photographer, then put a document on the table.

"This is a share transfer, made in April 1962. It records a transfer of 800 shares from Lombroso to EyeCo, Libby's company. Up until this point Lombroso owned a majority share in Libby's Kings Road shop, including copyright on the dress designs."

"This …" she waved the certificate. "This signs all that away, for a single payment of £2,000."

Across the room the photographer was snapping away; Jackson looking smug, waving the share certificate, Debbie's reaction, or lack of it, because she was keeping her face carefully neutral. Jackson's finger jabbed at the foot of the document.

"It's signed by Lombroso and Libby, and witnessed by Nick or Nicholas Patterson, can't really tell from his signature, who is listed as company secretary. And look at the date – April 10th, 1962. A few days before Lombroso was shot."

"What does this prove?" asked Debbie.

"Libby was in New York on April 10th 1962, so not in a position to sign anything .. and this is not Lombroso's signature. We had a graphologist do some comparisons, Lombroso was left handed. This was signed by a right hander. And Lombroso never received that £2,000. But someone else did."

Jackson reached into her bag for another photograph. Debbie recognised it straight away; it was of her first club in Magaluf.

"I sold that place years ago."

"But you bought it in 1964, once your dad had been cleared. We know he didn't pull the trigger, but who did? Who was it Debbie? Who shot him? Was it the mystery woman from the hotel lobby, who may have been a man in a wig. Libby must have known all about it, after all she was the one to gain the most. She got rid of someone who was blackmailing her, and picked up all those shares. We don't think it was your dad, but he had the contacts, and he knew about the gun. So who was it?"

Jackson began to collect the papers together.

"You've had an interesting life: showgirl, two divorces, bankruptcy. Always bouncing back, but we think you know the answers to what happened in that hotel room; you link all the strands together. The police were too stupid to notice. But they'll re-open the case if we give them the file."

Debbie had heard enough.

"You have nothing. Nothing at all, print this shit and see what happens. I couldn't care less and Libby's legal team will sue you to the skies."

She nodded to the three solidly built men who had appeared unnoticed at the far end of the bar. The photographer saw the danger and tried to pack away his camera as the men moved in.

"This lady is leaving," said Debbie. "She has a recorder somewhere, and her mate doesn't need the film in his camera."

With quiet efficiency the men restrained the photographer

and removed the camera film. Helen's Jackson's bag was emptied onto the floor, revealing a small cassette recorder.

"Word of advice," said Debbie. "Never get out of your depth."

Alex

It was a year to the day, and Michael picked up a small bouquet from the florist before heading down to the church.

The grave was in the new section of the churchyard, at the end of an avenue bordered by tall Poplars. The plot no longer looked brand new, and the small display of alyssum was well established.

Bringing his mother's remains back home had been a complicated business, involving an exhumation from the paupers' burial ground in Birmingham, and the reburial where she had been born and baptised, in Bishop's Castle on the Welsh border.

Michael had not intended to move to the area, but preliminary visits to check the location had opened his eyes to the unspoilt beauty of the small Marches town. He had no real ties to Totnes after the sale of Overhill, James and Edith having opted for cremation, and he didn't need a physical location to honour their memory.

It was, of course, James and Edith who had located his mother; James having made a series of visits to Somerset House as part of the preparation for Michael's adoption. James first traced the birth certificate, dated August 27th 1930, with the address given as the Mary of Magdela Home for Fallen Women in Birmingham. This led to Mary Ratcliffe, born in Bishops Castle in a ramshackle cottage that had long since ceased to exist. Her birth certificate read 1915, and the 1921 census recorded her living with her mother and grandmother. There were no men recorded in the household and Mary's mother was described as a scullery maid.

There were nothing to fill the gap between the census and the move to Birmingham. James's theory was that the pregnant girl was packed off once her condition was known, either because of the moral pressure, or perhaps even more simply because the household had not the means to feed a child.

Mary must have escaped the confines of the institution at some point, because Michael's first memories were of a back-to-back terraced street, of playing outside on the cobbles, and of a steam filled kitchen swathed in sheets and shirts, which was presumably how his mother scraped a living.

He knelt down next to the neat grave, and laid the posy next to the headstone, with its simple inscription: 'Returned Home'. Michael had no religious convictions, quite the reverse; he had a dislike bordering on contempt for the mummery and hypocrisy that characterised the Church as an institution. Churches as buildings were a different matter, and the parish church of St John the Baptist occupied a beautiful corner of the town, perfect for quiet contemplation. The local priest had been welcoming, unconcerned about religious observance, and helpful with the necessary paperwork. The inscription had been his idea.

At the committal in the churchyard the cleric had spoken of the importance of closure. Of achieving a resolution that would enable Michael to seal the memories and heal the remaining pain. Michael had nodded at the time, but largely in agreement about the importance of righting a past wrong.

Closure was a different matter. In the real world Michael felt that events were rarely concluded in the neat and tidy ways that were so common in fiction. Real life stories had loose ends, untidy consequences, puzzling gaps in understanding. Finding a proper resting place for his mother was important, but he didn't feel a sense of closure. That final resolution was still elusive.

The letter was on the sideboard, where he had left it that morning. From Debbie, a letter and two pictures. One was the party in Belgravia. Archie, surrounded by admirers, holding a copy of the Express, Debbie on his arm – Libby on the fringes, looking distinctly unsteady. Michael had last seen Debbie, thirty, no, forty years years ago. Yet the pictures conjured memories that were sharp as a razor.

Libby, and the long walk to her flat through deserted streets; the ease of their lovemaking, as if they had known each other for years instead of days.

Which we had, of course …

And then to be called away, to the kind of job he could never had turned down.

I tried to call, I sent a telegram, wrote letters …

Michael re-read Debbie's letter, with its bombshell news about the boy, another child seemingly abandoned by his parents. And then the second picture, inside a leaflet about a gallery exhibition in Wales. A grown man – Paul – an artist apparently – who had already won Debbie's approval. Michael examined the face of the man who had suddenly become his son. Was that a trace of sadness in the eyes? Had Paul been left to grow up wondering who he really was, always aware of being part of a not-quite family, no matter how wonderful his adopted parents had been.

I did not abandon you. She knew where I worked. She came to the office. Mrs Perceval would have found me and passed on a message …

Michael picked up the Belgravia picture again, focusing on the slim brunette on the fringes of the group.

You could have told me. I could have – would have – been a father to this boy. Which I intend to be, starting now.

Michael checked the contact details in the letter's postscript, then stuffed the contents back into the envelope. After leaving a message on Debbie's answerphone he rang a London number.

"Alex? Great … look, it's Michael Ratcliffe … yes, long time no see. I was worried you might be in France … any chance of dropping in for a chat?"

***

Alex Cross lived in Blackheath, south of the A2. After working as the southern Europe correspondent for a variety of titles, Alex had a brief spell in Paris as the BBC's Europe Editor before joining a London based research group as its director.

"They're funded by pro-Europe business interests, who were really worried about the eurosceptics, the Tory little Englanders and their opposition to the project, so we had a big budget. With Blair's majority that's going not a problem for a while, so I expect they'll lose a lot of their funding. Not my problem any more."

Michael has always liked Alex, they had got on well in Nice and stayed in touch after Michael moved to Singapore. He'd made a special trip back to Europe for Alex's wedding in Grenoble. Alex had stayed married, unlike many of his contemporaries, and looking across the table Michael could understand why. Michael wondered what mysterious chemistry enabled French women to defy the years with such apparent ease. Françoise had been in her early twenties on her wedding day, and did not look significantly older as she approached what must be her fiftieth birthday.

She'd chosen a Lebanese restaurant within easy reach of their apartment.

"Try the Sfeeha," she said. "It's very good here."

The food arrived, a range of dishes presented tapas style. There was a lot of catching up to do; Michael and Alex had last met five years ago, at the launch of Michael's second book. He'd not seen Françoise since the wedding. She quickly established Michael's single status, the names of his recent partners, and the circumstances of his meeting and break up with Libby.

"And you had no idea at all – about the boy?"

Michael had a mouthful of Kafta; he shook his head.

"And this woman Nicole, who has been ... une bonne fee ... good fairy?" she glanced at Alex for confirmation.

"Fairy Godmother," he supplied.

"Exactement," said Françoise, turning back to Michael.

"So .. this Nicole, did you know her? And it is a French name, she is French, No?"

"No, not as far as I know. I only met her twice, and even then we hardly spoke. She was a friend of Libby's."

Having established that Michael intended to see Libby the following day and then drive down to Wales, the conversation moved onto the death of Diana a few days previously.

Françoise wanted to know whether the Michael subscribed to the conspiracy theories rampant in the French press. Alex gave a warning shake of the head before being spotted by his wife, who elbowed him sharply in the ribs.

"Let him speak," she said.

"I don't know. No, really I don't," protested Michael. "It seems unlikely, but almost everything about the divorce seemed unlikely, and then she goes on Panorama and says it's all true. So I don't know."

Slightly mollified, Françoise allowed herself to be diverted onto the question of Alex's apartment, and whether it should be sold now that he was retired and they lived in France.

"But look," said Alex. "We're here, in London, because you wanted to see a show and do some shopping."

Françoise nearly exploded.

"You wanted to watch Chelsea," she said. "I would have been left alone in Paris."

"How are the boys?" asked Michael, in an attempt to move the conversation onto safer ground. This led to the relative merits of French and British universities – Alex and Françoise' sons being at St Andrews and Montpellier. Françoise didn't approve of St Andrews.

"It's so cold," she said. "And I don't understand what the people are saying. Even Alex doesn't, and he's Scottish."

"Only on my mother's side."

On the way back to apartment Françoise announced her intention to have an early night.

"I have an appointment tomorrow and you two will just be talking about work."

She ignored their unconvincing denials and, after ensuring that Michael had found the carefully placed overnight essentials, she said goodnight.

"She likes to listen to FIP radio, especially when she's over here," said Alex. He selected two glasses and waved a bottle of Jonny Walker Black Label.

"Still drowning it?"

Michael nodded and Alex produced a bottle of still water.

The second floor apartment overlooked the heath and was clearly Alex's comfortably sparse working retreat. The main living room had a military style desk complete with word processor, a triple seat green leather Chesterfield facing a huge TV, and two matching swivel armchairs. A Swedish style coffee table completed the furniture, though there was a small bookshelf next to the desk. Françoise had made attempts to inject some colour and style with fresh flowers and impressionist prints – which were, on closer examination, not prints at all.

"I'm not selling. Françoise would like to, she's never really comfortable over here, but it's a good investment and I like to keep some personal space."

Alex took a sip of Scotch and pick up a bound notebook from his impressively large desk. He sat down opposite Michael.

"So … I've done some digging. Spoke to a few people."

Michael edged forward on the settee.

"Your friend Debbie was on the nose about the story," said Alex.

"Helen Jackson has been hawking it round Fleet Street for some time. She was on the original Spotlight team at the Shield. It's clear that Libby was involved with an Italian gangster called Lombroso. He seems to have helped her set up the original business. How and why we don't know. But there's a strong sex element in there somewhere, with some very dodgy pictures. He may have been blackmailing her, the business accounts at the time don't stand much scrutiny."

Alex turned the page of the notebook and took another sip of scotch.

"In 1962 Lombroso is murdered, shot, just as Libby's business was taking off. The police investigation was the usual farce. It didn't help that Lombroso didn't allow anyone from the hotel to enter the room. So it wasn't clear what, if anything, was missing. The only certain thing is that he was shot with his own gun and that there was a large picture stolen. A triple nude from the bedroom."

"A triple nude?" Michael looked up in surprise.

"It was a poster size black and white photo, not a Rembrandt," Alex smiled. "The porters remembered it for some reason. The general consensus is that it was a gangland killing. Lombroso seems the type to have made lots of enemies."

Alex had noticed Michael's thoughtful expression.

"Bells ringing?"

"Not really. Taking the picture doesn't really fit with a gangland murder, does it?"

"Not my field," said Alex. "Or yours really, perhaps it's hanging on some scruffy bedroom wall in Tottenham. We'll never know will we?"

"And the Spotlight team?"

"They made the connection between Libby's business and Lombroso, no idea how. But the story never ran. Paul Hectre was the Shield editor at the time; he spiked it and the other titles were equally chary about the legalities. It didn't help that Jackson is convinced that Libby was involved in the murder – when she has a cast iron alibi."

Alex finished his Scotch, and waved the glass.

"Another?"

Michael shook his head. His own glass was still half full and he knew better than to try and match his friend. Alex poured another.

Michael tried to make sense of what he was being told. He couldn't match the girl from the party with the underworld figure Alex had described; still less with the playful friend from his childhood.

"Could this be just hype?" he asked. "Jackson making a connection that doesn't really exist. 'Young' is quite a common name after all."

"No. They stood it up. Jackson's partner at the Shield was a solid reporter: David Lewis, currently with the FT as their US editor. I've met him. The business angle is solid; it's the sex and the murder that makes it a difficult story to run."

"But without those it's not a splash is it?"

"Correct," said Alex. "Red tops' motto: no sex, no pix, no story. There are two recent developments. One is a High Court injunction from Libby's lawyers. Obviously they know that the story is being hawked around. Basically the injunction means that no-one can write the story, even in the most general terms, until after Libby's death."

"And the other?"

Alex leant back in his chair.

"My sources tell me that the trust that owns Libby's business is in discussions with another high street name about a takeover. That would make sense on all levels. The business has been treading water since Libby's illness. If this story does break it would be very bad news for the brand. Better to cut and run."

"Can they do that?" asked Michael. "Sell I mean, surely she's still the majority shareholder?"

Alex grinned.

"She set up a trust, and transferred her shares, probably as some kind of tax avoidance scheme. That works as long as you can still pull the strings, maintain control. But she's ill, so she can't do that. The trustees will be thinking about their bonuses and dividends. They will sell."

Michael drained his glass and stood; he had no desire for a hangover in the morning.

"Thanks Alex. Appreciated. Much more than I expected. I couldn't have done that, don't have the connections over here any more."

Alex looked meaningfully at Michael, at his glass and at the half full bottle.

"Can't persuade you?"

Michael shook his head.

"Françoise wouldn't like me in the morning."

"She quite often feels that way about me," said Alex ruefully "But I can usually win her round by midday."

Alex drained his remaining Scotch and picked up the glasses.

"But be warned. You know as well as I do that they'll run the story when they can."

"When Libby dies."

"Or if something else changes, the lawyers, for example. Or if they find the mystery woman."

Michael hesitated at the door to his room.

"The prime suspect," said Alex as he headed to the kitchen. "Who met Lombroso on the day of the murder. A tall blonde who may have been a man wearing a wig. No-one seems to know who that was."

Michael's hand was on the bedroom door handle, where it stayed for some time as his mind's eye re-ran the events of that long ago day on Kings Road, and the tall blonde girl who had given up her day off to help out.

St Davids

The summer holidays were over.

On the High Street the families with children had been replaced by grey haired couples and honeymooners, what the locals called the season of the newly weds and nearly deads.

Claire was smoothing down the beds at the Bailiff's House. She'd been there since 7am, cleaning the rooms as they had rarely been done before. Next on her list was a trip to Fishguard for the shopping, then back to the house for some serious food prep.

The frenetic activity had been triggered by Wednesday's phone call. Debbie had 'phoned the studio, hoping to speak to Paul.

"Oh – you must be Claire," said the confident voice. "Just the person I need to speak to."

It transpired that Debbie and Michael would be travelling down on Friday.

"This Friday?" asked a horrified Claire.

"Yes – didn't Paul say?"

No, Paul did not say

Claire had been under the impression that the visit would occur on some unspecified date in the uncertain future. After Paul's trip to see Libby in Teddington he had followed the advice in Nicole's letter and written to his father's publishers. With no reply after a month he had written to Debbie, who had promised to find Michael and make contact. In late August Debbie had indeed found Michael, and a week later she reported that a visit to see Libby in Teddington was planned, after which they would get down to Pembrokeshire at some point.

At some point! Like three days later!

"Anyway," Debbie continued. "Is there any chance you could book us in somewhere? Neither of us know the area and it's a bit late to get brochures or guides."

Claire thought furiously, trying to work out what kind of place they would expect and, more to the point, what was available.

"Hello – you still there?"

"Yes, just thinking about places."

"Anywhere will do, bed and brekkie, hotel, bunkhouse … wherever … I'm not fussed and I'm sure Michael will be OK with whatever you can find."

Paul was duly apologetic.

"She said they'd arrange something, but I didn't expect it to be so soon. And I have that exhibition opening in Tenby."

"They're both retired," said Claire. "Haven't got diaries full of work like us. Don't worry. You go to Tenby. I'll sort something."

The practicals were formidable. Claire was due a visit to her mother, she had holiday lets to prep and shifts booked at the Mariners. In a furious bout of 'phone calls Claire re-arranged the visit to her Mum, swapped her shifts, and booked the Bailiff's House. This had the advantage that it was roomy and comfortable, with a decent sized kitchen and two double bedrooms – and the disadvantage that it was by some distance the most expensive property she managed, and could only be booked by the week.

By early evening Claire was back at the house. She put pizza in the oven to warm, poured a glass of wine and flopped onto the deep and comfortable sofa. The Bailiff's House had been a farm, then a dairy, then a Victorian residence for at least three families in succession, one of which may even have been a bailiff. Prior to its reincarnation as a holiday let it had been known as the old dairy, which was still the name used by the locals. The house was in the centre of St Davids, with an unremarkable street frontage that was easy to miss. Claire often waited at the property for new arrivals, to ensure that their vehicles escaped the attentions of the area's enthusiastic traffic warden.

Michael arrived first. Claire saw the battered 4x4 circle twice round the block before pulling onto the parking space in front of the house.

On the doorstep there was a moment of mutual appraisal. Claire was not prepared for the resemblance; Michael was taller than Paul, but otherwise the similarity was remarkable: the crumpled clothes, the same easy smile, and the eyes – dark brown with a network of laughter lines that were deeper and more extensive.

"Hello," she said eventually. "I guess that you're Michael, I'm Claire, welcome to the Bailiff's House. I hope it's going to be alright for you."

The smile broadened.

"This looks fine – is this your place? Or Paul's? Debbie wasn't specific about where we'd be staying."

"It's a holiday home, bring your things and I'll show you around. Paul's studio is just round the corner, but it isn't big enough for guests. He's in Tenby at the mo', back tomorrow."

Claire led the way into the house and watched with some amusement as Michael opened doors and investigated cupboards.

"It's a big place for just me," he said.

Women were supposed to grow to be like their mothers, a thought that Claire found seriously scary, but she liked this older version of Paul.

"Ah," said Claire. "Well – Debbie's staying here as well. Sorry not have said, there are four bedrooms … I thought it would be OK."

The smile became a grin.

"Might have to put a lock on my door. Don't worry, it will be fine. We'll both be in bed at nine with a cup of cocoa."

In the kitchen Claire pointed out the range of breakfast food that she had bought in that morning, along with the freshly made pizza in case her guests arrived hungry. There was a bottle of white wine and some beer.

"Someone's been busy," said Michael. "Look, there's no need for you to wait up. My guess is that you've been working all day."

"Thanks, that's kind of you. What time would you like us to call round in the morning?"

"Don't know about Debbie, depends when or if she arrives, but I'm always up by eight – shall we say here at nine – that will give us time to catch up. I've not see her for … gosh, forty years."

Claire looked up in surprise.

"Didn't you see her in London, when you went to visit Libby?"

"No. It was all arranged on the 'phone. She did say that she'd try and meet me, but she was in Majorca and there were problems with her flight."

"So, you didn't know she was coming here."

"Yes and No. She said she wanted to meet, but she didn't say anything about coming to Pembrokeshire."

Claire hesitated.

"Do you mind … I mean, I've put you both in the same house."

Michael put a reassuring hand on her shoulder.

"Really, don't worry. If it's the same Debbie I remember she won't bat an eyelid about sharing the house. And I'm looking forward to seeing her – we have a lot to talk about."

***

At Paul's studio the next morning Claire discovered that her only clean clothes consisted of a crop top and a pair of three quarter length leggings. Neither left much to the imagination.

"They'll think I'm a tart. I don't even have any clean knickers. I've just put yesterday's stuff in the wash."

"You look fine," said Paul. "You're not a tart and no-one is going to be inspecting your knickers."

Claire ransacked Paul's clothes drawers and picked one of his shirts.

"Can I borrow this?"

Paul glanced up and grinned.

"Course you can, suits you."

Claire made a face.

"It does ... looks better on you than it does on me."

Claire's face crumpled and Paul jumped off the bed

"Sorry," he said as he offered a hug. "Empathy failure. You'll be fine ... really."

***

At the Bailiff's House Claire hesitated on the threshold. She was nervous, partly because of the inadequate wardrobe, but mainly she knew that the day was going to be incredibly important for Paul, yet she knew virtually nothing about her guests.

She found Michael in the kitchen with a half cup of coffee and the remains of breakfast.

"Good morning," he said. "Coffee in the pot if you want some. Debbie's not arrived yet."

"Thanks, Paul will be here in a mo. He had an exhibition yesterday – in Tenby. He has to make a couple of follow up 'phone calls."

Claire poured herself a coffee and joined Michael at a table strewn with the disassembled remains of the Times, Telegraph, Guardian and Mirror newspapers.

"Did you buy up the shop?"

"Old journo habit – first job of the day is to go through the papers. It's wall to wall coverage of the funeral."

"But that's tomorrow."

"They've got pages to fill."

Claire leafed through the pages.

"So sad. I liked Diana. Do you think this is the end for the Royals?"

"Doubt it, people have short memories – just you see, ten years time and it'll be queen Camilla."

"You've missed out The Sun."

Michael smiled a lopsided smile.

"There are limits."

Once again Claire was struck by the uncanny resemblance. If this was what her man was going to look like in twenty years time … she hugged the thought close.

Paul arrived. There was a brief moment of awkwardness as he stood half into the kitchen. Claire watched a range of emotions fly across Michael's face before he stood to embrace the younger man. Both were offering simultaneous apologies; Paul for being absent the evening before, Michael for the missing forty years. He took half a step back, his hands on Paul's shoulders.

"I had no idea, none – no clue that you even existed."

"You're here now; that's what's important."

Claire watched the two men as they appraised and appreciated.

"Why don't you two walk the coast path whilst I wait for Debbie."

Paul nodded, they'd agreed on this the previous night. He turned to Michael.

"That's if you have some reasonable footwear."

"Always in the boot, will I need a waterproof?"

"Not according to the forecast, " said Clare. "But I'd take one anyway."

"We'll head down to Solva," said Paul. "Perhaps take a look at the cathedral first."

"Sounds good to me," said Michael

"Meet you at the Harbourside," said Clare. "About one?"

Paul glanced at the clock.

"It's a good six miles, best make that one thirty."

Clare nodded, and the two men were gone.

***

Paul led the way, dodging holidaymakers on the narrow pavements. As they walked he offered a shorthand history

"St David is buried here … Wales' patron saint … the cathedral's origins are Norman, it was a busy pilgrimage site in the medieval era."

Paul paused to navigate round a clutch of Japanese tourists who were diligently photographing a tea shop.

Following the flow of sightseers they passed through a medieval gatehouse into the cathedral close. The building lay below them dominating the valley, with the ruins of the bishop's palace beyond.

"Doesn't look very Norman to me," said Michael.

Paul nodded his agreement.

"The guide book hedges its bets on that one, says it's 'eclectic'. A lot of the work is Victorian. The original building was woefully neglected after the Reformation; one of the bishops nicked the lead off the palace roof, another was accused of forging church papers. Do you want to go down … take a closer look?"

Michael shook his head.

"Not now, could we drop by your studio? I'm interested to see what kind of work you do … if we have time that is."

Paul nodded quickly.

"That's fine, no problem, it's just round the corner."

Paul walked back to the busy square, then down a side-street to an anonymous door. Paul's flat lay above a high street shop specialising in overpriced outdoor wear and popular with tourists who had been too optimistic about the weather. The studio was on the top floor and had been chosen for its north facing aspect and huge floor to ceiling window. On the way Paul had been enthusing about the quality of the light and he led the way upstairs expecting to hear a reaction, only to turn and find that Michael wasn't there.

Making his way back down to the flat he found Michael anchored in front of the Three Graces portrait.

"Ah, I see you've found the picture."

"Yes … who … how did this get here?" Michael's eyes never left the portrait.

"It's from Nicole," said Paul, slightly puzzled. There had been a distinct change of atmosphere.

Michael turned slowly.

"From Nicole?"

"Yes … she left it to me in her will. She wrote a letter; there was a book – Libby's biography – a dress from Libby's shop, some sketches, your wildlife book and a few of your clippings … this picture, and the money. That's Libby on the left, and Debbie I think. I don't know about the girl in the middle. I suppose it might even be Nicole."

Michael laughed.

"You guessed correct. That is Nicole, although I think this may have been the only time she modelled."

"You've seen it before then?"

"Not this version, but yes, I have seen the photograph before."

Paul looked at the picture, trying to fathom what was causing the all too obvious tension..

Because something is … surely it's not the nudity.

"Are you the photographer," he ventured.

Michael laughed again.

"No, not my thing, and anyway, this is a touch early for me. This was about 1949. I'd only just left school."

He stared at the picture, recalling that other studio and the party at Archie's house in Cheshunt Gardens. Archie's brother

Robbie; this was his work. 'For a commission', she had said. Michael shook his head, partly in an attempt to dispel the disquiet the picture had triggered.

"She didn't leave you anything else? Negatives or a package? Nicole that is." he asked eventually.

"No," said Paul. "Look … is something wrong? You seem unsettled. I could find the letter if you like."

Michael pushed the half formed conjectures out of his mind. It was neither the time nor place.

"No, I'm fine, really. I'd forgotten about the picture. It brought back some difficult memories. Let's go and look at your paintings."

***

Clair washed up the breakfast things, tidied Michael's newspapers and listened to a deeply daft Woman's Hour interview about the mountain of flowers left outside Buckingham Palace in memory of Diana.

She turned the radio off in disgust when the regal tones of the mystery interviewee started to pontificate about how the Queen was 'feeling the nation's pain'.

"Good for you, girl. Total garbage."

Claire glanced at the immaculately dressed woman in the doorway and immediately felt plain and drab.

"Hi. You must be Claire, jeez it's a long drive from London. I'm bushed, any coffee in that pot?"

Paul had said nothing about what Debbie looked like or wore, only that she was 'about sixty'. Claire had made assumptions based on that inadequate information and she was unprepared for the approaching vision, with the figure hugging red leather trousers and white silk blouse.

"The men are walking the cliff path to Solva," said Claire as she poured the coffee.

"I passed that I think. Not sure, twas all a bit of a blur by that time."

"You would have. It's about five of six miles down the coast. Little place with a harbour and a steep hill. I live there; there's a pub by the harbour. We're meeting them there for lunch."

"Six miles! Walking! Bugger that for a game of soldiers. The pub sounds a much better idea."

The cool grey eyes twinkled and Claire wondered if she was being teased. She fielded a series of questions about the house, Paul, how they'd met, her mother, her job …

"That going well, the job, working for yourself, making money?"

"It can get pretty hectic, especially in the season, but I like working for myself."

Debbie poured the remains of her coffee into the sink.

"Hold on to that. Rely on yourself, not on other people."

"That's good advice," said Claire, and then, in an attempt to stem the flow of questions. "Were you on holiday in Majorca?"

Debbie explained that she lived in Majorca, had owned two nightclubs and was on her third.

"Plus two ex-husbands. No plans for a third."

The feeling of being mocked intensified and Claire cast around in her mind for a new topic of conversation.

"I like your blouse," said Claire. "And the trousers … and … do you mind me asking … cos you look really well … and …"

" … not like a pensioner at all."

Debbie laughed, as Claire reddened.

"Well no … or yes, actually. Do you work out?"

Debbie grinned.

"No luv. I sit around all day drinking Sangria and eating chips"

Claire stammered an apology and turned way. In a futile attempt to hide her embarrassment she picked up a cloth and made to wipe down the table. Debbie stepped forward and took the dishcloth away, before enveloping Claire in her arms.

"Relax love. I'm sorry, I'm being a bitch. I'm not going to eat you. I'm a bit ratty after the drive."

Debbie stood back and did a slow pirouette and curtsey.

"I've been lucky … I dance, I always have, and dance is a really good way to stay fit. I don't stay too long in the sun, I watch what I eat."

She took Claire's hands in her own and made a careful assessment of the younger girl.

"And there's nothing wrong with your figure, so stop fretting."

***

The cliff path followed the sheer coast overlooking St Bride's Bay, dipping down to isolated rocky coves, before climbing back to skirt its way around abrupt dizzying drops.

They had just left a deserted cove where a new born seal was suckling from its mother and Michael was cursing his lack of foresight, having only brought one camera.

"September's the best time for seals," said Paul. "But there are things to see at any time of year."

Michael took a series of photographs of the seascape, before being distracted by a pair of red beaked choughs tussling over a large snail.

"It's amazing, I had no idea. I need to come back with a long lens."

"The light isn't always this good. We get damp and dismal days, especially in winter. That can feel quite claustrophobic. From November on there are hardly any visitors; a lot of the shops only open in season."

The conversation paused while they descended a precarious slope to a rocky beach. A convenient bench allowed a view out into the bay and an opportunity for Michael to take the conversation into deeper water.

"So, who were the Stannards?"

Paul detailed what he knew: Frank and Rosie, the cottage, sailing on the Deben in boats borrowed from the shipyard. In turn Michael offered the not quite mirror image of his childhood in Totnes: James, Edith, the Youngs – and Libby.

"You knew her before, in the war?" interjected Paul.

"She was an evacuee, just as I was. But her father took her back to London when her mother was killed."

Michael described the bombing and its aftermath.

"Eight children were killed, as well as Libby's mother and another parent. Edith – my foster mum – was lucky to survive. Libby and I were incredibly lucky, we had been playing in the valley. We thought we were going to be in trouble for being late."

Michael reflected for a moment.

"Libby was never the same after the bombing; she became very angry with the world, and wilful."

"And you never met after that, not until …" Paul hesitated.

"Until I got her pregnant?"

Paul winced and Michael smiled. He waited for an answering smile before continuing.

"It happened. You happened. No point in beating around the bush … we met at a photoshoot on the Kings Road. I didn't recognise her, not at all. We went to a party … the attraction was really strong, I felt I'd known her for years." He grinned again, "which I had of course. And we did take precautions … of a kind … things were different then."

"Nicole's letter said you were called away."

"I was offered a job, a real opportunity, but it meant flying out the next day. I tried to call her, but never got through. I wrote from France, but she can't have received the letters, in any case she never replied. I don't know why not. She knew where I worked; they would have passed a message on … I don't understand why she didn't tell me."

There was a silence broken only by the waves rolling onto the rocky shore as the two men contemplated the 'might have beens'. Michael was the first to move.

"Water under the bridge," he said, picking up his pack and returning to the path.

***

The pub in Solva occupied a prime spot next to the working harbour, with a fine view down the fjord like cove. Debbie and Claire had bagged an outdoor table before the rush. Claire had taken the opportunity to call by her flat, and was now dressed in her new ankle boots, designer jeans and matching top. Debbie had murmured her approval. They saw the walkers long before they arrived at the pub, and Debbie had the drinks ready and waiting.

"Hello stranger," she said as the men arrived.

"And Hello to you," said Michael.

There was a long pause; a silent and mutual appraisal, broken only when Claire distributed menus.

"The fish will be fresh, we saw the owner coming in with the catch."

"Good," said Michael, before turning back to Debbie.

"Seems a long time ago."

"That's because it is … forty years."

Michael turned to the others.

"The last time I saw this lady was at a fancy dress ball. She was dressed as a very sexy Red Riding Hood .. a costume she could probably still get into."

"Why, thank you kind sir," said Debbie, raising her glass.

"Was that your first meeting," asked Paul.

"No," said Michael. "That was a photo-shoot. Debbie was one of the models. Libby was the agency booker. Nicole was there as well."

"She'd taken the day off to help," said Debbie.

"I wasn't supposed to be there at all. I was sent as a messenger boy."

Debbie looked up in surprise.

"I didn't know that."

"It's true," said Michael, turning back to Paul and Claire. "I worked for an agency called Pattens, but they would not have approved of me taking the pictures. I would have been given the sack."

"But you didn't get sacked," said Debbie. "You disappeared."

The tone was light, almost playful, but the challenging eyes belied the surface impression. Claire watched as Michael turned back to Debbie, clearly holding back from an instant response. Michael made as if to speak, before turning away. Paul reached out a restraining arm.

"He didn't know," he said, with a forcefulness that surprised everyone. "We talked about this on the way down. It was a big job … too good an opportunity for anyone to miss. And Libby knew where he worked, how to get in contact. Michael wrote letters, sent messages … she never told him."

He looked directly at Debbie

"Michael never knew about me."

Debbie's gaze was still focused on Michael.

"She was crazy about you, couldn't wait to see you again. I thought it was daft, she'd only met you twice, but she felt she'd known you for ever. And then nothing. It destroyed her. The pregnancy was just the cherry on the cake."

She paused to allow the words to sink in.

"So what was the big job?"

"It was for The Sentinel, the national, you know?"

Debbie nodded.

"They flew me out to Gibraltar, then Cyprus." said Michael. "It was Suez crisis and very hush hush. I went in with the ground forces as a war photographer."

Paul nodded his support, then turned back to Debbie.

"It's all in Nicole's folder; the news clippings and photographs. He was on the front page."

Claire took in the tableaux: Michael impassive, accepting of the wrong that had been done, Paul fiercely loyal to the man he barely knew; Debbie in resolute defence of her friend.

I love you all

"We can't turn the clock back," she said. "We need to focus on the here and now. Michael is here for Paul. And as far as I'm concerned it's better late than never."

She picked up her glass.

"I'd like to welcome Michael into our lives."

Michael and Paul picked up their glasses. After a tiny hesitation Debbie raised her glass.

"Paul and Michael – Michael and Paul" said Claire. "Now let's get some food, I'm starving."

***

On the way back to St Davids Michael accepted a lift with Debbie, recognising the offer for what it was: a peace offering.

"We need to talk about Lombroso," he said.

Debbie kept her eyes on the road, weaving between parked cars as she climbed the steep hill out of the village, but Michael knew she was listening.

"I followed up the warning you gave me about Helen Jackson. She is still trying to push the story, and she's not the only one. At the moment the papers wont touch it because of the legal restrictions. But that could change."

Michael paused, waiting to see if Debbie would offer any kind of comment.

"And then there's the picture. The commission: you, Libby and Nicole."

"What about it?"

"Nicole kept it. She's passed it on to Paul. It's hanging in his flat."

Debbie swerved under the nose of an approaching tanker, crossing the carriageway into a lay-by and skidding to a halt in a cloud of dust. She turned the engine off and turned to face Michael.

"Nicole kept the picture?"

"So it would appear. It might be a copy."

"Jesus fucking Christ."

Debbie gathered her thoughts, choosing the right words.

"Was there anything else?"

"There's a suitcase full of stuff: clothes, books, clippings about Libby and me. I haven't seen it all … no negatives."

"Oh the silly fucking cow … don't suppose you have a fag. I've given up, but I could really do with one."

"Sorry."

Debbie released a long sigh. The hard exterior softened, for a second she looked vulnerable, frightened and old. She met his eyes.

"You know, don't you?"

"I worked some of it out, Paul supplied the remaining piece in the jigsaw. I didn't know about Nicole, how close she was to Libby. Once I knew that … well, the rest fell into place."

He placed his hand over hers.

"Paul doesn't know, and I'm not going to tell him. As for what happened; I'm not going to lose any sleep over Lombroso, but we need to do something about that picture."

Debbie squeezed the proffered hand in thanks.

"There are negatives," she said. "Jackson has some, and there may be others."

"I'd guessed that. Look … we can't do anything about the past, but we do need to protect Paul and Claire … and Libby, though she is probably beyond being hurt by anything printed in the papers."

"I don't want Nicole's name dragged into this," said Debbie. "Or mine come to think of it."

"If the story runs someone somewhere will join up the dots. First step is to get rid of that picture."

***

"Well, that went well."

"Yes," said Claire from the bathroom where she was brushing her teeth. She put her head around the door. "I was a bit relieved after what happened at the pub. But they were fine this evening."

"I should think so too, the food was fantastic."

Paul straightened out the bedclothes and kicked some socks underneath the bed. He considered whether to take his T-shirt off and decided not. He'd had too much supper. He picked up the latest Ian McEwan.

Claire reappeared and took in the recumbent figure, book and T shirt. She kept her nightdress on and jumped into the bed.

"Move up."

Paul edged over a fraction. A real double bed was high on their list of priorities for the money left to him by Nicole. Claire snuggled into his shoulder.

"It was nice of Debbie to offer me a job, do you think she was serious?"

"Why not? You're a great cook and a good manager. I'm sure you could run, what was it she said – 'a boutique hotel' – whatever that is. Question is whether you want to."

"I'll have to think about it," said Claire, who had already decided that moving to Majorca was completely out of the question.

"I think they must have had a long chat in the car. Debbie seemed a lot happier. There was a lot of flirting going on."

"Really?" said Paul. "I didn't see that; they are a bit old for that surely."

Claire rolled her eyes.

"Do you mind about the picture?"

"No, not at all. She seemed keen to have it. It's not my thing."

"She's got a really good body, even now, and she must be what … 70?"

"Surely not," said Paul, putting the book to one side. "Michael said that he was born in 1930. That makes him … 68. So, yes, I suppose she could be 70, but she doesn't look it."

"Neither of them look like pensioners. Do you think we'll be that good looking when we are their age?"

Paul recognised a loaded question when he heard one.

"I've no idea. They're both pretty active and they watch what they eat. They've been lucky as well. It sounds like Michael could easily have been killed in Vietnam."

Claire picked up the book.

"What's this about?"

"Obsession. There's a chance meeting and one guy becomes obsessed with another."

"Is he gay?"

"It's not that kind of love."

"Obsession isn't love," said Claire. "Nicole loved Libby, but she wasn't obsessed. At least I don't think so, but it's so sad … to love for all that time, from a distance, with nothing to show for it, nothing returned, nothing to hold."

She snuggled closer to Paul.

"I'm not obsessed by you."

Paul turned towards her and kissed her gently on the forehead. "That's a relief."

Claire rolled her fingers down Paul's chest.

"Do you really need that T-shirt?"

About the Author

Phil Revell is a mill town Lancastrian relocated to Shropshire: ex-teacher, ex-journalist, ex-charity director. His writing career began with 'She' magazine, and moved onto the nationals, including The Guardian, Times and Independent newspapers; 'The Three Graces' is his second novel.